Cilantro,
Not Coriander

a novel

John S. Munday

Plain View Press
P. O. 42255
Austin, TX 78704

plainviewpress.net
sb@plainviewpress.net
512-441-2452

Cover photograph by Jeffrey L. Wiles, a wildlife photographer who lives in Hopkins, Minnesota.

Cover design by Susan Bright.

To Fran, who insisted I go to El Salvador because she fell in love with the country on her first visit there, and who accompanied me on many of my sojourns to that nation named for the Savior of the world.

Contents

Prologue

When I saw the blustery, unexpectedly fierce cold of late March in Philadelphia, I pictured Bev holding her coat tight when she would come into the church tonight. I closed the curtain on the kitchen window of St. John's Lutheran Church and hefted two stainless steel ten gallon kettles in the sink to fill with cold water. I salted the water, then took ingredients for chicken soup from the refrigerator. I intended tonight's soup supper to moderate the raw weather for those who would come to the church. And to finally get Bev to try it. We were having a memorial service commemorating the eighth anniversary of the murder in El Salvador of Catholic Archbishop Oscar Romero on March 24, 1980.

Out of habit I turned on the radio, wondering if NPR's news would mention the anniversary. El Salvador's civil war and Reagan's fight against Communism in Central America kept the tiny Central American nation in the headlines. More likely another story about the Iran/Contra stuff, I thought. After I filled the kettles with water, I put them on the stove and unpacked the chicken. I hummed to a jazz riff on the radio as the NPR program went to a new topic. The news would be on soon. Pushing back the sleeves of my sweatshirt, I tossed the chicken into the sink, turned on the cold water and began scrubbing each piece with a brush.

I plopped a scrubbed and rinsed piece into a kettle. I'm a purist and I make the best chicken soup this side of Antigua, Guatemala. Some cooks start by briefly boiling the chicken, strain off all the water with the foam from the blood and grease, and begin with fresh water. "Not me," I will tell anyone who happens to see me cooking. "Scrubbed chicken soup is my specialty." Later, when the chicken is cooked, I'll fish out the pieces, cut the good meat into bite size chunks and put them back in. Celery, onions, and a short while before serving, some home-made noodles go in. So does more salt, some pepper, and chopped cilantro leaves. Not the coriander seeds that are the fruit of the same plant. Skin, fat and bones go into the trash.

The news came on before I finished the chicken. "My God!" I gasped when a reporter announced the shooting death of a young man from Philadelphia, David Stevens, in the capital city of San Salvador, El Salvador. "Not David!" I quickly rinsed my hands and ran to my office.

○

I dialed Bev's phone, then hung up when not even the answering machine picked up. I franticly flipped through the cards in the rolodex, wondering who I should call next. I left a message for Father Jimmy Simpson at St. Giles. We had collaborated on several events and went to Congress together once to lobby for ending aid to the Contras in Nicaragua. The priest had introduced me to David Stevens, just last fall, with his mother, Bev. I rubbed my face with both hands, as if I could erase the news of David's death. I dialed Bev's number again, then sat back. I had no idea what to do. I tried to think and only drew a blank. A big nothing.

I had other clergy friends but only two were Roman Catholic. Father Jimmy, and Padre Rafael in El Salvador. He didn't have a telephone. Rafael knew David, but did he know anything about the young man's death? I picked up a yellow pad, letter size ever since I went to seminary. The pages from legal size pads were too long for the files I kept. I flipped over the pages with my notes for next Sunday's sermon. *A blank page. That's what I need. Start over. Start yesterday over. Change history.* Keeping David safe is what I would change if I could. I hesitated, waiting for my brain to start working, willing it to make sense. I wanted to make a list. What list? *This is too much for me.*

I thought back to the first time I met David's mother. The truth is I remember every time I met Bev. Her eyes had been just the right rich shade of sparkling blue. I can still picture her smile, a strong but sweet jaw, her blond hair. *Poor Bev,* I said, stupidly, then pushed away from the desk. *How can I think of a smile. She's just lost her son.*

○

I went back to the kitchen, finished washing the chicken and turned on the burners. *Tonight will be a double memorial* I thought. *Bev would have been here tonight.* Moving to the butcher block, I began cutting celery. When I unwrapped sprigs of fresh cilantro, the sweet sharp scent brought the memory of a special lunch at a small cafe in Antigua, Guatemala, where I had spent some time in language school. I recalled when David went to language school there. Bev and I talked about the café and my chicken soup. She said one of her relatives, an aunt I think, used coriander seeds in some Swedish recipes.

I heard a knock. Father Jimmy Simpson stood at the door to the kitchen, arms folded over a Saint Joseph University sweatshirt. "Smells great," he said. Simpson was wiry, 5'6", a half-foot less than me. More compact than skinny, he covered his balding head with a Phillies baseball cap. His weather-beaten bearded face, one people tended to trust, soft voice, and placid unafraid blue eyes told of a life caring for the people in his parish. "You called," he said, moving into the kitchen.

"I've had NPR on. Nothing more about David," I said. "How is his mother? Have you gone to see her?"

"Just came from there." Father Jimmy paced back and forth, rubbing his hands on his pants. "She unplugged the phone. Said she didn't want any more bad news." He looked into the pot, then went back to lean on the doorway.

Neither of us can think of anything to say, I thought when no one spoke. I stirred the soup, tried to take comfort from the essence of chicken that now floated up in the boiling liquid. "Jimmy, this is scrubbed chicken soup. The recipe came from a little café in Antigua. I ate some as a cure for the stomach deal —Montezuma's revenge— and it took me a while to figure out how to duplicate it."

"In quantity, I see," Father Jimmy said, peering into one of the pots. "Gimme a taste?"

"It's the best," I said, handing Jimmy a spoon. "Fresh cilantro leaves. It is the leaf of the plant that has the flavor I associate with Central America, not coriander. The seed of the plant. Plus I make my own noodles from scratch. They go in last, once the celery and onions soften."

"I was with Bev this morning when the cable that confirmed the call arrived from the embassy. She called me right after she got the phone call. She didn't know who else would come."

"I'm glad she got you," I said, wondering if she even thought of calling me. "I tried to call her."

"It's hit her really hard." Jimmy began pacing again. "I helped her call her parents. And her in-laws in Florida. I had to." Jimmy's voice trailed off.

I couldn't picture the scene, calling grandparents to tell them something they never dreamed they would hear. Something I never dreamed I would hear. "Can you tell me what actually happened to David? All I heard was the news saying he'd been shot."

"Bev got a call at about 7:30 this morning. I was saying mass and I went to the house after. She told me the guy from the embassy told her that David had been shot and that details were still vague. Vague. What a hell of a word. All they told her was that he, David, was walking along a street, probably to go from his apartment to the Archdiocese offices where he worked. Someone drove by and shot him. Once. No one saw the license plate, if it had one."

I shook my head in disbelief, then stared at the priest. I had been on my way here at 7:30. Did she call me, then give up? "What kind of vehicle?"

Jimmy nodded his head. "White Jeep Cherokee. Blackened windows."

"She knows about death squads, you know."

Jimmy shuddered. "I answered the door when the cable came, and when I looked for Bev, she had gone up to David's room. She was standing by a decoupage David had made as a high school project when he was a sophomore. Using newspaper clippings. I'd seen it before when David showed it to me. It had headlines and news reports just from one bloody year. 1980. The year of the martyrs, he called it. Bev moved her hand across the newspaper proclaiming Archbishop Oscar Romero's murder. The headline is dated, March 24, 1980, exactly eight years ago. 'My son is a martyr,' she said when she saw me at the doorway. 'Just like Romero.' Then she took the frame down from the wall. 'I know your history, El Salvador,' she said. 'Look at all this, Father Jimmy,' As if I couldn't read, she named them, her voice rising with each one."

I could picture the scene because I'd also seen the collage. Bev had shown it to me, proud of her son's work. I told her I once met Ita Ford's brother at a solidarity meeting, I shut my eyes, picturing Bev reciting the headlines like a litany. I looked at the priest who stood as if in prayer. "She showed it to me one time when I went to her house." *What had been a monument to the deaths of others has a different meaning for her now.*

Jimmy frowned. "Her hands shook so badly I thought she would drop the thing when she came to December 2, and the story of how Salvadoran soldiers raped and killed the church women. Bev said she remembered when David had added this last article to the collection, along with the newspaper photograph of the women being pulled from the shallow grave while U.S. Ambassador White looked on. She told me how David had become obsessed with El Salvador."

"Do you know anyone in the Archdiocese in San Salvador? I know a priest, Padre Rafael, but not how to reach him." I shrugged my shoulders. "Maybe I could go through the Lutheran Bishop's office. I know him, too."

"No. I wish I did." Father Jimmy leaned on the counter by the sink. "I remember when David compared El Salvador in 1980 to a boxer being beaten by a bigger foe. He said he felt one tragedy after another slamming into the people. Like brutal body punches."

I stirred the soup, my stomach in knots.

"You should go see her," the priest said, breaking the silence. "She's talked to me about you." He smiled, adding, "Not in the confessional."

"There's nothing to confess," I said, not turning from the soup, "nothing at all."

◯

Father Jimmy didn't come back to St. John's that evening for the Romero memorial service. Instead he went to Bev's house, sat with her as she talked about her son. Consoling the bereaved is not something they teach in seminary, but the years in the parish had given him more experience than he wanted. And the death of a child, at any age, was always the hardest. Unnatural. And there are no magic answers to take away the pain.

The priest told Bev he had been at St. John's church, talked with Pastor Charles. She shook her head when he mentioned chicken soup, then shuddered. "I had some with David, in Antigua. Charles said his is as good as at the café. But I don't know. I was going to go there tonight, to honor Romero." She began to cry again.

Father Jimmy plugged the phone line back in, understanding why Charles hadn't gotten through to her. He answered the phone for Bev whenever it rang, checking with her before he gave her the receiver. She took a call from her mother.

"My mother wants to know if I am going to El Salvador to claim the body," Bev said after hanging up. "I should have told her he went down on his own and can come back on his own." She burst into tears. "I don't mean that. I'm just so angry." Jimmy said nothing. "My stupid husband died in Viet Nam, being patriotic, and now my son is dead in another rotten part of the world. The family tradition, dying for God and country. What am I going to do?"

The priest watched her contort her face, twist her body. "I don't see what you'd do for him by going down there. You will be busy with getting ready for the funeral. There are a lot of people to notify, I would imagine."

"I don't know where to start." Bev sat back on the couch, eyes shut, nodding slightly as if in conversation with herself. "I only know one thing."

"What is that?" the priest asked, a worried look flashing across his face.

"I have to find out who did this to my son. And why. I want answers. I want to know why someone could shoot David, take him from me. I'll bury him, but then I'm going down there."

Jimmy's mind raced, trying to find some argument to dissuade her. "You can't... "

"I can."

"Let me finish. You can't go to El Salvador alone. You need resources. Support. Talk to Charles."

After the priest left, Bev unplugged the telephone again when it rang. She took a long time to cry herself to sleep.

◯

After the soup supper and memorial service for Archbishop Oscar Romero, I put the dishes in the dishwasher, stowed the left-over chicken soup in the refrigerator. I tried Bev's number again, then began the walk home. This night my thoughts were not on the martyred Romero, but on David's mother's grief. I ignored the strangers and street people I normally speak to, those I usually see as someone I could reach out to with a word of kindness. Being kind wasn't on my mind.

I have to talk to her, I thought as I walked, faster than normal. I felt so frustrated that Bev hadn't answered any of the calls I made before and even during the event at church. *Just to express my sorrow.* As I continued to walk home from St. John's, I tried to bring back memories of David, feeling irritation that most of my thoughts were for the young man's mother. I could not imagine what I could say to her now, not finding words that made sense.

My house, townhouse really, is a two story stone building dating back to the 1920s, with oak floors and railings. When I arrived home, I went to my library, my place of solace, ran a hand over some of the liberation theology books. What would Padre Jon Sobrino say now? I had met the Jesuit at a rally in Washington, DC, and was impressed. Sobrino's less famous co-worker, Padre Jon de Cortina, also a Jesuit who taught engineering in San Salvador at the *Universidad de Simon Cañas*, had come to Philadelphia some two months ago, speaking to people who were planning to send a delegation down to El Salvador. I built an entire sermon on one statement de Cortina made. "If God is not with the people of El Salvador, God is nowhere." *That seemed so powerful when I applied it to down there, but what about now?*

I admit I read obsessively. I took the smallest bedroom for my own, rationalizing that all I did there was sleep. The largest bedroom, what should have been the master bedroom, became the library, because I needed the space and because it had a window looking out at the back yard. I built floor to ceiling bookshelves and filled them. One wall contained theology and Bible reference books, concordances and study guides. The Greek and Hebrew books and dictionaries sat on a shelf at shoulder level. I call it my God wall. The shelves that framed the window held the fiction. I buy and read a ton of novels. I admit I hide in the fictional world imagined by the wide range of novelists I like. Often I'd use a scene as a sermon illustration, not always of a positive course of conduct. The third wall contained more religious writings, mostly liberation theology. There was no book that could hold my interest that evening.

Part I

Cilantro

One

In October, 1987, St. John's Lutheran Church no longer proclaimed
the glory of God with much emphasis. Old philanthropic money
built the huge stone edifice in 1910 on the then edge of center city
Philadelphia. Once 2500 members called the church home. Now a
remnant of maybe sixty souls show up to worship in the chapel on the
second floor, above a kitchen, two offices and a small area for fellowship.
Seven rows of pews form layers of increasing semi-circles facing the
pulpit. When they sold the main sanctuary to a theater company, they
got its promise not to hold Sunday matinees before noon. Only the
massive marble baptism font had been carried up from the old sanctuary.
The manse had also been sold to a Christian Association affiliated with
nearby University of Pennsylvania. The money from those sales, in an
endowment trust fund, pays the pastor's salary.

I'm the new pastor. That October evening I stood near the organ,
watching as people filed in, a much bigger crowd than on any Sunday. I
had been installed as the pastor just a month ago, and didn't know the
congregation well enough to distinguish between members and those
whose interest in El Salvador brought them to the meeting.

St. John's became a "Sanctuary Church" in solidarity with refuges
from El Salvador under the leadership of its former pastor, who had
resigned to go to back to graduate school. Others in the church kept
up this interest in solidarity and the congregation occasionally hosted
visitors from El Salvador or Guatemala who would tell their stories of the
conflicts and the political strife.

I watched an older couple help each other to seats on the front row,
hoping, I supposed, to be better able to hear the program. I wished St.
John's had an elevator. The stairs were steep and older folks often rested
on the landing half way up. I recognized Jerry and Walter, two men from
the committee that decided to call me to be St. John's eleventh pastor. I
decided to greet everyone, play my 'match the name with the face' game.

Just before I had to go to the podium and open the gathering, a man
wearing a cleric collar and a Phillies baseball cap came in, along with a
woman and young man. They walked directly up to me.

"I'm Father Jimmy Simpson, of St. Giles, in Clifton Heights,"
quickly taking off his cap. "We're here for the dialogue. My church is a
bit conservative for this kind of thing. You're the new pastor?" he said,
offering his hand.

"That's me, Charles Silas," I said. "You've brought some folks?"

"Right. Sorry." The priest shuffled, made room for them to shake hands with me. "This is Bev Stevens and her son David. From St. Giles. David is a recent graduate from St. Joseph's University." Taller than the priest, David wore jeans, a white shirt open at the collar, and a light green corduroy sport jacket. The young man seemed nice, and Father Jimmy would speak well of him later, having encouraged him to take part in some of the activities at St. John's in the past. Bev wore a denim skirt and a white blouse, also open at the neck. They looked like mother and son, I thought. I said nothing for a moment, just admired her very blue eyes and her smile. Father Jimmy nodded and walked off to greet someone he knew. David and Bev stood there, waiting for me to speak.

"You don't wear a cleric collar? I don't know about Lutherans," she said.

"Most Catholics don't," I replied, regretting the words even as I spoke them.

"Let's meet the speaker," David said, taking his mother's arm.

◯

When Bev and her son walked to their seat, I went up to the front of the room to get things started, do my thing. I opened with a prayer, then introduced the speaker, José Clímaco. José wore white cotton pants and a long sleeve plaid shirt, and had just come from his community in El Salvador. His black hair and brown skin sharply contrasted with his very white teeth.

When I sat down, I made sure I could see the young man and his mother. They had taken a pew in the front, on the left side of the pulpit. I watched Bev watching her son watch José and wondered if we would make eye contact. She sat with her hands folded, resting on her lap. A Catholic posture, I thought.

José pulled a chair from the choir section behind the pulpit and sat down, surveying the group, smiling. "When I came into the solidarity movement, in 1978," he said, "I saw the future and it was terrible. The only people from the United States I knew were the army and missionaries from the sects like Mormon and Jehovah Witness in their white shirts and suits talking about God. God is very much respected in my country. They were so very far above us that we never expected to be on an equal level. Then came the solidarity workers dressed in jeans and sandals, and they were more like us. Now I can work as an equal with people like you and it is without prejudice."

David clapped, and others joined him. José bowed to David, who then asked, "Tell us about your community. Where is it? How did you organize?"

"The FMLN, the guerillas you know, suggested or invited us to move to *Santa Cruz* and we did. Fifty-two families settled there. It is a long and painful story that would take days to tell, but we are happy to be in *Santa Cruz*. We planted corn and built houses."

The dialogue went on for about half an hour, and then broke for refreshments. I walked over to talk with Bev again after the meeting. David stayed with José and the other refugees to talk with them in Spanish.

◯

"This is nice," Bev said, pointing at the group still talking with José. "My son is going to work with the Archdiocese in El Salvador. He's been to this church a number of times before. You're new, so I don't think he's met you."

"I would have remembered," I said, thinking that she would be the one I would recall. I looked at her, then away, not wanting to actually study her. "Are you worried about him being in a third world country?" I asked. "One that's in a civil war? "

"Yes. I'm scared to death."

"I've been there. It's dangerous, but gringos mostly can be safe if they take the right precautions. I will add him to our prayer concerns."

"Do your prayers come with a guarantee?"

"No. My view of prayer is complicated." And a subject I wasn't prepared to go into with her, or anyone, on a first time meeting.

"Oh." She seemed surprised.

"The last time I went was right after the October, 1986 earthquake. We visited the University and a guy walked by me and said, 'Get out of here, now.' and I told the group leader. We didn't go into the classrooms like we planned to do." The memory of fear came back, but I tried to hide it from Bev. She could see I had thought of something. "But another time on that trip we were in a resettlement in the country. We cleared a Salvadoran military check point and were inside this fenced in resettlement. There was a baby on the ground and I thought that I could pick that baby up and smother it, and my blue passport would protect me."

"That's sick." Bev moved away from me.

"What's sick is how I felt our government's presence let our people do whatever they want with full impunity. I would never hurt anyone."

"The image of the baby being smothered kept me from understanding what you were saying. I hope David gets the benefit of our government's power, though he says he won't." Bev moved again, trying to keep David in her field of view and still look at me while we talked. "My husband, David's father, died in 1965, killed instantly by a land mine in Viet Nam. David, just six months old, never knew the kind, gentle man, never had the love of a father as he grew up. I tried to keep David senior's memory alive for my son, using photograph albums, letters and stories to let young David carry on the memories of what might have been, what should have been."

She seemed so eager to talk. I stared at her, saddened by the long ago loss of a life's companion. Then she laughed, probably because I must have looked as serious as I felt.

"I became an activist against the war. Viet Nam war. The only time I took part in a civil disobedience protest, I brought David, carrying him in a tummy sack. He was this small," she said, holding her hands apart. The policeman almost didn't see my baby, then gave me a lecture about motherhood and sent me on my way. He couldn't arrest a baby."

"I guess not," I answered. "But he grew up quite nicely it seems."

"Thank you. He is my pride and joy. I actually felt shame for letting my grief for his father push me to take a chance I had no right to take. So I wrote letters, to Congress and to newspapers. I joined the Democratic Party for a while, served a short stint as a precinct captain. Then I quit activism. I went to work for a law firm in Center City, Philadelphia. I'm a paralegal." Bev looked at my left hand, noted the absence of a ring. "Are you married?" She looked away. "I don't mean to pry. I only asked because I tease Father Jimmy about his not being able to get married. Because he's a priest. I'm sorry," she said, giggling, then seeming to blush. "I really don't know much about Protestants."

"I was married, some time ago," I admitted, surprised at the question. I do come in contact with unmarried women in my work at the church and a few had made it clear they found me interesting, though not at St. John's, yet. I have not returned the attention since before my ordination. "We got married after we finished law school. She is a lawyer. We fell in love in our senior year. It took three months in a law firm, working with others I might add, for her to fall out of love with me. No children, thank God. Career came first. To be honest, it couldn't have worked."

"I'm sorry. About the divorce, I mean. I didn't know you are a lawyer and a minister."

"Don't be sorry. That was another life. I had many problems with the profession. With the justice system. She didn't like that."

"What firm were you with?"

"McMasters and Johnsen. We always joked about how it looked like a misspelled sex report."

"I've heard the jokes. I also know the firm. Her name isn't Silas anymore?

"She found someone else. A lawyer with a lot bigger income. I know a lot of lawyer jokes. His name is Johnsen. A partner."

"Is her name Elizabeth?

"You know my ex?"

"Yes. Well, professionally, at least. Would it help if I said I didn't like her?"

"No." I thought but didn't add that she didn't have to compete with my ex. "We had fights when I said I wanted to study theology, but that wasn't what broke us up. I wanted answers, and she didn't even listen to the questions. She went off with Johnsen, then I went to seminary, and here I am. This job takes all my time, and I have adjusted. To living alone, that is."

"I am sorry," Bev said, touching my arm. "Being a widow is not much help in understanding divorce."

"Neither is being Catholic," I said. I wondered where the conversation was headed. She didn't seem forward, just interested or curious. "How are you handling David's interest in El Salvador?"

"David is so enthusiastic, I just have to go along for the ride." She pointed to him, clearly engaged in his conversation with José. "I feel okay about his wanting to help people."

I nodded, then looked back at David. "I normally don't talk this much about myself," I said.

"I'm glad you did. Maybe David's excitement about El Salvador is contagious." She touched my forearm gently, reassuringly, then went to join her son.

I circulated among the crowd, being pastoral. I kept my eye on Bev, noticed how animated she seemed while talking to Father Jimmy. In time Father Jimmy collected his parishioners, waiving to me as he left with them. A moment later Bev came back in, hurried over to me.

"David is leaving next week for Antigua to go to language school before he goes to El Salvador." She looked at me as if I understood.

"I spent a month there. Lots of fun," I replied, wondering why she came back to tell me that. "It's a tourist place in addition to the language schools and they are really the way to learn the language. One on one."

"I asked Father Jimmy to take us to the airport, to see David off." A tear formed in her eye. "He has a conflict. The archbishop or something. David suggested I ask you to take us."

I wanted to give her my handkerchief, but didn't. I didn't want her to be embarrassed that I noticed, so I pulled out my pocket calendar and pretended to check out my availability on Wednesday. I was available. "Next Wednesday?" I asked. She had wiped the tear.

Yes."

When I nodded, she asked, "You can take us?"

She gave me her address, told David who had joined her, and they set the time for me to pick them up. Later I found myself whistling the words to the *Darktown Strutter's Ball.* I'd use my car, not a taxi.

○

On the day David left for Guatemala and language school, I felt a heavy shroud of silence as I drove the young man and his mother to the airport. They both sat in the back seat of my car. From time to time Bev hugged her son, stroked his hand. David stared ahead, as if he wanted to see the future.

I dropped them at the door and parked, knowing Bev would need someone once David boarded the plane. When I got to the gate, they were hugging, and I held back. The flight began to board, and for a moment I thought Bev was going to board with him, but they parted, slowly. She stood near the doorway, finally wiping a tear.

After the door closed and the plane taxied onto the runway, Bev just looked out the window. I put my arm around her, surprising myself at least, and feeling her sense of loss.

"I already miss him," she said, waving to the memory of the airplane as it lifted off. "Thank you for being here for me. For us. For me and David."

Bev leaned on me. Her warmth seeped into my shoulder and chest, her perfume almost narcotic. I could feel her breathing, felt the sobs rather than heard them. I felt a different kind of intimacy, not sexual but not innocent, as though she was sharing her soul. Sweat formed on my brow and I tried to freeze the moment. Then she moved away.

○

When I met with the call committee of St. John's Church for an interview some months before they called me to be the pastor, they had already reviewed the dossier that the Synod staff had made available to them. The questions were very much to the point. Jerry Shields, a biochemist by profession and chairperson of the call committee, wanted

to know how I felt about my prior work as a lawyer and whether it helped
or hindered my work as a minister in a church.

I'm glad you asked that, I thought, but didn't say because I saw the
question as an opportunity to head off some problems if I did take this
call. "First thing that has to be clear," I said, "is that I am on inactive
status with the Pennsylvania Bar and I will not practice law or give legal
advice to anyone in or out of the congregation. I got out of law. Law is
very competitive, and quite different from the ministry." *If they only knew
some of the dirty play that goes on.* "Most preachers I've met talk about
justice, you know, the statue where a blindfolded woman holds out the
scales of justice, and they hold their two arms out straight, pretend they
are balancing the two trays, and then end up even. Preachers think that
is justice."

"Isn't it?" someone else asked.

"Not at all. In the legal system there is a balancing of the two sides,
as lawyers put evidence on their client's side and try to remove evidence
from the opponent's side. Justice is blinded by the cloth across her eyes
so that she is impartial and does not favor either side. When all the
evidence is in, she will have the blindfold removed and one side will
win. The scales won't be balanced and one side will have more evidence
than the other. It could be a lot, where, say, a jury finds the defendant
guilty beyond a reasonable doubt. Or a little, like in a personal injury
case where both sides were negligent to some degree. But one side wins,
having a bit more evidence. A 'scintilla' is the legal term, which means a
tiny amount of something. When the 'something' is evidence, it only has
to be the smallest amount that can be measured."

"All that's interesting," Jerry said, "but what is the point?"

Ah yes. What's the point. I looked at the members of the committee,
hoping to see a glimmer of light in someone. "The point is that some
ministers think that both sides are right and that being Christian means
giving in to everybody. And lawyers don't."

"I'm not sure I know what you mean," Jerry said.

None of them did. "It means that I'm a minister, first and only, but
I know that justice demands the resolution of the conflict. I'm not
going to argue in a sermon that we should forgive those who promote
racial injustice or that this church should ignore the findings of the
denomination on Central America, since that is a big topic here at St.
John's. May I quote an Anglican?"

"Why not?" Jerry answered.

"Archbishop Desmond Tutu, of South Africa, says, 'Not taking sides
is taking sides.' Another way to say what I mean is that, as the liberation

theologians say, 'God has a preferential option for the poor.' If God takes sides, so can I."

"We understand that," Jerry replied. "We have a history here at St. John's of being concerned about social justice issues," Jerry added, as if he wanted to leave the subject of law. "We see you do too, which is why we wanted to meet with you."

I still wanted to finish the point. "Look. A lawyer wants the client to win and that means the other side loses. As it should be. In ministry, as I see my work in the church and in society, I am different than most clergy because I am not afraid to take sides. But, I'm also going to call on the sick, and counsel couples who want to marry."

"I have a question," asked a man named Walter who had been sitting quietly. "You are divorced?"

"Yes I am." I wondered if Walter would have the nerve to ask a more personal question.

"Are you in a relationship with someone now?"

"No."

"The reason I ask is that sometimes the minister runs off with the choir director, or something."

I laughed. "Walter, I'm quite aware of those things. But it happens to married clergy too. In fact one of my classmates at seminary told me she was having an affair with another seminarian, even though both were married to someone else."

"What did you do?"

"I told her to end it and to confess it to her pastor."

"Did she?"

"She said she did, but I have wondered how she could be ordained after that. But you asked about me. I don't plan to embarrass either myself or this church by becoming involved in a romantic affair with the choir director or anyone else."

"What is your thought on adultery?"

I began to think that Walter might be fun to have around if I got the call to be the pastor. He's not afraid to ask me about what he wants to know. And should ask, I added to himself. "My thought is that I accept and agree with the denomination's policy or rule that single clergy are to remain celibate." I thought for a moment, wondered if I should add that this applies to heterosexuals and homosexuals? "By the way, that applies to straight and gay clergy. And so you don't have to ask, I'm straight."

"I was not going to ask," Walter said.

"I don't believe it is appropriate for single clergy to date members of his or her church, and I won't. I will not. But I do enjoy the company of women and will occasionally have what might be called a date, or at least a time together to do something enjoyable. Like dinner out, or a concert."

The rest of the meeting became safe. Shields, as committee chair, returned the conversation to his dossier and the questionnaire from the Synod. Decently and in order, as Lutherans sometimes say, time passed and I received the call and was installed as the pastor of St. John's Lutheran Church in September, 1987. In October, I helped organize the meeting with José Clímaco from Santa Cruz, El Salvador. That is when I met Bev and David,

○

Ten days after David left for Guatemala, Bev came to St. John's for a worship service. When I saw her come up the stairs into the Sanctuary, she reminded me of a lost puppy, searching for something familiar in a place she didn't know. Do I take in strays, I wondered? That is my job as a minister, I reminded myself. I could see she felt a little out of place.

"I'm Catholic," she said, after returning my greeting. "Is it okay if I just sit through the mass? Or worship?"

"Sure, but if you sit with Evelyn—tall woman with big glasses and a ponytail," I said, pointing, "just do what she does. She's nice to talk with, been to Salvador," I added, happy to see Bev nod gratefully.

At the last moment before the service began, I ducked into my office for a book I had been reading. When the time for the sermon came, I arranged my notes, looked out at the congregation. Bev seemed to be praying silently. I thought back to my first ever sermon and how nervous I was when I stood in the pulpit. When I looked out then, I happened to see a man with a broad grin, looking, I thought, right at me, nodding when I began to speak. I took encouragement from him and actually preached fairly well for a first time. I later learned he was looking at his girlfriend in the choir behind me.

I glanced out at the congregation and began to preach. I used the book to talk about a Jesuit, Padre Jon de Cortina, who lives in the north country of El Salvador. I said, "Quote. Padre Jon writes that we quote 'can go to El Salvador with a bit of morbid curiosity, to see poor, oppressed peoples who are unjustly dealt with on a national and international level, and the trip can be a good lesson. It can be instructive. On the other hand, if we visit or live in El Salvador with an open heart, a heart free of prejudices, and not feel we have the solutions to their problems in hand—if we simply wish to accompany the people of this land in their death and resurrection—the result will be an experience that transcends the physical experiences we encounter, to be transformed into an experience of life, of hope, of God.' Unquote. I normally don't read that much," I added when I stopped. "I believe that each one of us in this church today, here and now, can live with an open heart, a heart free of prejudices."

When the time came for the congregation to partake in communion, I held up the bulletin, pointed to and read aloud the statement that St. John's Lutheran Church offered the Lord's Supper to all baptized Christians who wish to participate. When I spoke the words of institution and held up the bread, then the wine, I thought that Lutherans and Catholics aren't that far apart on what they both believe communion to mean. And, unlike many Lutheran churches where the elders distribute the elements, I insist that the congregation come to the altar and receive the bread and wine on their knees. I watched Evelyn take Bev by the arm, encouraging her to come up with her.

After worship, I stood at the door to the sanctuary, shaking hands and speaking with each one in the congregation as they filed out. When Bev came up, I shook her hand, suggested she join the others downstairs for coffee. "You've come all this way. Have a cup with me."

Two

When I caught up with Bev downstairs after the worship service, she held her coffee cup in two hands like a chalice. She seemed so serious when she asked me why I didn't end the reading of the gospel with "The word of the Lord," or some special sentence the congregation could respond to. Then she told me my stole wasn't straight and reached up to pull it where she wanted it. "You fiddled with your ring during the sermon. Tell me, why do Lutherans call it a sermon instead of a homily?"

"Did you ever hear of the homily on the mount?" I replied, trying to be funny.

"So you think you're Jesus Christ?" she replied, quietly laughing at last.

Was she finding fault so she wouldn't have to say what was really on her mind? Am I even in her radar? I wondered.

"Anyway, I'd like to read that book you referred to."

"Stick around, and after I do my pastoral duties with a few more folks. I'd be happy to loan it to you. Then you'd have to come back again."

Later when I showed her the book, I told her that the author was a Presbyterian who had been on the denomination's 1986 Task Force on Central America. Bev wanted to know why a Catholic priest wrote a forward if the author was Presbyterian. I took the book from her, opened it. "It's part of having that open heart, like Padre Jon said, 'If we simply wish to accompany the people of this land in their death and resurrection. It will be an experience that transcends the physical experiences we encounter, to be transformed into an experience of life, of hope, of God.' I believe that. Has David been transformed? Has he written to you?"

"Yes. He's even used those words. Thank you. I think about him all the time. I also meant to thank you when you named him in the pastoral prayers."

"I do that every Sunday, even when you aren't here. How is he doing?"

"He's still at language school. In Antigua."

"I've been there, for the same reason. *Hablo Español.*" She gently took the book from me, began paging through. "I have an idea for you," I said. I put my hand on her arm. I was standing close enough to smell her perfume. I took my hand back, too quickly. Bev looked me in the eye, then down at her arm. "Actually," I said quickly before she could speak, "I have two ideas. Why don't you go to Guatemala? Spend a few days with David. Antigua is a great town. There's a café where they make the best chicken soup in the world."

"Chicken soup?"

"Right. With cilantro leaves that remind me of Central America. I'm trying to duplicate it here." I shrugged, adding, "I like to cook."

"I like chicken soup," Bev replied.

She didn't seem to be thinking about whatever was on her mind when she picked at me. Maybe she just misses her son.

"What's the other idea?"

"Dinner. Out. At a restaurant. Us." *Good Lord I hope I don't spoil things.* "I like being with you."

Bev looked away, stepped back. "Where would I stay in Guatemala if I went there?"

"With David or with a local family he finds for you. I see you're back to the first idea."

"Well I have to try the Antigua chicken soup so I'll know if yours is as good, like you say. Maybe you'll have a third idea someday and want to cook some for me."

◯

The thought of cooking for Bev stayed on my mind, a sort of floating feeling of niceness without any complications. Still, I decided a public place might be better for a first time together. The Saturday after she came to St. John's, I picked up Bev at her suburban home, drove back to Philadelphia to a restaurant near St. John's that featured Mexican food. I parked in the lot behind the restaurant, hurried to open the door for Bev. I resisted the urge to take her by the arm as we walked to the front entrance.

Neither of us had said much on the drive, other than polite comments on how the other looked so nice that evening. I dressed casually: open jacket over chinos, button-down shirt, no tie and no clerical collar. She wore a denim skirt and a hand-embroidered blouse she said David had sent her from Guatemala. I helped her with her chair, then settled at the restaurant table across from her.

"I say, you look nice, In fact, you look quite nice. Special." I looked at her, tracing her outline with my eyes, surprised at my boldness. I even enjoyed the sudden thought that I might, some day, do the same with my hands. *I am really attracted to her*, I thought, and began to understand the seriousness of my feelings for her. *It isn't that I just need a woman. But maybe I need this one?* I tried to dismiss the thought before I blushed, picking up my spoon, polishing it with my napkin, tapping it on the tablecloth.

"Thank you. I don't get many compliments." Bev arranged the
silverware and china, unfolded her napkin. We both looked at the menu
as silence seemed to separate us. Bev ordered a margarita and I ordered
a Corona. When the waiter brought the drinks, I pushed the lime
wedge into the bottle, put my thumb on the mouth of the bottle, turned
it upside down. The lime slowly drifted through the beer. "Mexican
tradition," I told her, clinking the bottle on her glass as she raised it to
offer a toast.

"To Mexico," she said. "and El Salvador." Her son was never far from
her thoughts.

"And Guatemala, where David continues to study *Español.*"

Bev cleared her throat, leaned forward, resting her elbows on the
table. "You are Lutheran. A minister."

"Right." *She talks about religion a lot. Jimmy said she had a strong faith. I
wish I had asked the priest if it was too strong.* "I am ordained by people who
are part of an unbroken chain of Christians who have had hands laid on,
in their ordinations, all the way back to St. Peter, or maybe James, the
brother of Jesus."

"This is impossible."

"Why?"

"I'm Catholic."

"Lutherans are reformed Catholics. And reforming."

"You're divorced."

"That's one thing we Lutherans have reformed."

Bev pushed her chair back, stood up, motioned to me to stay seated
when I started to rise, "Well, I like the fact that you have manners." She
stood in front of me, ignoring the other diners. I watched, also unaware
of others in the restaurant. "When David's father died, in Viet Nam,
I felt so alone, hurt so bad. After a while I dated. Some. No knight in
shining armor came along to rescue me, and my baby. Men don't seem to
get too interested in other people's children. Speech is done. I wanted to
say that." Bev sat back at her place at the table.

The waiter brought the food before I could think of a reply. I watched
her pick up her fork, gently, delicately, as though she didn't want to
disturb the rice that she eased into the refried beans. She mixed them,
lifted one over the other and stirred, and I imagined that she was testing
to see if we could mix well. I waited until she tasted them before I spoke.
"Bev, as far as your speech, well, I enjoy being with you. But I'm not
rushing into something. I know you have a strong faith and I wouldn't
change that. What if I go to mass with you and you can come to St.
John's whenever?" I just could not keep my eyes from looking into hers,

and she seemed to be returning the gaze, as though we only had eyes for each other. *All we needed is mood music*, I thought.

After a long moment, Bev shut her eyes, made balancing motions with her hands as if weighing her thoughts, or feelings, then held up her left hand. "On one hand, besides no longer wearing my dead-twenty-plus-years husband's ring, I enjoy being with you. I am glad you understand David's, and my interest in El Salvador. We probably like the same books or movies, mostly, and our friends would accept us. I almost said, 'as a couple.' Don't interrupt. On the other hand, I don't see how we could be more than friends. Well, what I mean is, I don't see how we can get past the religious issues."

"I pray we can." I felt frustration rising. I talk with people all the time who come to St. John's Church from other denominations. So often they learned their religion as a child, in Sunday school or, as most Catholics did, in a parochial grade school. I try to help them see that they are no longer children and should seek some adult understanding of their faith.

"I pray the 'Our Father" and you pray 'The Lord's Prayer' and we can't even agree on the name."

"The words are the same for both," I countered.

"We have the Eucharist, and you have communion."

"Same bread and wine."

"I'd be an adulterer if I married you." She frowned, I think at the thought of being an adulterer.

"Because I'm divorced? What if we lived together unmarried?"

"I'm serious." Bev opened her purse to get a tissue, drying the tear that ran down her cheek.

"Why don't you talk with Father Jimmy?"

"I did. He said the church, the Holy Roman Catholic Church, is clear about me marrying someone who is divorced. No can do. He also said that ultimately it is up to my conscience. He did say he would not refuse to give me the Eucharist at mass."

"Did he also tell you that the biggest difference between Catholics and Protestants is that Protestants pray directly to God, not through an intermediary. Have you prayed to God, Bev?"

The conversation seemed to drift after that, as if both of us had said more than we meant to say. I wondered why we were even talking about marriage and divorce. We ate, though Bev poked at the enchiladas, played with the mixed rice and beans on her plate, more focused on looking at me than what she had for a meal. For the first time, I began to imagine what it would be like to love her, physically, as well as being partners for life. But I still didn't understand why such a serious topic of conversation had dominated the meal. *I've never believed in love at first sight*, I thought, then forced that thought from my mind.

When the waiter cleared the table, I had an idea. I reached over to take her hand. "What is the absolute most important aspect—value, belief, practice, whatever—of the Catholic church for you? What is the most important part of you being Catholic?"

"Oh, I don't know." Bev shook her head as I named those I thought might be important to her. Virgin birth, or the assumption of Mary into heaven without dying, or the Pope's infallibility.

"What about not being allowed to use birth control?"

"Don't be funny, Charles."

"Abortion? Death penalty? Celibate clergy?"

"You're arguing, like a lawyer, not a minister."

"No, Bev, I am not. I also am not trying to convert you. I want to see if what you most treasure is something either that the Lutherans have also, or I agree with even if we don't have it."

"You aren't joking?" Bev asked. "Okay, I think the most important thing about being Catholic is the Eucharist."

"Why?" I said, grateful that she was finally taking me seriously.

"Because they can prevent you from taking it. They can issue a 'something' that says you can't come up to the altar and the priest can't give you the host. Excommunicate. I can't imagine being cut off from that."

"Is there a hearing first? Can you tell your side of the conflict? Can you appeal?"

"See, you think like a lawyer."

"No. No," I said, feeling frustrated. "I'm thinking like a human being created in God's image. In Protestant words, we sometimes ask, 'What would Jesus do?' when we have something we can't understand or don't like. Look, I know Catholics aren't suppose to have communion if they are in a state of sin, but why don't the priests withhold communion from all the married couples who don't have a kid every year? Everyone knows they are using birth control, including the priest."

"It's a matter of conscience, I suppose."

"Did you and David's father use birth control? I mean, not when you wanted to get pregnant."

"We did. I did. He knew, of course."

"Did you confess it?"

"No."

"Then why worry about my divorce? No, I don't mean 'worry' because, well, this is all about the hypothetical..."

"Like, if we continue to see each other?" She sat back in her chair, folded her napkin on her lap.

I did the same, as if to complete a separation.

"Charles, when I told you no one took an interest in me when I was raising David, that wasn't quite true. Once, no, really twice, I met someone who I thought might be a partner. Someone I might marry. The first guy was divorced. I asked him to have his marriage annulled." Bev squeezed her eyes shut. "Anyway he got mad, said I couldn't ask him to make bastards out of his two children. He stopped calling." Bev laughed, pointed to herself. "Dumb me. And the other one," she said, as though she was entertaining me now, "when we talked about the church's position on divorce, he actually got religion. He went back to his wife. They remarried."

"Well that did some good, for them at least." I played with an idea, of suggesting that since my own marriage had been a civil ceremony, maybe it didn't count in the Catholic church.

"I heard later that they divorced again. She didn't want him anymore." Bev sat back, as though satisfied with the result. "Neither did I, after all."

○

After dinner, I drove over to Fairmount Park, then along the Schuylkill River. I had no place in mind, just wandered through some nice parts of Center City Philadelphia. Bev and I had stopped talking, I supposed because we were thinking about what we had opened up at dinner. I went over the conversation in my mind, and didn't have it sorted out. Bev fiddled with the radio, pushing each of the buttons as if to see what music I liked. "Maybe we don't like the same music," she said. "Maybe you should take me home."

"At that suggestion, some men might ask, 'your home or mine?' but I know that isn't what you meant."

"You are so clever, asking the question without risking a refusal. Let me make something perfectly clear, as a former president is quoted as having said. I would appreciate it if you would take me to my home, and then you can go to your own house."

"Hey, don't get mad. I sure don't want you mad at me."

"You make me nervous sometimes. You are too clever with words, and I don't always know how to respond." Bev folded her arms across her chest. "Look at all we talked about tonight. Heavy stuff, for a first time out." When I slowed the car and looked at her, she added, "Okay, first date."

We had talked about heavy stuff, and I could not figure out why. I liked this woman, found her attractive but in some way so vulnerable. The image of the lost puppy came back to my mind. I wondered why we didn't talk more about David. I asked several times what he liked in school, if he had a girlfriend. It's like she doesn't want to share him with me. Or if she shares him, she may have to share herself? Or if she shares herself, she might have to share him?

"Bev, the Episcopalians have an answer to our problem."

"What is that? I've never met an Episcopalian."

"They use a book in their worship service called the *Book Of Common Prayer*, which, an Episcopal priest told me, is much different from a book of common beliefs. There are those in his church who are as Catholic as you are and others who are as Protestant as I am, or more so in both of our cases. They get along just fine with common prayer. Like I said, the words are the same in the Lord's Prayer and the Our Father."

"I like that. We can worship together, at your St. John's or my church, St. Giles." She didn't look convinced.

"Same God."

"I'm not coming to St. John's tomorrow," she announced.

"St. Giles and Father Jimmy?"

"Yes, as a matter of fact."

"When you see him, say 'hi' for me. Are you going to tell him we went out? Dated?"

"Using words again," she said, looking away.

We stayed silent as I drove the last few blocks to her house. I walked her up to her door, staying one step behind, deciding not to take her arm. "Bev, I really wanted this evening to end on a positive note. I really like being with you." When we reached the door, I stepped back. "When can I see you again?"

"I don't know. I have to work out this religion thing."

"I want to see you again." I leaned on the porch rail, no longer steady, not daring to touch her, even on the arm. I wanted to hug her and hold her.

"It isn't about what we want."

"Why not? It isn't like I'm asking you to go to bed with me. All I have said is that I like being with you. I haven't even tried to kiss you."

Bev stared at me, stepped back, then moved up, pulled herself against me, kissed me. "See," she said, hurrying to go inside. "I'll call you," she said, closing the door and snapping the lock.

○

When Bev shut the door and turned the lock, she hurried down the hall, not wanting to see or be seen when Charles went to his car. She didn't consciously think that if she saw him she might ask him to come in, but forced herself to damp down her feelings. She rubbed her lips, reminded herself she had kissed other men. She appreciated that he is different, smart like some lawyers she worked for. She thought Charles is nice, like Father Jimmy.

She went to David's room, put her hand on the collage he had made in high school of the 1980 assassinations in El Salvador. Turning from that horror, grimacing, a sob escaped from her throat, startling her. In her bedroom she stood at the small table at the wall opposite her bed as if standing before an altar, her place of honor for her son. She picked up the photo from her wedding, comparing herself then and now, comparing her husband to David, then to Charles. She no longer remembered the physical touch of her husband, or the feelings she had at the wedding. His death had carved a deep hole in her heart, so deep she never found anything to fill it back. At times she described the hole in her heart as being like a scrap heap, a land fill. All the rotten stuff went in.

She knew that her devotion to God had, over the years, helped her to replace each hurt feeling, each flood of tears, with reverence for God, for the Holy Family. In the early years, Bev made the stations of the cross her personal pilgrimage, reading, then memorizing the fourteen scenes where Jesus' road to death became her path to healing. "Woman, here is your son," she quoted from John's Gospel. She felt she had done the same thing. Jesus gave his mother to the disciple, and he took her home with him, after that. Where was Joseph? had been her early question. Did Joseph go off to do something patriotic? No. Only her husband did that. She had David, and now he's off to do the work of the church.

In time she forgave her husband, and while her memory of him didn't fade, the love did, unreturned, and the pain went with the separation from love and being loved.

She found Charles 'interesting,' and she believed he was right about religion. He showed a lot of respect for the Catholic views, and while he didn't exactly say that religion isn't about keeping people apart, just keeping them honest, she was sure he thinks that. She knew she didn't know if she was ready for him. Or for anybody.

○

I drove home from Bev's house in kind of a daze, half elated and fully
confused. This night I had no thoughts other than for Bev. Inside, I sat
for a long time in the leather chair in my library. Most of the time I talk
to myself as though God is listening in, hoping some of God's thoughts
might enlighten me. I realized that I can't let my thoughts about her,
about the two of us, crowd God out. I ran my hand over the creases in
the leather of the arm rest, tracing a path that went nowhere. Not in
circles and not back where I started. We started.

After a prayer for guidance, I reminded myself that people do have
relationships that are decent and proper. I glanced at my watch, and I
picked up the phone on the side table. I dialed Bev's number, listened to
the rings. When no one answered, I hung up. I burned the kiss into my
memory, trying to recall the smell of her hair, the touch of her hands on
my cheek. A week went by, and then Bev did call.

"Hi Charles," she said when I answered the phone. "I'm going
away. Far away." Before I could respond, Bev laughed. "I'm going to
Guatemala. Antigua. To see David. And taste some chicken soup."

"When you get back, I'll make you some even better." I fussed with
helping her get ready for the trip, gave her lists of what she should take
with her. When I took her to the airport, I felt the distance already,
sensed her need to be with her son. I dropped her at the door, didn't go
in, couldn't even mention chicken soup.

Three

When Bev arrived in Guatemala City, David met her at the airport and took her on a tour of the capital. She breathed the pollution of Guatemala City, was jostled on the crowded streets, besieged by vendors in the craft market, startled by the contrasting mix of indigenous and Latino dress, and became depressed by the obvious poverty. The ride down the steep hill to Antigua on an overcrowded bus frightened her, especially when David pointed out the big sign, *peligroso*, which he translated as 'dangerous' and began pointing out crosses along the side of the road marking where someone had died.

In Antigua, she stayed with a family who rented rooms to the many students at the language schools in town. Mother and son spent a day as tourists, with David serving as tour guide at a craft market, a silver mine, and a museum exhibiting what it claimed was an original oil painting of Christopher Columbus. David talked about his hopes for the work in El Salvador, and Bev talked about everything else to avoid thinking about the danger in a country engaged in a civil war. She even mentioned that she had gone to dinner with Charles.

"He's cool, Mom. He's been here to language school and he's been to El Salvador. Padre Rafael, who I'm going to work with, knows him. Charles is cool."

Bev sensed an approval from her son, though David quickly went back to talking about El Salvador. They entered an empty church that afternoon, the *Iglesia de San Francisco*, which dated back to the mid 1600s. They paused when David translated some of the notes pasted on a board at the entrance, slips of paper saying ¡Gracias! to the Lord for a new job, a healed relationship, a healthy baby.

When Bev sat on the front pew, resting her tired feet, David startled her by jumping on to the altar over the low, stone communion rail. Standing in the pulpit, he looked down at her. "Remember, Mom?" he asked. "We were together when it happened, watching TV, when the newscaster reported that Archbishop Romero had been shot while saying Mass in San Salvador."

"I remember." *How could I not?* she wondered. Bev could still picture the news photographs of the bloody, crumpled man lying on the altar steps of the small Chapel of Divine Providence, the bullet having torn into his chest just as he reached for the chalice for consecration. The wine, which she believes becomes the blood of Christ, mingled with Romero's blood.

"Do you also remember that I memorized the homily Romero preached the Sunday before he was murdered? Listen, I can recite it in Spanish now."

David's voice reverberated strongly, huskily, through the empty church, then rose to a passion-filled closing crescendo. When he concluded his Spanish rendition, he hurried excitedly to his mother's side. "I'll translate for you," he said, and delivered it again —this time in English— the fateful words Romero had aimed at the men of the army and in particular to the ranks of the Guardia Nacional, of the police, to those in the barracks. " 'No soldier is obliged to obey an order against the law of God. No one has to fulfill an immoral law. It is time to recover your consciences rather than the orders of sin.' " David took a deep breath, trying hard to do justice to the famous moment. "Picture it, Mom. The place is packed, overflowing, and the service is being broadcast live, not only in El Salvador, but in Costa Rica, Nicaragua, Venezuela and Brazil. There's a big delegation of U.S. clergy present. The applause is already building to a deafening pitch when Romero delivers that incredible finish: 'In the name of God, and in the name of this suffering people whose laments rise to heaven each day more tumultuous, I beg you, I ask you, I *order* you in the name of God: Stop the repression!' "

"My son," Bev said when he finished. "Always a little different."

"What do you mean?" David asked, not in the least concerned. His mother was smiling.

"Just that I'm very, very proud of you," Bev said, assuring him. "A lot of mothers have sons who memorize sports statistics. My boy's hero is a martyred priest."

○

Did I fanaticize about Bev while she was gone? Not in the sense that I imagined we made love, but I conceived of conversations we might have had. But didn't, of course.

"Am I being stubborn," I would have asked her, "honoring my promise to the church to remain celibate?"

She would reply with a sensible question. "What do you council the couples that come to you to marry them?"

"Depends on if they are already living together or not. I'm seeing a trend where most couples live together." I imagined saying that as a hint at what I tried to avoid thinking about.

"If they're not living together?" she would ask, putting emphasis on the living, as though she wouldn't think about it either. Or so I imagined.

"I suggest they wait," I would tell her. That ended more than one fantasy.

Another daydream variation was, "Are you being stubborn, using divorce as a reason not to let our relationship develop?"

She would shake her head to say no. "I don't like that word. Develop. Into a one night stand? Into marriage?"

None of these imagined conversations went anywhere in terms of helping me see what I should do, even a little. At home the day before she called, I sat in my library, not even glancing at the stack of books on the desk. So, I went to St. John's, knelt at the altar for one hour, prayed. I've said my understanding of prayer is complicated. In one hour of prayer, I didn't ask for anything. I also didn't hold anything back.

I read the Prayer of St. Francis that starts out "Make me a channel for your peace," and continually places others first, ahead of self, like "to be a comfort than to be comforted." An hour later I had not any better thought, so I placed her first, ahead of self. That sounded good, but I wondered, what if she wants a relationship? Or doesn't? I felt calmer, more ready to trust St. Francis than myself.

◯

At the airport, I walked slowly to the gate, checked the monitor half a dozen times, and wandered about, not able to sit. Bev flashed a brilliant smile that lit up her whole face when she saw me, seemed to bounce as she walked up to me. She dropped her carry-on bag, and pushed herself into me in a hug. I put my arms around her, held her tight. Neither of us seemed to want to separate. I spoke first. "I missed you, but, really, I hoped you had a great time. Of course, I wanted you here with me, too." I talk too much. "Did you have fun?"

"I did. David did a great job as tour guide. When he picked me up at the airport, we went on a bus filled with Guatemalans wearing that colorful clothing. When we came to a big hill that descended into Antigua, he translated 'Peligroso' as meaning dangerous. Then he pointed to all the crosses and flowers along the road, said they were crash sites. Oh, Charles, it's such a different world down there."

"Different and dangerous, not only on the highway," I said, finally separating but holding on to her arm. She couldn't get the words out fast enough and I had no chance to remind her that I'd been there too. I could picture the long, steep hill, and the crosses, remembered seeing bicyclists trying to climb it. "Welcome back," I said. I felt real gratitude for her safety. *Gringos* are mostly safe, especially with a young man like David. I picked up her carry-on, held her arm as we started to walk to the baggage claim area. *I'm in no hurry,* I thought, *and I sure liked that hug.* Walking slowly, I found it difficult to take my eyes off her. I had a loopy grin like a school boy. *She looks crazy too.*

After we put the luggage in the car and started the drive home, Bev put her hand on my shoulder. I felt the excitement of her touch surge through me. I even sighed out loud, and wished the feeling would never go away. I made every effort to keep my shoulder still as I drove her home.

Bev continued to talk excitedly about her time with David. It seemed like she wanted to describe every waking moment, needing to share what she saw and did with him. When we reached her house, I carried the suitcase in, hesitated in the living room, not wanting to just walk into her bedroom. At least, I told myself, I shouldn't. *I'm acting like a teenage kid.*

She saw my hesitation, and pointed, "The bedroom is down that hall. I'm going the other way. To wash my hands."

I stood waiting after I came back to the livingroom. When Bev came in, I waved to her. "Sit next to me," I said, as I sat on the couch.

Bev sat on the couch, but at the other end. "I think I'm too glad to see you," she said.

"I'm not too glad. Just very glad." I thought about what I had learned doing chaplaincy work in seminary. *I learned a lot about boundaries, and not kneeling at the bed of a woman in a hospital. At my office at church, I keep a window and a door open, even if it is just a crack during the most confidential work, because I understand the power of sexuality. We are, or I am, close to crossing those boundaries.*

"We should talk about us." She frowned. "Or am I assuming too much."

"No. I still remember the kiss, what, eighteen days ago? Seems like a lot longer than that."

"Our first kiss. I kissed you, and," she held up her hand as if in grade school asking to be called on, "you kissed back. Is that why I felt excited when you held my arm when we walked through the airport? I don't mean excited. Thrilled. Happy." She frowned, then grinned, then frowned again, flip flopping.

"There is an attraction between us. To be frank, it is sexual. In part," I said, "but it is a whole lot more than sex. I'm no bargain," I said, shrugging.

"I'm no bargain either," she said. "Or were you going to say that I'm not attractive?"

"Not at all, my beauty. What I mean is that there is something else that is happening and the sexual part is, well, more like mating than simply having a lust for each other. But sexual attraction is part of it. I said I'd be frank." I studied her, looking for a reaction as she sat, motionless, like a photograph of someone I once knew. I felt suddenly nervous, as though I had been taking advantage of her. For some reason I imagined talking with my guardian angel, a hold-over from my youth.

I didn't do anything.

But you want to.

No, I would never take advantage of her. Of anyone.

You are thinking about her. About what it would be like.

Nonsense.

You did. You are thinking about a relationship.

Nice word, that.

"Let me say this," I said, having made a decision. "I am attracted to you, in a hundred different ways."

"I know." She frowned. "It's mutual."

"Well I am enjoying the attraction and I don't want it to end, especially not the wrong way. I have to work through some things."

"I do too," she said, frowning again.

"Let's work through them together. Let's start by...." I let the words trail off. I didn't know where to start. A kiss or hug might start what I couldn't or maybe wouldn't stop. A cold shower would only lead to turning the hot water on and inviting her in to join me. I had no words. Talking about sex had spoiled the energy, put a different kind of tension between us. "I'll go."

"That's best," she said, no expression on her face. "We'll work it through. I think, maybe, it might be worth it. But not tonight."

I let myself out.

O

When he finished his language studies four months later in early March in Antigua, David Stevens went south to El Salvador to begin working with the Archdiocese in El Salvador's capital city. In Guatemala City, David found the international bus, took a window seat. The only *gringo* on the bus, he spoke Spanish to the others, some of whom from the highlands of Guatemala only spoke a Mayan dialect. Wearing jeans and a blue knit shirt, keeping his backpack close to him, the others on the bus stared at him, curious as to why a *gringo* would ride the bus.

After a while, the other passengers retreated into a patient waiting, and David leaned back to enjoy the panorama of mountains and volcanoes, lush valleys. Through the open window, fragrant smells from the vegetation were a stark contrast to the smell of garbage and bus fumes back in the capital. He watched workers drying coffee beans on the pavement near the plantations. He tried to keep track of the number of different indigenous cloth patterns he saw, having learned in Antigua that over 26 different and distinct Mayan cultures still existed in Guatemala.

After the bus crossed the border into El Salvador, and David had his passport stamped next to the visa he had obtained, he marveled at how the landscape stayed the same and the people looked so different. The constant presence of the military and armed check points also served as a reminder that he had entered a very different country. People back home assume that all Central American nations are the same, but David would learn that they are as different as New York, Alabama and Oregon.

David had learned the history. In the early 1700s, the natives in El Salvador had been pacified by forced conversion to the Christian faith by the Spanish and others who followed the Conquistadores. Wealthy families took title to large parts of the region and built haciendas. The church claimed to be saving souls, converting heathens, and the wealthy, who controlled the church through it's money, remained aloof and apart from the indigenous people. Rising in society through one's own merit could not happen in El Salvador. Faith was a tool, like any other.

By the 1890s the fields of the haciendas produced export crops, and only the difficult, higher soil remained for subsistence farming. In 1932, when 30,000 indigenous people were slaughtered in the massacre called *La Matanza*, the owners grabbed more of the land away from the peasants. Almost over night the indigenous dress disappeared, out of fear of another massacre, and Salvadorans became Latinos. The appearance of indigenous people vanished.

In the 1970s, the seeds of revolution that were planted by Marxists in the 1950s had flowered, though the conflict remained hidden. Fidel Castro's Cuban revolution spread into Central America, more so in Nicaragua. The oligarchy, or fourteen families, as the rulers of El Salvador were called, built up a military and police force with aid from the United States, claiming to fight Communism. The church, also against Communism, worked in tandem with the land owners and those who exported the coffee and other crops.

Peace Corp workers from the United States worked in the small cities and towns but they stayed out of the struggle for land reform. By 1978, the civil war had erupted, dividing every aspect of the country, including the church. The oligarchy owned most of the land, controlled the political structure, and had great influence over the church.

Revolutionaries joined together to form a coalition of left wing political ideologies, took up arms. Those who were in the church also took sides.

History told David only part of the picture of the land where he would serve. He knew that he would be entering into a revolution that included the church. Romero had tried to eliminate private baptisms for the wealthy, he had learned, believing that one enters into the church in community, not set apart from the poor. Authority struck some priests like a whip, lashing them into submission. Other priests took up a gun to join with those who resisted those in power, seeking change for their own benefit.

Though David tried to insure his mother that he would be safe working for the archdiocese, he had no illusions that anything could make him safe. No matter what he did, one side or the other would see it with their own ideology. He prayed, and many of his prayers were conversations with God, for the opportunity to make a difference. Romero's phrase, "Everybody can do something" came to him as a driving motive. Poverty and injustice exists all over the globe, he knew, and his choice was to live and work with the people of El Salvador." Romero had called him. More than once David repeated what Romero had said about his own life. "If they kill me, I will rise up in the people of El Salvador." David claimed to be one of those people.

Eventually David's bus descended the last mountain and entered into the capital, San Salvador. David noted the even greater presence of the military. He also saw the poverty, especially in the city itself. Cardboard boxes that once held refrigerators and other appliances for the wealthy became shanties. Rather than being depressed, David felt affirmed in his belief that he had a call, to help those who were oppressed.

From the bus terminal, David took a taxi, one of the hundreds of yellow painted Datsun B210s, still running after serving their time in the United States, then exported to Central America. He arrived at the offices of the Archdiocese of San Salvador. David could think of little except beginning his work with the poor. He would make a difference, he prayed. David also met Padre Rafael Anaya Chávez, who would be his mentor in working with the poor and the displaced.

O

All that time while David improved his Spanish, Bev and I didn't work it through. She came to St. John's a few times, whenever we had a program on El Salvador, and once to worship. I went to Mass at St. Giles once, spent more time talking with Father Jimmy than I did with Bev. I understood, without saying so, that she didn't want my input.

In March, before David settled into his apartment in San Salvador, he called his mother from the Archbishop's office to let her know where he was and how she could get in touch with him, at least indirectly. Bev then called me, told me who David would start working with. She said she already knew about my knowing Padre Rafael when I told her I knew the priest who would be supervising her son's work. So, she and David talked about me.

I invited her to go out for dinner, promised to tell her some of what I knew about Padre Rafael Anaya Chávez, who is a revolutionary priest, though he himself is nonviolent. We went back to the Mexican restaurant where we had our first date as she called it, but we took separate cars.

○

I had met the Salvadoran priest, in 1986, on my fourth trip, at a Catholic church unofficially named 'San Oscar' after Monsignor Oscar Romero. The two of us went for a walk, talking ever so guardedly about the role of the church and our duties as clergy to their flocks. I explained the Lutheran polity, of the Synod Council, made up of clergy and lay people in equal balance, serving with the bishop. Rafael told me about the base Christian Communities, where Liberation Theology was used to cope with the conditions of the civil war.

We had come about four blocks from San Oscar, the church where Rafael stayed when in the capital, A boy, no more than nine or ten came up, asked if he could shine our shoes. I had my running shoes on, but Rafael agreed. We kept silent now, because one never knows who sells information, even young boys. The rhythmic snap of the shoe shine rag sounded efficient in the hands of the shoeshine boy. In front of the priest, a bougainvillea vine bloomed scarlet, rain drops on the trees glistened in the sun. A mixture of burning garbage and open flowing sewer dominated the air.

I watched Rafael say a prayer out loud for the young boy shining his shoes, moving his own head just a bit with the rhythm of the strokes of the brush, then he looked away, still busy with his own thoughts. The bad smell was gone, replaced by the fragrance of the polish. Is it so easy to make things seem better when they are not, I wondered. Rafael smoothed his hands over his faded tan slacks. "I will be able to wear black again," he said, "when I no longer have to deny who I am by how I dress. At least I can keep my shoes shined."

We talked more on that visit, and kept in touch by letters hand carried back and forth by others working in the solidarity movement.

Someone going to any city would simply mail the letter once they cleared immigration and customs in the U.S.

○

At dinner I reminded Bev that David had obtained a stipend position with the Archdiocese offices in the capital with Rafael's help. The Catholic Archbishop, Monsignor Arturo Rivera y Damas, was no Romero but he did let a lot of the work Romero started continue and David had now become part of the organization that distributed relief supplies. She knew that, of course. She talked about how David's job would be helping to deliver food and desperately needed medical supplies. When his Spanish improved more, he would assist in translating and providing background lectures to visiting delegations from the United States and Canada.

After dinner we walked to the parking lot. I took her hand in mine, felt the gentle squeeze in reply. We stood at her car, still holding hands.

"Father Jimmy talked to me after you left St. Giles."

I thought about asking if it was in Confession, but knew better. I hoped that what she had on her mind wouldn't be bad news.

"He asked about you. And our relationship."

"We don't have one," I said. "But we should." I surprised both of us by saying that, I think. "We should at least talk about it."

"I know. Do you think God is doing this to us? Or is the devil tempting me? I wish I knew. Father Jimmy isn't against us seeing each other."

"What we do together would not be his business," I said, feeling anger at how religion had gotten in our way, not brought comfort. I thought of King David, in Israel, when he took another man's wife. I wasn't trying to do that. "There is so much evil in the world, and we don't need this. Why don't you ask David," I said, desperate to find an ally.

"I couldn't do that."

"Bev, look at us. We're standing in a parking lot, talking about something that hasn't happened, may never happen."

"Charles, the elephant in the room, or this parking lot, is right there in front of you."

"You're in front of me, Bev."

"Right. Last time you said it. We're attracted to each other and we're both aware of what it would lead to if we saw each other. It almost did."

"It probably should have. At least we could deal with it. Let's go somewhere to talk. Just talk. Better yet, let's start dating, getting to know each other. See a movie. Let's see if we can work out our relationship together."

"What kind of movies do you like?"

I wondered if she was considering a date with me. I said, "Adventure, romance."

"Did you see *Out of Africa?*"

"Yeah, two years ago when it came out." I rubbed my chin, chuckled.

"What's funny?" She was smiling.

"I don't know," I said, stalling. "I just remember when Robert Redford's character says to Meryl Streep's character, 'We know how we feel, so lets lie down and get on with it.' Of course they didn't get on with it, at least not in that scene."

"Are you suggesting we know how we feel?"

It looked like she remembered the scene. "That would presume too much."

"Presume what? That I'd lie down with you?"

"No, that would presume I know how you feel. I'm barely able to sort out how I feel. About us."

"Do you know how you feel about me?" Bev reached out for my hand, rubbed her thumb on my fingers. When I didn't speak, she pulled her hand away. "You've done it again. You have us talking about going to bed without asking me. You're trying to get me to ask."

"Would you go to bed with me?" I stepped back as I spoke, not sure of her reaction. "If I asked, that is."

"There you are again. No. Not if you ask. I want to go home."

"Next week, at St. John's. It's Romero's eighth anniversary of his death. I'm making chicken soup. Come. It starts at 7 P.M. Then we'll talk. In my office."

"Maybe. Oh, yes."

"I have a surprise for you."

"What?" she said, taking her hand from mine.

"I'm thinking of taking a delegation to El Salvador. I want you to join us."

"And see David?"

"Yes," I said as she hugged me. I held her, then helped her into her car.

Four

Padre Rafael received his Holy Orders in 1975, ordained by Archbishop Oscar Romero. Rafael said his first mass in the Chapel on the grounds of the Divine Providence Hospital where Romero lived in a small apartment.

After he began his clerical duties, Rafael had considered advanced study, perhaps traveling to Rome, even having an audience with the Pope, at least John XXIII. But the young priest never did. By 1979 the war imposed so much stress on his flock, he put off his own dreams and lived for those who called him Padre. When Romero was assassinated in 1980, in the same sanctuary where Rafael had been ordained, all that remained for the young priest was to follow his calling, serving the people of El Salvador.

Rafael worked hard, keeping in touch with the refugees who fled the conflict, learning the new theology of Liberation from the Jesuits and, while he was alive, from Monsignor Romero. Rafael expected God to exercise a preferential option for the poor, reading in the Bible of how God alleviated the suffering His people endured. He would pray often for the patience to wait for God to help the people of El Salvador, and remind himself that Monsignor Romero had personally told him that he, Padre Rafael, was God's agent for peace.

He would do his best to help David join the ranks of those who sought to do God's work. After he helped David get settled in San Salvador, the two of them joined a delegation going into the countryside to bring food and supplies to a repatriation camp.

○

As he waited, the old man, Alejandro, looked up at the sun, willing it to cross the horizon and bring the time for his son Rafael to arrive. A delegation normally gave him pleasure, and he enjoyed watching the gringos squirm as they began to see the reality of extreme poverty. Finally the sound of a truck straining up the road to the center of the community interrupted Alejandro's thoughts about the past. He felt a tinge of anxiety, and hope that his son, the priest, would not argue with his daughter, the guerilla. Vitalina was bolder now, meeting with the delegations that came to visit. Slowly he stood up, stretched his legs to get the circulation going.

Moving carefully, trying to work out the stiffness in his back and legs, Alejandro began to walk to the center of the community. By the time he reached the center, he could see the driver, Antonio, skillfully navigating the last half mile of the twisting, descending road, crossing a stream, past women bathing and washing clothes. The delegation had arrived at the village of *Santa Cruz*, with its 500 inhabitants.

Smiling boys and girls ran alongside the truck. Alejandro could see his friend, Ruben, point out the school and the offices of the Directiva, the governing body of the community that Ruben led. Two excited youths directed Antonio to park in the middle of the village. People shouted greetings, eager to talk to Ruben and Antonio, to hear the latest news from the outside. Children swarmed over the truck, unloading it and moving supplies into storerooms. Finally Alejandro waved to his son, Padre Rafael, when he and a young gringo got off the truck bed.

Amid the confusion of the arrival, a woman from the community divided the delegation into small groups to be taken to lunch, then on a tour. Later the Directiva would meet with them. In Santa Cruz, hospitality came first. The visitors must take time to share a meal. Alejandro motioned for Padre Rafael to come forward. The old man greeted his son, shook his hand, grinned and offered his hand to the young man from the United States. Rafael introduced his father to David Stevens, adding that David had just joined him to work with the Archdiocese in San Salvador.

Rafael and David walked with Alejandro silently to a house near the center of the village. The priest spoke quietly as they walked. "Papa," Rafael said, "we barely escaped a patrol. It is getting more dangerous all the time."

"Humph," the old man said as they reached a building. "Tell your sister to protect you." He waved his hand to dismiss the thought. "I want you to meet Ricardo and Lucinda," he added, introducing them to a man and woman standing by the door. "They've made us some lunch. It's expected that you eat," he added for David's benefit.

David tried to take in everything he saw. So many things were new to him. He wondered why no one said anything about the women bathing, barely clothed, down by the stream as they drove in. He had expected much more modesty.

The house nested neatly in a grove of second growth woods forming a crescent behind its back. Stumps and a few low spots showed where other trees had been removed when Ricardo built the house. The walls were made of woven poles, branches and sticks, with a door centered in the front wall. The thatched roof extended out over the front, covering a porch where a small table fabricated from limbs sat on one end. A blanket hung down, blocking the door and shielding the inside. Smoke from the kitchen a few paces away from the house itself spiraled upward to low clouds that still filled the sky, keeping the temperature down and the humidity up.

Lucinda bowed politely, then went to the kitchen, bringing back plates of tortillas, beans and a small piece of fresh cheese for each of them as they sat on the porch. The seats, sturdier than David had expected, had been made of branches tied with rope.

The bench creaked as David leaned back. He pushed the beans on his plate with a tortilla, and gratefully accepted another piece of fresh cheese. They ate, with Ricardo talking occasionally about crops and store rooms, his face briefly showing pride. Lucinda said nothing, even when she served the food.

O

Santa Cruz lies hidden, nestled among the steep terrain of the mountains and volcanoes. Paths twist serpentinely amid the high and low ground. Corn is planted on every hillside, growing skyward even when the ground slopes arduously. Young men growing up in the Salvadoran countryside learn how to plant corn on every part of the land, no matter how steep, testing severely their powers of endurance, for to slip is to face certain injury, even death. But when these young men are drafted into the army, they forget how to walk the sloping sides, remembering only that they might fall. The campesino doesn't laugh at the soldier who can no longer tend the crops; the combatant, in turn, does not destroy the corn in the field.

After lunch, Rafael took David for a walk. "We're going to see where the corn is grown," he said, implying much more. On the trip from San Salvador, the two of them had talked about David's fatherless childhood. When David mentioned Pastor Charles, Rafael told of how he had appreciated the time Charles spent with him when he had come on a delegation. David laughed and told Rafael how, in Antigua, his Mom said she worried about the fact that he's Protestant and she's Catholic.

"Maybe in name," Rafael had said, "but I can tell you that Charles and I are closer theologically than the churches we're ordained in."

"I wish my Mom could understand that. Even Father Jimmy sees what Charles is like."

Now the talk would be about El Salvador. The path from the community extended out for several miles along the tops of the hills, turning one way then another way, following the contours. "Visitors are expected to inspect the crops," Rafael said. "Come with me."

As the two men walked along, still very curious, David paused to look inside a storeroom. One pallet, partly loaded with seed sacks, sat near rolls of fence wire that the delegation had just brought. Rice and beans were stored in sacks along the back. "This is a two-week supply," Rafael said. "They are lucky to have this. The army usually confiscates food, claiming it's for the guerrillas."

The path dipped into a small hollow where pigs were kept in crude pens. "Why do some pigs run free while others are penned up?" David asked.

"The ones that run free are scavengers and belong to the community." Rafael pointed to one pen with two pigs. "Those are my father's. We have some things we own, some are for everyone."

"So you pen up what is yours?" David said, as though he had tricked Rafael.

"We are responsible to feed what is ours," Rafael answered. The priest made the sign of the cross. "You will learn not to be so judgmental if you want to survive down here."

They left the hollow, climbed a short rise and began again on a ridge. The way got steeper and narrower, evolving into a single pathway, sides falling off sharply. Corn grew in rows even on terrain too steep for David to imagine planting on it. When he and Rafael reached a ceiba tree, massive yet hanging precariously on the peak of a hill, he saw a woman sitting in the shade. Dressed in black military fatigues, she sat beside a tattered bag and an AK-47 rifle.

She introduced herself as Vitalina, not giving her last name. She had a strong, clear face with intense, piercing eyes. She nodded as Rafael and David reached the shade of the tree. Rafael passed a canteen of water to her.

"The sun is still hot," Vitalina said as a greeting. "It is nice to be able to sit under a ceiba tree. *Gringo*, do you know that the fibers around the seeds of this tree are silky. My people use them for stuffing pillows."

Rafael laughed. "There is little shade in our reality, Vitalina," and no pillows," he said. "Now that we have come back to our village, the sun makes our work hard, but it also makes the crops grow." Rafael sat to one side, on the edge of the shade. "I'm glad you could come. David is from Pennsylvania. He wants to talk to someone who will tell him about the conflict from the FMLN's point of view." Turning to David, he said, "This is your chance. Vitalina is a soldier, a muchacha, a guerrilla."

"You are another finder-of-facts from the churches in North America?" she asked.

"He's my friend, Vitalina."

Vitalina shook a finger at the two men. "I watched you both come up the hill along the path, talking and pointing, like two brothers going into the field. Do you remember the Bible story of two brothers in a field? Cain and Abel?" Vitalina laughed, and reached over to slap Rafael's knee. "You are nonviolent, of course, and will be even if it kills you. Am I right, Rafael?"

"I have to be. It is the only way."

"It is not the only way I have seen in this country," David said. "There are some men who are taking another way."

"Why do you want to meet some of those men?" Vitalina said. "How about a woman? There are many women in the mountains, also with guns. I'm a soldier. I carry a gun. The army kills everyone: women, children, grandmothers. I shoot back."

"Vitalina," Rafael said, "David has come to work in the Archdiocese, for the people of El Salvador. That's why he wanted to talk to you."

Vitalina turned to David. "You are young, for a gringo here. But not young for those I fight with. And against. She pointed to Rafael. "But, Rafael and I have been arguing about nonviolence for a long time. He's right, you see, but I need a gun for courage. I can't trust God. Still, Rafael is alive, even after being captured twice."

David nodded, happy to be part of the banter between the Salvadorans. He studied the gun Vitalina had set aside, but did not dare to even touch it.

"Vitalina, tell David about the mountains. I've already told him about my being captured and the telegrams and calls the internationals made. They saved my life, and they did it by voices, not with guns. Vitalina, tell us both how shooting will bring peace."

Vitalina pointed to the sky. "The pilot prays when he gets in the airplane to drop bombs. The army says it could win the war if they ignored just a few more human rights."

"Yes, Vitalina," Rafael said, "and the FMLN says it will get the support of the people in the final offensive. Both sides think they can win simply with greater violence."

"Rafael," David said. "Sometimes what we think are simple solutions turn out not to be solutions at all." He had heard the arguments for war, for peace, and agreed with the priest. Violence is no solution, he believed.

"Must it be complicated?" Rafael said.

"That isn't the choice," Vitalina said. "It's not easy versus complex. Real peace would mean real change, like land reform, honest wages and medical care for everyone —not just the rich. No more shopping trips to Miami on the weekend for the rich while people starve at home. Here in El Salvador, the change must be great."

"I agree," Rafael said. "When we challenge the ones who capture men and women and they become disappeared, never seen again, we echo what God said to Cain. We are asking, 'What have you done?' and sometimes we ask soon enough to prevent death. Sometimes not." Rafael hesitated. "We priests say God is in the poor. We say, everywhere you look in the Bible, God is proclaiming that there should be justice. 'Where is your brother?' God said to Cain. We ask about our sister, our mother and father? Where are our children?'"

David shifted on the hard soil. "There may be a God saying there should be justice, but God isn't going to bring the dead back."

"Their blood cries out," Rafael answered, "just like from Monsignor Romero and all the others who have been killed."

"So you say, Rafael," Vitalina said. "God sees, and the blood cries out to God, but nothing changes."

"The ones who murder must change," Rafael replied, "not because of more guns on the other side, not because of telegrams, and not because military aid might be cut off. People who persecute others must repent, change their lives. What they do is wrong."

"Rafael," David said, "there is homicide everywhere. For that matter, I am reminded that we are approaching 500 years since Columbus arrived and the conquest began."

"David, have you been to Tikal? In Guatemala?" Vitalina asked, then went on when he nodded that he had been there. "It's a thousand years old and there were human sacrifices back then."

Rafael interrupted her. "Listen to me," he said. "It isn't the most popular way to see God, but the church has told us we must not kill. We have talked about it and prayed and studied. I believe that Cain would have been punished for murdering his brother Abel, by God even, if God would have us take the life of anyone. The killing has to stop."

Suddenly, as Rafael spoke, the sound of airplanes filled the air, followed by the beat of helicopter blades.

"Get down," Vitalina said. "We're being attacked by the military. In spite of what we think about God, more innocent people are about to die."

○

The planes circled, firing machine gun bursts near the target, then into the village's perimeter. When the first sound of the firing began, Rafael grabbed David and pulled him down the slope, away from the ceiba tree. "Stay low," Vitalina said. "If they see us out here, they will have a target to practice on. Stay down. You can inspect the damage later."

David did as told, listening to rather than observing the attack. He kept checking his watch, cursing how minutes, even seconds, seemed like hours. Finally, the shooting stopped. The planes circled one last time and flew off, heading back toward San Salvador.

David jumped up. "I need to get to the village. To see the people. I never thought...."

"You must be careful going back." Vitalina inched her way up to look. "Rafael! You can't be caught out here. Soldiers are coming to search. Find a place and pull some debris over you. Take a nap," she joked. "Hide. I must go."

David leaned forward, seeing a double column of soldiers marching toward the village, entering each house on their way.

Rafael slipped over the side of the hill, working toward the village, holding on to corn stalks.

Vitalina began to run, bent low, on the path away from the village.

"Vitalina!" David shouted.

"What?" She paused, looked back.

"I want to talk to you again.

"I'll be back."

David watched her disappear into the corn stalks.

"David," Rafael said from his hiding place. "You will be safe going back. Go. Tell them nothing, but that your delegation had safe conduct passes. Ruben has them."

"What about you?"

"Fear not. I am going to spend a few hours with my sister. Did I tell you Vitalina is my sister?"

"Padre."

"It's fine. Go back. Tell my father, Alejandro, that we are safe."

O

Even as David started back, two A-37 dragonfly airplanes descended over *Santa Cruz*. They fired rockets directly into the community. Four screaming explosions from fragmentation bombs marched like stones skipping on water toward the wall of the old church where many of the people had huddled. Shrapnel and rock flew from the smoking wall. A path later measured at 16 meters wide and eighty meters long lacerated the earth. Trees were felled and holes blown in the ground. Rocket shards killed a man from the village who had been holding his 2-year old daughter. The child and three others died with him. Metal fragments embedded pieces of their bodies in the wall.

A trail of destruction led from the direction of attack straight to the one wall of the old church. Machine gun fire had also ripped through the zinc roofs and wooden sides of nearby houses, killing and wounding those who chanced to be in the path. When the deafening sounds of gunfire and bombing had stopped, a helicopter beat down on the village like a metronome, accompanied by the fading sound of A-37 Dragonfly airplanes.

By the time David reached the community, the cadence of lockstep marching troops grew louder—a background to the crying children and the screams of those who had been shot or had seen their closest loved ones destroyed. Gingerly at first, until they saw the soldiers were not attacking, then in a rush to help others, the villagers sought out those who most needed them. Initially, the soldiers would not let the villagers and church workers care for the wounded, who numbered seventeen. Most of these had been hit by bullets or fragments from the rockets, and needed skilled medical help. Leaders of the community began to protest, insisting the wounded be given medical aid.

The screams of the injured and outraged reached a crescendo. Amid much shouting, an older nun who worked and lived in the village applied a tourniquet to a woman whose arm had been shattered, then loaded her into a jeep. As she started to drive out of the village, soldiers shouted for her to stop. Several raised their rifles, waiting for an order to shoot. Women swarmed in front of the men with the guns, placing themselves to obstruct their line of fire at the jeep as it drove off. Others began shouting, "Come look at our wounded. See what you have done." The officer in charge hesitated, knowing he would have to kill everyone in the village if he ordered his men to shoot. His orders were to search, not destroy, and the jeep soon drove out of sight as his men awaited his order. "Let them go," he said, more concerned with what his superiors would say than with the safety of the village.

As the soldiers lowered their weapons, David found some of the women in the delegation who were with the mother of two slain children. "Are you all right,?" David asked them.

"Don't worry about me," one said. "These women need help."

David walked over to a bench that had been overturned during the raid, pulling it upright. His hand shook as he traced his finger over the gash where a bullet had gone though. He sat on the bench, staring blankly.

◯

The older nun came back twice with the jeep to drive more of the wounded for medical attention. On her first return, taking the delegation nuns with her for help at the clinic, she told the delegation that the soldiers had returned to their base. The second time the sister came back, she gave Alejandro a message to pass on to *Señor* David. The note, written on a scrap of newspaper came from Vitalina, and read, "In two days, go to the bar at the Hotel Alemeda at noon. Someone will offer you a beer."

David destroyed the note he got from the nun, thinking that, at least for now, he'd have to learn to be clandestine, like Padre Rafael. Then he found the priest had come back to work with others in the community, already doing repairs. David joined them at work. Physical labor, sweating and silence, made the time pass. He lent muscle to pull bullet-chewed boards off shacks damaged by machine gun fire, and caught his hand on a sliver. "Just what I need," he said, watching the blood flow from the tear in his flesh.

"There's blood everywhere in this hell-hole nation." Rafael paused, holding a plank while a man named Fidencio nailed it in place. "Sometimes, like now, I despair." Fidencio just pushed his straw hat back and hit the nails harder. Older than the priest, he had known him as a child and knew what he really thought about killing. Fidencio liked Vitalina's approach better.

David felt sadness at the thought. "Despair?"

"I don't know. Maybe my faith is weak?" The priest appeared to wilt.

"It might be you who gets hurt," Fidencio said.

"I hear about non-violence from the priests," David said, "and from many of the others. Do any of you really understand it?" He continued to hand boards up to Fidencio, mixing words and deeds, trying to cope with actually being so close to death and destruction.

"Meaning? said Rafael."

"Do you, Padre?" Fidencio echoed.

"OK, then," David said. "Non-violence is a response to violence. Bad things like not having enough food while the rich spend their money on toys in Miami or a veterinarian caring for the landowner's dogs while a child dies, needing a doctor. Aren't we talking about systemic violence as well as specific acts like this bombing?" David frowned, hearing himself spout the expected.

"What do you propose?" Fidencio asked, not expecting any practical answer from this newcomer.

David wondered if he should even speak in the face of all this destruction. "Many priests here say it's oppression" frowning again at the expected language. "Not just Padre Rafael. Mandela in South Africa calls it racism. Martin Luther King, Jr. preached non-violence and it killed him. The people of El Salvador are facing first-class terror, from death squads killing people and the military bombing today."

"David," Rafael said, cautiously, "if we respond to that violence with non-violence, we might be killed."

"I understand that is a possibility, but . . ."

"Do you really, David? It's the only way I can picture it ending."

"Are you saying you're ready to die, Padre?" Fidencio stepped back, hands on his hips.

"That's something I haven't figured out. More to the point, I'm wondering if I'm ready to kill? My sister does. It won't solve the problem. Killing never does, and I know that. But it's a whole lot more appealing right now than dying."

"What are you going to do?" David asked for both of them.

"Finish fixing this house. You can help if you're careful of the splinters. There's blood enough here."

◯

Two days later, back in San Salvador, David left his apartment and met up with Padre Rafael. At noon they planned to go to the Alemeda Hotel. Someone was to offer to buy David a beer. As they walked, the priest noticed a white Jeep Cherokee slow, pull to the curb near them. The blackened windows kept them from seeing who was in the truck. The passenger window came down. "God! No!" David screamed and pushed the priest aside. The bullet from the truck slammed into David's chest, killing him instantly.

A young man, Saul Flores, saw the shooting, then called the police.

Part II
Not Coriander

Five

When I finally went to bed, still unable to comprehend that David had died, I tossed most of the night. Every time I shut my eyes, I imagined Bev sitting so still, almost like a statue. I knew she would be crying, but I couldn't picture that. I had no idea how to comprehend the pain she felt. David was her whole life.

I woke the next morning and tried to put David's funeral out of my mind. Tried. All I could think of was standing at the coffin in a panic. I did the same thing I criticize other clergy of doing, trying to find magic words that would make it seem okay. There aren't magic words at a time like this and I would be careful not to try. I didn't even know when David's body would be sent back to Pennsylvania, or if Bev would have a public funeral. Father Jimmy would do a good job. Funerals and memorial services were what I use to measure the ministry of clergy. If they could do that well, the other things would take care of themselves.

That David would die doing the work of the church bothered me a lot, not because I knew David, though that did make it very personal, but because it meant that the violence was worsening. And because I could feel Bev's pain, if only partially. I rubbed my face with both hands, trying to erase the images of death I had seen in El Salvador. The only advantage the poor had was the solidarity of the North Americans, and if they were killed, it wouldn't be long and the movement would die. All the time I tell people about a three-legged stool, of the guerillas who fought in the mountains, and the church of liberation theology, mostly the Jesuits and some progressive parish priest since Romero was killed, and solidarity support from internationals like David. Now, for me at least for a while, the stool was broken. I don't even know if I can go to El Salvador on the delegation next month. Facing a place where church people were killed had become personal now.

I dialed Bev's phone number several times before I got through, a sign others were calling. A busy signal was better than no answer. I didn't recognize the voice when a man answered. He asked me who I was, why I was calling, then told me Bev couldn't possibly want to talk to someone connected with the solidarity movement. The line went dead. Dazed, I retreated to my library feeling a new sense of loss. I slumped in the leather chair, put my feet up on the ottoman. Moments later the telephone rang.

"Charles," Bev said, "I heard what my father said. It isn't true. God it isn't true. I can't reject what David loved."

"Can I come over? Can I do anything to help?"

"Father Jimmy is coming over tomorrow around 2 o'clock. Why don't you come then, too. But don't expect me to make any sense."

"I know. Or I think I know only a hint of what you are feeling. I am so terribly sorry for what happened."

"So am I," she said, then I heard her tell her father to relax and let her finish the call. "I have a question," she said when she came back on the line. "Should I go to the airport when David arrives? I mean, his body…" I could hear her sob, then take a deep breath. "No one seems to think it is a good idea. The embassy has shipped him home. I guess they're good at that. My father says I should wait for the undertaker to finish. He says I should be getting ready for the funeral."

"What I know is that you should do what you think is right, not what others want you to do. Don't regret not doing what you feel in your heart you must do. Maybe you should just talk to the undertaker. I could take you."

"No. Yes. I'll do that. My parents can take me. I'll call the funeral home now. I gotta go. Come over tomorrow afternoon."

○

At the appointed time, I pulled my red Dodge to the curb behind Father Jimmy's black Volkswagen and another car I assumed belonged to her parents. I let the motor continue to run while I listened to the end of the newscast on the radio. *David is no longer news.* I looked at the two story white house in Suburban Clifton Heights. The shutters had been painted dark green last year. I remembered Bev telling me about her painting adventures when I saw her at a meeting at Father Jimmy's church. Her church, too. I caught sight of an older man along the side of the house, raking leaves from last fall. *Her father?*

Bev bought the house almost eleven years ago when she wanted David to have the chance to go to a better high school than the one near her apartment in Philadelphia. Her commute to center city took about the same amount of time, and she enjoyed the neighborhood. When David went to college, living on campus at Saint Joseph's University even though the home was only ten miles away, Bev cut the grass and shoveled the snow. She had a flair for decorating and often had projects laid out, works in progress she called them. I shut off the motor. Thinking about her life before David's death made no sense any more. "Forever different," I muttered as I got out of the car.

I took my time getting to the front door, not certain of what I would say. I wore my cleric collar and a herringbone sport coat. *I know enough about grief not to say the wrong things, like how God has a plan. God doesn't.*

God didn't pull the trigger. And God didn't need David more than Bev did. I didn't know what I would say, however. *I'm not her pastor.*

○

Inside Bev's house, Father Jimmy had seen Charles pull up, watched him pause, then take his time coming to the house. "Reverend Charles is here," he said to Bev. "I'll get the door." Bev didn't respond, just continued to sit in the rocker by the fireplace, facing the door but not looking up. "I can't stay long," the priest added at the front door.

"How is she?" Charles said quietly when he saw Jimmy.

"As good as we could expect," the priest answered, pointing to the livingroom. "She saw her son late yesterday at the funeral home. Just after they took him out of the body bag. Before they embalmed him." Jimmy seemed upset as we walked over to Bev. She looked up, then waved for us to sit. We both chose the couch that faced Bev's rocker. She had a rosary in her hands, but just played with the beads.

Bev's mother and father came into the room, avoided looking at either of us. "We're going for groceries," her father said. "Will you be alright?"

"I'll be fine," Bev said. "I'll be just fine. They're going to tell me why God let David die and then I'll be just fine." Her parents left without saying anything, still not looking at us.

"Bev," Jimmy said, "we don't know why God let David die."

I cleared my throat, then said, "Father Jimmy and I don't totally agree on this but I don't think God had anything to do with David's murder. An evil person did."

Bev leaned forward, putting the rosary on the table beside her. "I've already told Father Jimmy I want to find this evil person and make him pay. And pay."

I leaned back on the couch, off balance by her fire.

"You have to bury your son first," Father Jimmy said, standing. "I'm going to the church to get ready. The viewing begins in two hours. You will want to get there early, too. Your parents can bring you?"

"I'll be there, Father. Right now I just want to sit, and try to get myself under control."

"You'll do fine, my dear," the priest said, then he blessed her and let himself out.

For a while we sat silently, each lost in thoughts or emotions. I know I struggled with one unspoken question after another, fearing any talk about David would further upset her, yet knowing that her only thoughts were about her son. I studied her, almost like I was taking inventory, checking to see what was broken. *Even in grief she is so pretty. I wish I could help her. Somehow take the pain away.* Then I mentally punched himself. *I know better. She will miss her son for as long as she lives. She will hurt until she stops loving David.* That would never happen. I stood up, frowned, cleared my throat. "Can I tell you what I know about grief?" I asked. "Not what you are feeling because only you know that, but about grief generally?"

"Sure. Tell me I'll get over it. Tell me I can have another son."

"No, that's nonsense." *There are no answers for her now.*

Bev showed her exasperation with me. "How do you know so much about grief? Or think you do?"

"My brother died when he was thirteen and I was eleven. In a car accident."

"I'm sorry for your loss," Bev said, still staring at me.

I remembered how those words of being sorry for a loss were spoken by so many cops on television shows, followed by a direct interrogation that contained little compassion.

"It's not like a son dying. You don't understand."

"I know, but I saw my own mother suffer so much, and I know she would understand, as you call it. It's really one of the major reasons I went to seminary. My mother found comfort in a bereavement support group, but not until years later. Back when Harold died there weren't any."

Bev rushed into my arms, pulled herself against me as if she wanted to push our spines into one. "I am so sorry. You know what a total mess I am, just like your mother. I'm so sorry."

I let her cry, stroked her shoulder softly. I never really understood mom's grief, and that hadn't changed. All I knew now was to be there, to let her cry. Finally she sat down, ready to listen.

"Here's what I know. The death of a child, at any age, is the worst loss anyone can suffer. More than a parent or even more than a spouse, though if that is your only loss it is terrible. I know you know that. And there is grief work that needs to be done. No one can do it for you."

"What is grief work?" She seemed interested.

"Over time you will experience many quite different emotions. You will be angry, or sad, or depressed, or full of anxiety. Not in any order either, and one emotion may dominate for a while. You need to talk about how you feel. A pastor friend in Minnesota told me that you have to let the bereaved talk. Not let, but encourage them to talk, long after we might be tired of hearing about the death."

"I don't know much about how he died. Just how he lived."

"That's good, Bev. The good memories are part of the grief work.

When they come, and they will, they will stay with you. And the bad memories, like the phone call you got yesterday with the tragic news, will fade."

"I can hear that voice every time the phone rings. 'Mrs. Stevens, I have some bad news.' Talk about understatements."

"That's what I mean. You need to talk about how you feel."

Bev began rocking the rocker, slowly as if she was processing what I had said. "My parents don't want to hear anything about El Salvador, and that was so much of David's life. They don't want me to go down there."

"Did you tell them you wanted to go? When?"

"After. I want to go to El Salvador to see where David lived. I want to meet his girlfriend, if he had one. His other friends. The people he worked with. I want them to share him with me."

I thought about saying it would be dangerous, then didn't because she knew better. Her son was shot dead. How much more dangerous than that could it be? I also thought about my delegation, in just one month. Would she be ready to join that group? Would I myself be ready?

"Father Jimmy told me I couldn't go to El Salvador alone. I told him to find resources. Support. He said you could be that."

Could I? Would, should I take her to El Salvador? Should I follow her around while she looks for memories?

"Will you? I'm asking you for your help."

I had to pace. "I've been preaching to you about how you should do your grief work. Yes, I will help. I am going to restructure the delegation. You should come along. I'm not sure how the others will take it, but I have to help you. Together we will find out what we can about David, though I'm not promising what we find will be pretty. But, I want you to know I think it is too soon to go."

"Tomorrow is not soon enough."

"Well, when the shock wears off you will feel even worse. I suppose going to El Salvador won't change that."

Bev stood up, a bit unsteady from the rocking chair, then walked over to me. "You represent what my David tried to be," Bev said, resting her hand on my arm. "I don't mean my son would have been a minister. In solidarity."

She looked like the old sadness had come back. "You knw, my husband didn't have to go to Viet Nam. He didn't have to leave me with a baby and nothing else. I blamed him for being irresponsible. And David did the same damn thing. Only David used religion instead of patriotism. They both meant well," Bev said, starting to cry.

I put my arm around her, pulled her to me, hugged her. I stroked her hair at the back of her neck. "Bev."

"Don't," she said. "Just let me rest against you. I am so very tired." In time we separated, and I left so Bev could get ready for the evening visitation.

◯

I don't remember driving back to St. John's. I tried to understand my feelings for Bev, from the first time we met, through the infrequent, casual meetings, even the times I took her to dinner. She was attractive, intelligent, funny, serious, and we both lived alone. The prospects of that changing now seemed so remote, so unimportant.

I drove to the church, picked up my messages, and unlocked my office door. I called two parishioners who were ill, then picked up my yellow pad. The sermon for tomorrow wasn't working. Normally, sermons came easy. I read the texts for the week, using the lectionary. Then I'd do some research, trying to find out what those verses said back when they were first written. What was God saying to the people of Israel or the followers of Jesus? I drew conclusions, decided what problem was being faced and how God guided them to the answers. Often, repent came to mind. Then I read the texts again, asking this time what the Bible said to the people of this church on this day, with today's problems. Again I drew conclusions about what the contemporary scene. Then I read them again, asking what the congregation should do about the situation as I had described it. This how I understand liberation theology, following practitioners like Leonardo Boff, Gustavo Gutierrez, Jon Sobrino and others.

While I worked, Jerry Shields stuck his head in the doorway. He came around from time to time, I guess because he felt responsible for the call committee hiring me. "When is the wake? You're going, right?"

"Yeah, it's at 6 P.M., and the funeral is tomorrow in the afternoon because it's Sunday, of course."

"Such a shame," Jerry said. "Can I come in? Just for a minute."

"Sure," I said, leaning back, wondering what Shields wanted. *It better not be about Bev.*

"Have you written your sermon for tomorrow? I mean, have you something to say about David Stevens dying? His death?"

"I'm not done. And it's not an eulogy. Not political either."

"Why not? You know the kind of people who would shoot him are the very ones we send guns to. My tax dollars killed Stevens. David."

"Remember the sermon I preached where I quoted the Jesuit, Jon de Cortina where he said, 'If God is not with the people of El Salvador, God is nowhere.' I'm wrestling with that."

"You believe in God. Don't you?"

"Of course. Why else would I be angry with him? It would be easier to preach about government policy and civil wars, but this is deeper."

"How?" Shields said, getting up. "That's what killed him."

"In some ways, probably yes. But we don't know enough yet. Maybe someone shot him by mistake, thinking he was a priest. Who knows? But it did happen, and I want to see where God is at this time, in this city, with the people of St. John's church. With you. With me. Where is God?"

"I'll be listening for the answer. Anyway, I know you've taken this hard. Knowing the mother and all."

I just looked at Shields until he left. Then I sat, asking myself where God is. *But God didn't kill David. A man or at least another person did. Is God confronting that killer, demanding a response. Is this like Cain and Able? Do I quote Genesis, Chapter Four, verse something? 'What have you done? The voice of your brother's blood is crying to me from the ground.' Is that true?* I picked up the study Bible I use for my sermons, began leafing through, stopping to read a few verses. *If I believed in divine intervention, the verse to use tomorrow would pop right out.*

The telephone rang, interrupting my feeble thoughts. Father Jimmy wanted me to be prepared to speak at the funeral, not a sermon but a testimony of the solidarity movement and what it meant to David, and what it should mean to those gathering to honor him. When Jimmy hung up, I turned to the Book of the prophet Micah, to my favorite verse in all the Bible, in chapter six, and read, "He has shown you, oh soul, what is good, and what does the Lord require of you but to do justice, love mercy, and walk humbly with your God." Micah was a prophet of the Old Testament, a second career prophet after being a farmer, like I had a second career after being a lawyer. *Maybe Micah knew something back then.* I finished the sermon, then got ready for the wake.

○

As I expected, the line outside the funeral home extended for almost a block. I ignored the full parking lot and turned on to a side street. I had my clerical collar and black suit on, wanting to be high church Lutheran for the viewing. Several people I knew called to me, and others offered to let me go ahead. Clergy should wait too, I decided, and thanked them. The cold March evening fit my mood, taking on the icy wind as a penance.

When I finally got inside, signed the guest book as the Reverend Charles J. Silas, I began to feel more anxiety. I couldn't yet see Bev or Father Jimmy. I looked carefully at the two posters someone, probably Bev, had made of photographs of her son. One picture caught my eye, of a baby being held by a soldier. *She's right. He does look like his father* I thought when I compared the soldier to recent pictures of David. Next to that picture was the one I took of Bev with David at the gate just before his flight left for Guatemala. I remembered Bev's dress. Bev had also brought the poster David had made in 1980.

Inside the parlor, I saw the casket, open, the young martyr lying in repose. I saw how Bev stared at the people as they approached the casket, as if to verify the honor each one gave David. She also met each person's eyes when speaking to them. I watched her mouth "thank you" when anything was said.

Bev's father, who had been sitting with his wife next to Bev, got up, walked over to me. "My daughter thinks I should apologize," he said, "for not letting you talk to her."

"That's alright. I understand."

"No it isn't alright. She has no business having anything to do with that damn country or anyone who has been part of the mess she let her son get involved with. My grandson. He'd be alive today if she had talked sense into him."

I turned so Bev's father had to face me and Bev couldn't see us argue. "I hope you aren't tossing guilt on her at this time. She needs support, not second guessing."

"You damn priests all think you know so much. You don't know anything about decent Americans."

At that moment Father Jimmy came up and took the older man by the arm. "He voted for Reagan, Charles," the priest said, guiding him back to his chair. "There are a lot of people here who want to pay their respects to your grandson. Greet them."

"Let go of me," he said, taking his seat.

I moved to the casket, knelt by David. I touched the rosary David held, noted the Salvadoran painted cross resting on his chest. *We prayed together David, and worshiped and worked and joined in the struggle. God rest your soul, mi amigo. Now I must face your mother.* I stayed on my knees, eyes closed in prayer. *God, if I can, I want to help this woman through her grief. God willing.* Finished with my prayers, I went to greet Bev.

○

The ten steps from David's coffin to the chair where Bev sat became a mile. I looked quickly at my feet, thinking stupidly of moccasins, then back at her. I felt the walls close in on me and sweat ran down my forehead. I don't remember saying anything to her, and later she reminded me that I only said, "I'm sorry." Her father grumbled something I didn't catch, then Father Jimmy took my arm.

"Bev," he said, "I want to talk to Pastor Charles about the service tomorrow." He led me away, and told me that he was sorry but the family, Bev's father really, had been making a scene about anything connected to El Salvador. "He flipped when I said you were going to speak about David's work down there."

"What does Bev want?" I asked, knowing that planning funerals brought out conflict in families often, and I felt that Bev, the young man's mother, should have prime consideration. "Is it important to her to tell the gathering what David was doing?" And why?"

"I asked her that," he said, "and she wanted to know if it was important to you." Father Jimmy gave me his most pastoral look.

I glanced over at Bev, who was talking with someone, receiving and giving comforting assurances. Her father was staring at me. "No. I don't have a need to say anything tomorrow." The tension between father and daughter clearly wouldn't be resolved with words from me. I thanked Jimmy, who went off to talk with others. After sitting for a while, I left, went home, cried.

○

At the funeral the next day at St. Giles, I sat in the back and on the left side of the church. I had on my black suit and clerical collar again. An usher mistook me for a priest. When the ushers brought Bev and the family in, she walked ahead of her parents, as though there was a distance between them in spirit. She wore a black dress with a matching jacket, and a black hat with a veil that masked her grief. The hymns were comforting, though not ones that I knew. Catholic hymns, not Lutheran, and the memory of our talks about religion came back.

No one spoke for the family and Jimmy's meditation affirmed the good that David did, as an altar boy, in high school as a swimmer and a fine student. Jimmy talked about his fluency in Spanish, and looked right at the family as he called David a martyr in the long traditions of the church. He named Archbishop Romero, reminding everyone that March

24 would now have a double memory for Christians in this part of the
world. I thought he looked at me as he used that ecumenical word.

The procession out went directly to the cemetery, eliminating any
reception line. At the grave, I guess I finally noticed David's father's
parents, holding each other as if braced against this new storm in their
lives. They knew Bev's pain, knew so much of the mourning process.
David is twenty-three, will be that age forever, and that's how long his
father has been dead. I hoped they would stay in touch with Bev, just to
sit with her, affirm what she had to say, over and over. They could help
her see that how she felt is what others also felt.

We all went back to St. Giles for a lunch in the fellowship hall. I sat
with some others from my church who had come because they had met
David at events at St. John's. They were full of questions that I had no
answer for. Evelyn Gillespie, who had helped Bev take communion the
first time Bev came to St. John's, suggested that I call someone in San
Salvador to get more information. Someone else wanted to know if we
were going to cancel the delegation.

When I looked up at the head table, Bev and her parents were gone.
Father Jimmy came over to me, said that she wanted to leave. "Charles,
she said she'd call when she could. Her parents aren't being too helpful,
but they at least tolerate me. The mother keeps asking why God let this
happen."

"You can't answer that," I said, feeling defensive.

"I know. Anyway, thanks for understanding. And thanks for coming,"
he added, nodding to the others at the table.

I went back to the grave before I left.

Six

The next day I picked up the phone in the church office on the third ring, a habit from my law practice days. It made my parishioners think I'm busy, not sitting by the phone. "St. John's Lutheran. This is Charles."

"Are you busy?"

"Hi Bev," I said, almost overwhelmed with relief at hearing her voice. "Somewhat. What's on your mind?" I paused, listened to her soft breathing. "Hello? Bev?"

"My parents went home, thank God. Then a load of firewood got delivered. I can't even lift a match the way I feel. Can you? Can you help stack the wood?

"Why not? I have a new member coming in soon, then I have to see two people at the hospital."

"That's okay."

"I'll be over after that. Is that okay?"

"I said it was okay," she said, then hung up.

○

When Charles arrived at Bev's house he went right to the pile of firewood where the delivery truck left it. Bev came out briefly, unlocked the door to the cellar, pointed to where she wanted him to stack the wood. Then she went inside. Bev chose to sit at the breakfast room table in a chair she rarely used herself. It gave her a view of the back driveway near the garage. She watched Charles moving the firewood, stacking logs in the wheel barrow and hauling the wood out of sight to the basement steps. To the bowels of the house, she told herself. Each load represented another evening before the fireplace, another night without David, looking into the fire for some answers.

At that moment, she didn't believe there would be enough firewood in the world to give her what she wanted. She stared out the window, no longer following Charles' movements, instead remembering last night's phone call with her father, when he asked why she was crying. Her sharp reply, "Because David is dead!" opened the distance between them more. She ignored his reply of wanting to know the particular circumstances, what special memory had come to mind. She told him he wouldn't understand.

She peered out the window at Charles. Half way done, she thought. For a moment she felt pity for him, for his wanting to help a messed-up person like herself. He's struggling too much with the firewood. I should ask him to rest for a while. Instead, Bev sat, watched Charles until he finished. She went upstairs to lie down, as though she had been doing the work.

Charles waited in the kitchen, not disturbing her. He was prepared to wait. When she came down, Bev insisted on going to the cemetery to put more flowers on David's grave. "I need to go," she told Charles, and he took her.

○

At the cemetery, we stood together, silent, our shadows from my car lights on the still-settling grave. The footing for the stone had been installed, but it would be months before the proper monument would be ready. "He's not there," Bev said. When I put my arm around her, she added, "He's in heaven. I know that."

In the stillness, as I felt her body shaking from tears, I spoke to the grave, "Where ever you are, David, I promise. I will take care of your mother."

"He heard you," Bev said, and, after a while, we left.

Back at her home, we sat in front of the fireplace and the faltering flames that failed to warm the morbid chill I knew she felt deep in her bones. The distance between us on the couch seemed impenetrable. The room now felt too big and too empty, lifeless. Finally, she spoke of not understanding God's motives.

"Neither do I," I said.

"So what *do* you understand?" she asked, pulling David's high school sport letter jacket around her. She had piled up some of his things that he didn't take to El Salvador, as if to find him in the memories and physical contact with his things.

"I'm sorry. I'm afraid I know more about the motives of people than why God acts or, in this case, didn't act."

"Then *you* should know why someone killed David."

"The problem is, we don't have the facts. Just what they told you."

"I don't believe them."

"We could try to find out why David died," I said. Bev could see me watching her carefully. Bev offered an almost imperceptible nod of agreement. What I said were words she needed to hear. There could never be peace for her until she learned what had happened, or at least exhausted all avenues in the search. Her need to know ran soul-deep. She knew she would become obsessed with tracking down her child's killer.

"I can't tell you how I feel," she said. "You won't know it's not revenge but my need to make sense of life. I'll hunt relentlessly, even decades, until my grave rises up to claim me."

"Even if we don't learn everything," I said as I got up and stoked the fire, "we can try."

Bev sat quietly, surrounded by keepsakes and reminders of her son, tears again rolling down her cheeks. She could no more control those tears than rein in the wind. "Charles," she said, "I'm not much good to you now."

"Don't say that." I moved to her, wrapped my arms around her, not knowing how else to offer comfort.

"I'm not. I just can't feel anything but pain."

"I wish I could take it away. The intensity will ease up, of that I'm sure. Time heals. Staying busy helps. And you'll always have your memories of David." I knew I shouldn't be saying anything.

"But not *him*. Not until I die."

"Bev . . ."

"You say we could find out what really happened?"

"We can try." I wondered if I had dodged a bullet, or maybe it just hadn't been fired yet.

"I know I can't have David back." Bev paused, swallowed hard, and pressed three fingers against her quivering lips. "But if I understood why he died, if his death meant something, then maybe I could settle for that."

I let go of her, let her sit back on the corner of the couch, pull David's jacket over her legs. She seemed to get more comfort hugging herself than anything I could do.

"I'm going to El Salvador."

"Sure. With our delegation." I wondered what she was really saying. "We agreed. I'm working on the arrangements."

"I don't need them. I went to Guatemala alone. Why do I need them?"

"You had David in Guatemala, had a limited, though nice, agenda of visiting your son for a few days. In El Salvador you know no one, don't speak the language."

"I know what delegations do. They go to meetings and hear compelling stories from oppressed people, and talk about solidarity, then they go home to their normal, safe, middle class life. I don't need that. I don't care about that stuff any more."

"It's what David did." I wanted to hold her, squeeze her until she agreed. "Listen, Bev. I called someone in El Salvador. She didn't want to talk, out of fear that the call was monitored, which it probably was, but she did say that the priest I know, Padre Rafael, had been with David that morning, and that they were to take part in a commemoration."

"For Romero. I knew that."

"Right. And she thinks we need to talk to Padre Rafael."

"We?"

"Bev, I don't know what the future holds for us. But right now, even the fact that we enjoy being together isn't important. If I were you I would want to know what happened, what really happened to David, and you have said you want that."

"Charles. Are you saying you will help me? Really help me?"

"Yes."

"When I had David, my son, my anchor of sanity in this ugly world, solidarity didn't seem so bad. No," she said, pausing as if to find the words, "don't tell me you'll be my anchor. It isn't the same."

"I would never presume to say that. What I wanted to say is that you have David in your memories, and we are going to El Salvador to gather more of them. You are doing the grief work. I'm just a resource. The nice thing is, I want to be more than just a resource."

"Maybe some day, but not now. Go. You have work to do. Get that delegation organized for me. I'll go with you."

O

Of course I knew the unacceptability of a death like David's causes a disorientation in grieving persons that prevented them from functioning normally. Life no longer makes sense, and even simple tasks seem impossible. Bev desperately needed help. I vowed to provide it. I called daily, came over three or four times a week, took her on errands on days she didn't have the strength to go herself. Being there, I had learned from life at home after my brother died, and from my work in the parish, is the only thing we can do early in a person's grief. In time, when she reaches out to other mourners, she'll really begin to heal.

One day I took Bev to the grocery store, taking the list from her quivering hand, reminding her what she had gone there to buy. Another day I accompanied her to the hairdresser, not explaining to the beautician why we left after only five minutes, Bev in tears and the whole shop staring.

Before the fatal bullet in San Salvador changed her life, our lives really, I had begun to dream that coming home to her would be the highlight of both of our days. I pictured us sitting in our favorite chairs, anxious to share the day's events, not worried that dinner might be getting cold. Not any more. Now, after parking my car in front of her house and saying a silent prayer for strength and guidance, I would cautiously cross the threshold of the unexpected. Then the search began: a game of hide-and-seek Bev didn't know she was playing. The hunt might lead me to her bedroom, finding Bev kneeling in front of the open cedar chest rearranging David's baby clothes, saved twenty years for the grandchild she would never rock to sleep, or sing a lullaby to, or cuddle in her arms. Another time Bev would be curled up by the breakfast room window gazing outside almost catatonically, "seeing" a different backyard where David and his friends played catch, and tag, and marathon Monopoly games, and shared problems, secrets, and dreams peculiar to pre-adolescent boys.

Some days I had to stay away, busy with ordinary ministry to the congregation, keeping up my work at the church and in the community. The dream of being home with Bev around-the-clock had been banished from my consciousness. When I looked at her, she seemed so vulnerable, and I could not hug her, hold her. I couldn't do that. Her bereavement became a private agony, something she could not share.

A few times, Bev would stop in at St. John's Church when she went out. She would try to run an errand, then need to talk to me to calm her down. One time she came into my office and I told her, "I got some black grouper. I went to the Reading Terminal. Great seafood."

Bev looked around, like she expected to see a fish on my desk. "What's special about black grouper?"

"Just wait. I coat it with Old Bay seasoning, then fry it in olive oil and a little butter."

"Sounds good," she said. Bev looked weak, as though she couldn't remember how to stand. She moved over to the chair in front of my desk.

"Your tongue will think it is in heaven."

"Heaven? Do Lutherans believe in heaven? I mean, not just for tongues?

"Sorry, Bev," I said quickly. "Poor choice of words. Extremely poor."

Bev looked at me, hopefully saw my contrition. "Sorry. There is so much in this world to be sorry for. David and I often talked about El Salvador and the tragic lives of the poor." She made a fist, as though to shake it at me. "You didn't mean anything. At least you talk to me. I should shake a fist at my parents. It's me, not you. Remember, you said I had to do my grief work. Dealing with heaven is part of that. I just can't see David in heaven, looking down on me, seeing me cry all the time. My parents won't let me cry. I told them not to come over anymore."

Bev did talk, however, mostly rambling speculation on why and how David died. Feeling and sounding miserable, her words were still punctuated by occasional great sobs, Bev seemed beyond consolation when she wondered about her son. I tried to answer her, to comfort her, knowing that saying nothing was probably best. I listened long after there was anything new to hear. A few times, unable to fathom the depth of her pain, I offered suggestions —as the minister perhaps— and quickly wished I hadn't. She was drowning in grief, beyond self pity, disoriented, spiraling downward into an abyss.

At dinner one evening, I said, "I can find someone who understands."

"Now I'm one of your bleeding heart projects," Bev snapped.

"You're the liberal," I snapped back, then winced in regret.

Another wave of pain flowed through Bev as she sat, silent, unable to deny what I had said. I knew she had to be thinking that she's the one who let him go.

"Charles, back when he and I were alone, when David helped out with our expenses, just the two of us, giving me money from his paper route, we were into causes. Issues. 'Looking for justice' I used to say. Now, I don't need his money. It doesn't matter that I don't need his gifts. I went to her, put my arm around her. As the immediate tension subsided, she said, "I know my grief is keeping me from seeing you as I had before. I had a thing for you," no humor in her expression. "I kissed you first. Remember? But I'm not a project," she said. "Looking for justice has never been that. Now I can't even do that for David."

"What I want to do is to introduce you to someone I know whose son died."

"How?"

"Car accident," I said, frowning.

"No. Introduce me to the mother of a murder victim. In fact, do that for me in El Salvador."

"I would help you."

"If I let you," she said, pushing me away, then pulling me to her, hugging me, as if she was trying to hurt me with her strength. Later, I learned that Bev spent all night looking at David's letters.

○

A month later, though it seemed to Bev to be a lifetime, Charles picked her up at her home and drove her to St. John's. The delegation was meeting for the last time before the trip. Jerry Shields, acting as the logistics leader of the group, announced that there would be no hotel for this group. He had happily accepted an invitation for the delegation to stay in a church in San Salvador. Such an arrangement would bring them closer to the people. Salvadorans have a great respect for the church, he affirmed, and tended to frequent church grounds both to socialize and to seek refuge from dangers of the street.

Bev shook her head at that notion. No one should consider a church a safe haven. The sanctity of the church or, for that matter, world opinion had not been a concern when Archbishop Romero was cut down in the Chapel of Divine Providence. Yet Bev did know Salvadorans used the churches, even when they were aware they were being watched, just as Romero continued to preach after being threatened.

Bev half listened to the talk about the logistics. Her mind wandered off to chicken soup in Guatemala with David, to the void in her heart. When they talked of money for food and medicine on this mission of mercy, she tried to imagine David would be there to help direct the aid. But he wouldn't be there. He could be leading this, she mused, suddenly overwhelmed with an injection of reality that once again plunged her heart to the bottom of the earth. When Charles put his hand on her arm, she jumped, then realized she had been breathing rapidly. Calm me down, man, she prayed, but get ready to take me there. I am going to the land they call *The Savior*. God, and you, my unlucky resource, are going to have all you can deal with.

After the meeting broke up, Father Jimmy Simpson walked over to where Bev still sat, ignoring the others who were excitedly talking about the trip. Jimmy hung back a moment before speaking to Bev. "How are you, Bev?" he said. "I haven't seen you at church as often, though Charles has brought you to the Saturday mass. I want to repeat my deepest regrets regarding David. I've known him for a long time. Do you know your son spoke warmly about you, about how lucky he was having a mom like you?"

"Not so lucky," Bev said.

"I disagree. It's not the length of a person's life that counts, but what he accomplishes in the time allotted. Christ himself didn't live to a ripe old age. David followed Christ's teachings and paid the ultimate price. Our hope is to make sure it wasn't in vain."

"He would still be here if he didn't follow so well," Bev said, grabbing the priest's arm for support. "Will Christ bring him back to me?" She looked around for Charles, didn't see him.

"He's over there," the priest said. "Charles cares an awful lot about you."

"How do you know?"

"He's my friend. And a nice man. I'm giving him time, and advice, just like he's helping you."

"Father, I had no idea."

"Oh, not as much help. He just needs someone to listen. We all do, but Lutherans did away with Confession."

"What?"

"Well, confession to a human. So Charles and I drink coffee. Sometimes we have breakfast. I wanted to talk to you privately to say I believe Charles is good for you. As a friend and as that resource you made me promise to find. He is an honorable man, and there aren't many of us left." His laugh went unanswered.

Seven

The craft market in the Capital, San Salvador, occupies a full city block, bordered on all sides by small shops selling commercial goods. Inside the market, crafts and souvenirs are offered from tiny, crowded stalls by vendors ever alert for new faces, especially gringo tourists. To the right of the main entrance, food and consumer goods are displayed while the craft booths beckon on the left. Each side leads to the other, intertwined in a network for those who had no access to the mainstream of retail commerce. Most vendors are poor, and a good sale to a *gringo* could be income for a week.

Other business is transacted at the market as well. A constant, confusing flow of people facilitated the spread of news and gossip, the delivery of messages, the making of plans. As all markets do, this place has its share of intrigue. A surprisingly enlightened Salvadoran army officer once remarked that Wall Street is where the richest of the rich conspire, and the craft market served the same purpose for the poorest of the poor.

Saul Flores moved unhurriedly from stall to stall in the market, nodding to vendors and customers alike. His jeans and knit tee shirt loosely fit his tightly muscled frame. Smiling, not unlike a politician working a crowd, he was acutely aware of those around him. Confident and assured at the age of twenty-two, he was careful not to linger too long with any one person or at any single spot.

Saul glanced at his watch every few minutes and kept moving, hoping the individual he looked for would be on schedule. He realized that those who were searching for him would learn through their informers of his presence at the market; they might even be on their way at this moment. It would not be good to be found here. When Saul spotted Daniela, he moved quickly to intercept her.

Pert and pretty and shy, Daniela Ramos carried tortillas from her mother's *tienda* to sell at the market. She wore a faded yellow cotton dress, neither concealing nor displaying her good figure. Her blouse was closed at the neck. Saul put a hand on her arm. "Daniela, try to get to the church tonight. We can find some time together."

"I want to." Daniela returned his greeting touch. Both of them seemed to freeze for a moment.

"Yes, of course," said Saul, finally. "Padre Rafael is anxious for us all to be together." He moved closer to her.

"Not in public," she whispered, stepping back.

Saul laughed out loud for those who watched. "Say, maybe you could start a big business with those tortillas. You could be the Salvadoran McDonalds."

"Don't tease, Saul."

"I'd like to stay and tease you all morning," he said quickly. Come to the church tonight."

"You better go." Daniela looked around, suddenly aware. "Be careful. I'll be there tonight, when it is safe."

Saul quickly left, just another man in the crowd.

◯

A white Jeep Cherokee sat parked, halfway between the San Salvador craft market and the National Cathedral, its motor running, its windows black, like an indifferent cat ignoring a bird. People on the street knew the Cherokee well and averted their eyes, fearing the occupants would see and remember them. Two patrolling National Guardsmen saw the vehicle and crossed the street to avoid walking past it.

The two women weren't so lucky. Rosalita Menéndez and Daniela's mother, Alícia Ramos, turned a corner and were upon the parked Cherokee before they noticed it. Rosalita, a heavy woman with dark, indigenous features, saw it first, gently took Alícia by the arm, and continued walking. "Don't look up," she said. "We have to be careful. There is the Cherokee."

Alícia, who was slim like her daughter, startled in fear. "Is it the one that killed the gringo? David? Can we tell? Rosalita, I must know."

"No! We can't tell," Rosalita said, pulling on Alícia's sleeve. "This is not the time, Alícia. Please. If they recognize us we will be in great danger. They have already seen my white scarf."

"I don't care." Alícia tugged and strained to break free of her friend's tightened grip, but Rosalita, much stronger than Alícia, wouldn't let go. "This is why I came to you. You're a Co-Madre. You work with those who confront killers. Help me, Rosalita."

"Please. Not yet."

"They killed my husband, They took my Miguel last month. I found him dead. You know that." Alícia said, no longer struggling against her companion. "How can we wait?"

"They are too powerful for two old women. Later. When we have enough support. Others must help us. Please. Now would be suicide."

The women crossed the street, and after a moment, made their way past the Cherokee, stopping several times to look at a vendor's goods, trying to see if they were being watched. Then two soldiers wearing the

uniform of the Treasury Police of the Salvadoran Government got out
of the Cherokee and began to approach the women as they reached the
market. Rosalita and Alícia darted into the aisles leading to the crafts,
looking over their shoulders as the soldiers moved faster, as if to intercept
them. Rosalita puffed and labored to keep pace with the now terrified
Alícia. They broke into a run when they were out of sight of the soldiers,
weaving between booths, vendors and customers, Alícia leading, Rosalita
struggling. They hurried out a side entrance, and crossed the street to
enter a music store.

The Cherokee pulled up at the exit. After seeing a signal from the
truck, the two soldiers got back in. The one with the deep pockmark
scars spoke to the man who had been sitting in the back seat. "We could
have had them, Señor."

The Colonel sitting in the back nodded, "True enough. But they
aren't aware of that. Now I know where they'll hide when they have what
I want."

O

Also that morning, Arturo Chacon came to the craft market to find
his friend Saul. His jeans were torn, and two of the buttons on his shirt
were missing, exposing a slight paunch. Arturo had known Saul for as
long as he could remember. The youth felt pride that Saul might some
day become a priest like Padre Rafael, who had sent him to the market.
Saul always looked out for other people, Arturo thought. The young
man went to the market, taking the long way, with extra buses and two
changes in direction. This is silly, he thought. If they find out I went to
the market, what does it matter how I got there?

By the time he reached his destination, Rosalita and Alícia had
fearfully returned to the market from the music shop across the street
from the side entrance. "Arturo," Alícia said when she saw him, "it is not
safe here any more. We were followed by soldiers in the white Cherokee."

"So lucky you escaped," Arturo said, looked around, cupping his
hands together. "Were they the ones who took Don Miguel? And
murdered the gringo?"

"I think so," said Rosalita. "We were lucky. We went out the side."
She adjusted her white scarf, again proud to wear the emblem of the Co-
Madre.

"I wanted to confront them," Alícia said. "I thought the Co-Madre
could call to account the evil one who killed my husband. Rosalita said it
wasn't the right time." Alícia wrung her hands, glared at her friend.

"Our chance will come," Rosalita said, "but not without many, many more of us." Rosalita pressed her hands on her stomach, as if to seal her words to Alícia.

"You wouldn't be here to talk to me if you challenged that one, for sure." Arturo shivered. "I'm trying to find Saul. Is he here? Have you seen him?"

"He isn't here any more, Arturo," Alícia said. "I don't know where Saul went, but it isn't safe to be here. I have to go now, with more corn. Now that Miguel is gone, we need so much."

"And you, Arturo," Rosalita said. "Leave as soon as you can. Go to the church."

Arturo waved to them both, and continued his search through the market for Saul. Perhaps, he hoped, someone had a message for him. Arturo ambled down an aisle and turned a corner. Witnesses later said he offered no resistance. Two Treasury Police officers grabbed and held him, loudly proclaiming that he was under arrest. Two other policemen stood by with automatic weapons ready; no one in the market dared interfere. The Colonel stood facing him, smiling, then jabbed him in the stomach with his nightstick. The policemen carried Arturo to a military truck. Silent prayers were said in the market as people went back to their lives.

O

The Colonel's men took the captured Arturo to the Treasury Police building not far from the United States Embassy, near the road to the city of Apopa. The facility fills the entire block and is protected with high walls and roll after roll of razor wire. Colonel Juan del Norte, a protégé of the now deceased Lieutenant Colonel Domingo Monterrosa Barios, held command of the Treasury Police. Previously, he served in the security forces for most of the 1970's.

Del Norte had been working in the streets of San Salvador under Monterrosa when his enthusiastic barbarism caught the appreciative eye of Major Roberto D'Aubuisson. At D'Aubuisson's request, he joined ORDEN, an organization of paramilitary forces supplementing the army and the three security agencies —the treasury police, national guard and national police. Members of ORDEN received training from U.S. Special Forces with assistance from the CIA and U.S. Military. The School of the Americas at Fort Benning, Georgia, served as a second home to some.

The colonel began carrying out the personal wishes of D'Aubuisson, who left the army after the October 1979 coup. D'Aubuisson took key intelligence files and reorganized ORDEN as the Democratic National

Front. Del Norte felt pride in his association with the Major, as many called him. He often praised D'Aubuisson for his efforts to save the country from Communists. The colonel reported to him until early 1980, when he transferred to the Treasury Police. Even now, from time to time, he performed favors for him and Arena, the political party D'Aubuisson founded. In the Treasury Police, del Norte learned many secrets from those he interrogated.

Del Norte watched two soldiers drag Arturo through the gate of the main building into the lobby, a square room with a worn and torn set of four plastic chairs and two couches with tarnished metal arms. The lobby served as a waiting room for the few people who entered on their own initiative. Nearby lurked an office for interrogation where the non-political prisoners were brought for preliminary questioning. Those lucky ones saw concrete block cells and round turrets at the gate.

The blindfolded Arturo didn't see the lobby. The soldiers roughly took him to a holding cell. They sliced and cut his clothing as they stripped him, then left him to stand, naked and barely conscious, still weak from the beating he received when arrested. Handcuffs held his hands behind him, digging into his flesh. He could hear screams, cries and moans coming from other rooms, and tried without success to keep his mind free of memories of friends who had been captured and tortured before him. Images of bodies he had mercifully helped bury resurrected their ghosts in his mind.

For an hour Arturo stood waiting, alone except for the voice of a guard yelling from where the sound of a door being slammed shut had come, warning him to remain standing. Arturo shifted his weight as he stood silently, trying to rest. When the guard came to the door, it sounded like he might come in, and Arturo stiffened. Once, as Arturo pulled back from the sound, the guard cursed him. Each time he heard a noise at the door, he shuddered.

Finally Arturo heard the door squeak as it opened, and the sounds of flesh on flesh and wood or metal on flesh became louder. So did the screams. Three guards of the Treasury Police came in, along with the Colonel. "It is time, you worthless scum," said Colonel del Norte.

The Colonel walked directly up to the blindfolded Arturo, driving the end of his dark, polished nightstick into the pit of the boy's stomach. "You have had time to think. Tell me where is the one named Saul. Where is he?" A shot from the club punctuated each sentence. "We know he comes to your church. You are his friend, no? Where is he hiding?"

The blows were even and always in the same place. Arturo gagged, almost vomiting. Bile rose in his throat as he whispered, "I . . . don't . . .

know. I told you. He comes. He goes. I haven't seen him lately. No one talks about it. I don't know anything." The blows from the club resumed. Arturo began to choke. "Don't . . . know" he gagged through the vomit spilling from his mouth and down his chest.

"You have soiled yourself. Now you must be washed." The Colonel motioned to the guards. "Bring him to the tub. He stinks."

Two of the guards pushed and dragged Arturo from the cell into a larger room down the hall. He could barely breathe from the pain. He felt certain he would not survive this day. Prayers formed in his mind, begging Jesus to save him, entreating for a miracle he knew would not come.

They took him to a large, waist-high tank formed out of concrete blocks. Water flowed into the tank from an overhead faucet, and the floor sloped unevenly to a drain. The guards pushed Arturo against the cold, hard tank, splashing water on him. "I'm telling the truth," he cried out.

"You must stay clean, you swine." Colonel del Norte punched Arturo harder this time as he nodded to the guards who quickly forced Arturo to bend, pushing his head under the water. He thrashed and struggled but could not raise his head and get air. Finally, he lost consciousness. The Colonel nodded again and the guards pulled him from the water.

They held him as Arturo coughed and fought for air and a clear breath. His stomach heaved, and he vomited again.

"I said, stay clean, swine." Colonel del Norte hit him again, starting the process over. This time Arturo barely regained consciousness, and no longer could vomit. His heart gave out during the fifth drowning ordeal, his body slumping into the water.

The Colonel stepped back, no longer interested in his latest victim. The guards stood patiently, holding the dead young man, waiting for orders. "This one gets taken to his church where he prayed. It will be easier for them to prepare him for his funeral. His reward for telling the truth." Colonel del Norte marched from the room without looking back.

○

Less than half an hour after Arturo died, two men dressed as civilians tossed his naked, bruised body from the back of a white Dodge pickup truck. A third, still wearing a damp uniform of the Treasury Police, drove the truck. Arturo's body bounced on the cement sidewalk just outside St. Oscar's Catholic Church, rolled over twice and came to rest at the base of the front steps. A woman passerby witnessed what happened and ran screaming into the church.

Rafael, stunned and heartsick, instinctively began to administer the last rites, once again using prayer to fight the tragic obscene death of yet another innocent young man. It took every effort for the priest to keep his balance. Sweat formed on his brow and his stomach churned. Quietly, prayerfully, he administered to the body, feeling his own guilt for having sent Arturo to the market to find Saul. His eyes welled with tears as the happy, idealistic youngster's smiling greeting flashed before his eyes. A chill ran down his spine as he thought of the dead he had buried. Now Arturo. This is too much, he thought, slumping in despair, everything they did just leading to more and more death.

Rafael called out to two of the other young men of the church who stood by, in shock over the death of their friend and co-worker. He spoke to them rapidly and intently, almost whispering the last few words. "Do you understand?" When they nodded, the priest added, "Go now, I will have him ready when you get back. Be careful. Very careful."

Saul had come out to the street with Rafael, and rushed to the body of young Arturo. "Padre, I'm so sorry," Saul said, when he had the chance.

"It's escalating," Rafael said, rising to his feet. "It appears that anyone with even a slight connection to our work at this church is not safe." The priest saw that Saul had questions, but cut him off. "For now, the boys will take Arturo to the funeral home. I must make arrangements." The two boys carried Arturo on a blanket, a makeshift stretcher. Rafael waved Saul away, pointing to the church. He could not face Saul now, knowing that this death put everyone in danger. "I should have known. They eliminate—kill—witnesses. The priest went inside to the altar in the sanctuary. He sat in the front pew, unable to pray, unable to think, desperate for a way to end the threat of more violence.

One by one the members of the youth group came up to their priest, knelt before him, asked for a blessing. Rafael assured each of them that their efforts to comfort the poor in the midst of a civil war was what God had called them to do. He did not say that God would protect them, just that they should be careful.

Rafael began to pray his rosary. "Holy Mother of God, pray for us sinners now and at the hour of our death." How can a youth group be a threat to the oligarchy?

Eight

When I drove her to her home, Bev talked about needing to meet
Padre Rafael in El Salvador. "I can barely live with my grief, Charles,
and there is no way in the world I can ignore this," Bev said, waiving her
notes on the delegation preparation in my face. "How well did this Padre
Raphael know David? Maybe they were like father and son," she said, as
if her imagination would bring David back. "I thought for a long time
that he should have had a brother or sister, too. But I was single so long."

"I know, Bev, but David had you."

"I have to see this priest. Rafael," she said, almost shouting.

As Bev talked, I considered the rational aspects of traveling with a
delegation. I slowed the car, pulled over to the curb. "I didn't talk with
him alone more than once or twice, but David once told me that there
are still a lot of poor people. He was at a meeting at St. John's. I am
sad to say, I said, 'There will always be poor, particularly in the cities.
Sometimes, I envy you and your compassion. Just don't let it kill you.' I
remembered those words during the meeting tonight. I felt physically ill.
Besides, Salvador is even more dangerous now."

"Charles," Bev said, turning my face to hers with her hand. "Someone
killed David, why not shoot you or me? Or anyone?"

"Bev."

"Why not slaughter the whole damn miserable country?"

"But Bev," I didn't say we shouldn't go. Just that it's dangerous."

"Dangerous? For me the only danger is if I let your damn fear keep me
from talking to these people. I don't care about my life right now."

"I'm sorry."

"You better help me find out the truth. I don't care what you..."

"Stop," I said, gently taking her hand. "There is no reason to make
this into an ultimatum. I just need to process the trip. I can't let you go
alone any more than you could stay home. Agreed?"

"Sure. But listen. I don't have any energy for anything or anybody. I
can only think about David. What I could have—a slice of the life he had
chosen to live—maybe will give me some of my sanity back."

"I see that. The trip offers hope," I said, "for some answers. The press
has made David practically into a criminal the way they describe the
solidarity work he did."

"David is a good person. Was good. Oh Lord."

"We're going."

"I'll hold you to that promise, Reverend Silas." Bev took her hand
from under mine to make a handshake. Bev looked away, now not able

to meet my gaze. "My only son has been murdered, and so I ask you. What will I become?"

I said nothing to this, for me at least, unanswerable question.

◯

I became absorbed in the last minute details and then it was time to depart. Father Jimmy came to see Bev off, and to offer a blessing for the whole delegation. The two of them talked, oblivious of the rest of us standing near. The priest blessed her separately, prayed that she would be safe in El Salvador. I wondered if we would be safe when David certainly hadn't been. Jimmy prayed for him, I knew.

"Will my delegation be in less danger than if I went as a tourist, Father?" Bev asked.

"There is some safety in numbers, Bev, Jimmy said. "But you're right. No, these others could not protect you. The government will know you are there. The way I see it, possibly even in that god-awful land, the bad guys, if you will, might think twice before attacking a delegation. Reagan wouldn't like it, for one thing, not if it caused trouble in Congress getting support for military aid."

She had been looking at the priest as though she didn't know him. "Why are you talking about safety? You should be worried about my finding justice."

"There may be no justice in El Salvador," I said, taking her arm. "Time to board. Say goodbye to Father Jimmy." In the background we could hear the attendant announce the flight.

Bev held tightly to my arm, let me guide her through the boarding ramp. I had wanted to remain separate from the others, not interested in their talk of crossing borders in solidarity, so I splurged on first class tickets that gave us that space. As we took advantage of priority boarding, Bev began to talk. "I can hardly wait to meet Father Rafael and Saul. They'll know what happened. Or they'll introduce us to others who do know. I want a clear picture of where David died. I want to stand on the very spot."

"You'll do that," I said gently. Bev, sitting by the window, began a retreat into the unreachable gloom of her most intimate thoughts. She knew she had become obsessed about being where David died, and I of course would take her to that place. The authorities had so far given her nothing, with indications of providing more of the same. When I told her about calling the U.S. Embassy in San Salvador, and talking with Special Consul Roberts to arrange an appointment, she got angry when I told her Roberts advised us not to come. "I have the police report," the diplomat had told me. "I'll send it to you by courier." When it came, with a translation, courtesy of the embassy, she didn't learn anything new. A drive by shooting. Vehicle and occupants unknown. No witnesses, which meant that the people on the street had not come forward, probably for good reason.

The flight droned on. I found myself watching Bev. She seemed so small, sitting by the window, curled up under an airline blanket. She abruptly reached for the call button.

"What's wrong?" I asked.

"I want another blanket."

"I'll get it."

"Stay relaxed, Charles."

"I want to make you comfortable. It's no trouble."

"No one can make me comfortable," Bev replied. "No one can make me . . ." She looked at me. "I'm sorry. I miss David so."

"Another blanket, please," I told the stewardess when she turned off the call button. I shifted constantly, as we talked. Ice melted in our untouched drinks.

"How unfair is it to be murdered," Bev asked, "when David was only trying to help the people down there? How could this happen?"

I was silent.

Bev went on, "I can hardly wait to talk to the priest." We'd agreed not to say his name in public.

"We'll do that. We'll do whatever we can. Everything we can."

"I know," she said, in a voice barely intelligible over the vibrations of the plane. Bev sank lower in the blanket. She pulled the other blanket closer. "My problem is not about the danger," Bev said as she withdrew. "I was going back to El Salvador anyhow."

I took Bev's hand.

"The Lord will help us."

"The Lord should've worried about not letting David get killed," I said, not hiding my doubts that prayers are answered.

"Fine thing for a minister to say. It's hard enough that David is dead. I need my faith."

"And I need answers. From El Salvador, and maybe from heaven as well." I had to shut up.

"And you know we might have to wait until we get to both of those places before we get those answers."

"El Salvador is first," I said as the announcement came that we would be landing soon. As the stewardess collected our glasses, I was still shaking my head at the thought that heaven might be next.

As if she could read my mind, Bev said, "We go together, Charles. Through immigration."

Silently I thanked God, or her, for showing just a touch of her sense of humor, then took her arm to leave the plane.

○

The delegation gathered outside the terminal, tossing suitcases, duffel bags, rolled-up sleeping bags, and back-packs into a waiting pale blue pickup truck. Jerry Shields herded the group to a red Toyota van parked near by. Bev and Charles sat in the front seat with Antonio, the driver. The others packed into three bench seats behind them. Jerry jumped on the back of the truck to stay with the luggage and reassure the delegation that someone would watch their belongings. The pickup looked a lot newer than the battered Toyota.

The drive from the airport inland to the capital city of San Salvador is generally uphill. Unless one has a powerful vehicle, the grade is steep enough to slow the trip considerably. The journey is enjoyed by those who savor their arrival into a tropical country with exotic vegetation and volcanoes on the horizon. Others resent seeing soldiers standing at points along the road with guns ready. The trip is simply endured by most. Occasionally one sees peasants along the side of the road pulling huge loads or carrying bundles on their heads A few are seen waiting for a bus.

Bev sat quietly in the van as Antonio accelerated through the gears. David had come here with so many expectations, so full of energy. He wanted to understand this life. Now maybe he had his answers, but far, far too young. His mother should know these things first. She leaned forward. At least she could look closely at the soldiers idling by the airport and the bridges, wondering if they were police or army, if there was a difference. Could any of these be the one who shot David? Would she know if he had killed her son? I am going to look right into the eyes of the one they say did it, she thought. A mother has rights, at least at first.

Bev felt on edge, her imagination flooding with images of David being threatened by one danger after another. But fantasy had nothing to do with what she saw at the first of the two toll booths placed between the airport and the capital. Some forty soldiers loitered by the gate, their automatic weapons held loosely, carelessly, without concern for their deadly potential. The soldiers were young, 13 or 14 years old, with blank, ignorant I-don't-give-a-damn expressions. Life, each face seemed to say, means nothing to me. Bev followed the casual aim on one of the barrels:

it pointed straight at Charles. She pressed her lips tight together to keep from gasping. Bev found herself praying to God to intervene, prevent any more deaths. If the soldier squeezes the trigger, she told God, he will take two lives, for I shall surely die too. Guilt filled her heart again as she waited, hardly breathing. Why had she permitted David to come to a hell-on-earth country where child-soldiers held the death of innocent people in their uncaring hands? Existence would be impossible for her if Charles also died because she allowed —no, insisted— that he bring her here.

Bev, scarcely breathing, didn't dare even glance at Charles. Seeing her fear might cause him to react in some way that might spook the boy soldier. Nor could she look directly at the callow youth who kept the rifle pointed at Charles. Her eyes were riveted on the gun itself and the thin brown finger curling itself on the trigger, loosening, curling itself again. Trained with methods that use humiliation and degradation, even being forced to kill their own parents if they object to the compulsory draft, this barely big enough to carry a gun warrior would not hear her plea. At last the barrel drooped downward toward the dusty, cracked cement pavement. Had the crisis passed? A fellow soldier lit a cigarette for the boy, laughing at something he said.

O

When later Bev told me about her fearful encounter, I suspected that I might have "challenged" the soldier, possibly by looking him in the eye. "Rule Number One," I knew from other travel, "forbids eye contact with anyone in uniform. Look at the ground. The sky. A tree or a car. Anything. But never into a soldier's eyes. He'll see it as disrespect or even a challenge of authority." The conversation occurred that evening.

Back at the toll booth on the ride in, however, when the gun no longer posed a direct threat, Bev turned to me, exhaled deeply, and took one of my hands in both of hers.

Somewhat surprised and very pleased, I continued to keep my hand in hers when the van left the toll booth.

After a few miles, the Toyota pulled past an old sugar cane truck laboring up a hill. I spoke softly. "This is the road David took when he came here."

"I remember," Bev said. "I have all his letters."

"He wasn't into guns at all."

"I remember that, too, Charles."

"I was thinking about one he wrote to our church, a simple note about feeding the people. Nothing risky, I thought. Then."

"He's gone, and won't come back no matter what we do, but we can remember him and what he said."

She let go of my hand. It looked like the terrible dark despair had returned into Bev's heart, crowding out her feelings for me. "I'll be honest with you," she said. "I don't have any reason to keep on living with this pain."

"I don't like to hear that."

"I don't care if I get killed."

"Your death won't bring David back. In time you'll get over it."

"I can't."

We sat for a while, looking out at the road. "I don't mean get over it," I said, knowing I had blundered again. "I mean heal, with scars but no open wounds."

"I feel like an open wound."

"I don't want you talking about dying."

"Don't you want me to let you know how I feel?"

"Yes, tell me. Just don't feel that way." I realized the moment the words were out of my mouth how foolish they were.

"Sure." Bev said, arms folded across her chest.

○

The church where the delegation would be staying had been unofficially renamed St. Oscar in 1981, in defiance of a hierarchy who would not properly see Archbishop Oscar Romero as a saint for many decades. Rafael lived a clandestine life there, working with the priest assigned to this parish, also using the church as a base for his work in the countryside. He spoke quickly with the staff, making sure that extra food would be on hand. The small amount of money spent feeding the delegation would be multiplied by the generosity of the group. Rafael checked the refrigerator to be sure there was adequate cold soda and beer. After the delegation gave the money they had in their budget for the poor, God willing, they would also give of themselves.

Rafael assigned the privacy of the small office next to the Sanctuary to David's mother for her room. Two cots were set up, side by side, behind the desks that he shoved against the now locked outside entrance. Pictures of Pope John XXIII and Monsignor Romero looked down from the wall between the room and the Sanctuary. The room had a flush toilet and a shower, without a curtain. Although the door to the sanctuary could be closed but not latched, the room provided the private space Bev needed in her grief. The rest of the delegation received larger rooms on the lower level, one for men and one for women. These good souls from Philadelphia would adjust, he knew, and be so busy taking in the poverty they wouldn't remember where they slept.

Rafael went down the back stairs, looking for the youth group. Seeing one of the boys, Rafael called out, "Fernando. Are the others back from the airport? I want to talk to them about Arturo's funeral. It won't be safe for us."

"Not yet, Padre." The boy hurried to the priest. "We're all so sad about Arturo. He suffered so much. Someone asked why God didn't protect him."

"What did you tell him. Or her."

"I just said what you say. God doesn't cause evil. Bad people do."

"That's right, Fernando. There is much evil in El Salvador, and much dying."

Fernando paced back and forth, then tried to change the subject. "It is fun to see if the gringos will trust them with their baggage, or if they recognize them later when we tell them about our liberation."

"And the rest? Where are they?"

"Padre, they're just standing around."

"Where are they standing? Are they watching the embassy again?"

"Of course, Padre. No, Padre." Fernando shuffled his feet, then brightened. "They're not watching, just standing around. Padre. We know." Fernando shifted as he stood. "When will we meet with the delegation? When is that going to happen? Will they go to Arturo's funeral? "

"Soon. There is one more thing, my young friend. Did Saul go to the airport?"

"No, he said he would find you in the park. Didn't you see him?"

"No." The priest thought a moment, not quite feeling the terror just beneath his consciousness. "So. Do you understand?"

"Sure, Padre."

"These are the lucky ones from North America. They will at least see how their neighbors hunger and thirst, and suffer and die, what those who are safe in the U.S. do not see. They will hear and touch and smell, and they will know just a bit of what our people endure."

"They will learn the Gospel, won't they, Padre?"

"Yes, Fernando." Rafael paused. "Keep in mind that the woman who came to find out about her son's death already knows much pain. She will need space. As she learns about poverty and helplessness, perhaps she will learn hope."

"That is the gospel, too. You taught us that." Fernando knelt before the priest. "I'm going to the park now, Padre."

After receiving a blessing, Fernando left to find Saul, happy for
the chance to talk to his priest, one to one. Fernando was from the
countryside, where Rafael once had a church. Ten years ago, Rafael had
also been his priest, before the bombs fell.

Not long after Fernando slipped out the back of the church, the
delegation arrived from the airport. The staff took them in, and helped
them find places to put their luggage. Rafael stayed in the background,
waiting to observe the group. He wanted to see David's mother. Then,
after she rested the night, he would talk with her.

○

After we arrived at St. Oscar's church, we met as a group, had dinner
of rice and beans, with tortillas, and complained about the flight while
having a second beer after the meal. Bev fussed a bit at not meeting
Padre Rafael, then shrugged in resignation as though nothing ever went
right in El Salvador. A young man in jeans and a knit shirt and a young
girl in a faded yellow dress took the group down to the lower level and
I took Bev's bag and mine into the room they had shown her earlier.
"These two are ours," I said, dropping one bag on each of the two cots at
one end of the room."

"Didn't they say 'boys in one room and girls in the other' or did I
miss something?"

"You need space from the others. They're not on a mission. Besides, I
need my Ghandi practice."

"You stay away. I know the story of Ghandi sleeping with naked girls
to prove his resistance to temptation."

"Right." I move my cot as far away from hers as I could, then left the
room. When I came back, she was asleep under a sheet. I lay down on my
cot, fully dressed. In time I fell asleep.

Nine

The next morning, sounds of children laughing woke me just as the sun came up, filtering in through louvered windows. Bev continued to sleep on her cot, seemingly relaxed and temporarily at peace. I realized I hadn't actually told her that I love her. This isn't the time, and if I put my feelings first, she'll run from me. I had to take comfort in simply being there with her in her grief.

I got up, peered out the window, looking down on a path where people walked to school or work from a shanty village just in sight along the edge of a ravine. Bev woke when I moved some luggage. "I'm going to breakfast," I told her. "I'll shower and change when you are done in here."

"I'll be along soon," she answered.

I walked behind the altar to a large, open air room, nearly as big as the sanctuary, located behind it, sharing a common wall. The upstairs room formed the center of the daily activity of the church from the kitchen, just off the side entrance to the sanctuary, to the laundry tubs at the other end, near the stairs to the lower level. A long table extended near the common wall, partly under a tin lean-to ceiling, just out of sight of the unfinished portion of the roof that opened to the sky. In the open area one could see the stars and moon at night and, sometimes, military helicopters flying over.

Jerry Shields sat at the table quietly reading a Bible and eating an orange. He wore jeans and a rugby shirt, plus sandals. He pointed to the coffee pot as I reached the table.

Evelyn Gillespie sat sideways at the table, denim skirt tucked under her knees, eating a tortilla and waiting for a chance to talk. She had tied the tails of her oversized white shirt at her waist, sleeves rolled up to her elbows.

"Good morning," I said, easing my legs over the bench seat near the coffee. "How did the night go for you folks?"

"Fine," Evelyn said. "I slept good. The coffee is hot, but the tortillas are stale."

"Good morning," Jerry added, looking over the top of his wire rim glasses. "Don't mind me. I'm just reading." He hesitated, then said, "I looked in on you three times last night."

"Three? I only heard you twice," I said, returning his gaze until he looked down at his Bible.

I poured coffee for myself, then for Bev when she entered the room.

Evelyn looked at Bev. "Did you hear the roosters all night? And the helicopters this morning? I was out in the courtyard when one flew over. The guns were pointing down!"

"There is nothing to shoot at if they point up," Bev answered.

"What?" Evelyn asked, then frowned. "Don't be silly."

Bev stood by the table, unsure of what she would do next. "Oh, I'm so out of it."

"Sit here, Bev," Evelyn said. "You need to eat."

Bev's eyes had puddled with tears and her hands trembled. She sat down again, turning to me. "My son is dead," she said loudly. "And no one, not God or anybody, can fix that. I went to bed thinking about David. I woke up thinking about him. He's all I can think about."

"There's a lot of misery in El Salvador, Bev," Jerry said. "Not to take anything away from your grief. I'm sorry. I just don't know what to say."

"I don't mean to sound harsh," Evelyn added. "but you do know you are hardly the only mother in this country who has lost a son. There are tens of thousands more, and many of these children died prolonged, terrible deaths. A bullet would have been a kindness to some of the victims."

"I don't know those mothers," Bev said. She took a tissue from a pocket, wiping the tears away. "I should care about the victims here," she said, sighing, "David did. Maybe I should meet them. I don't know. David was trying to help them."

"That might be a good idea," Evelyn said.

Leaning back, Jerry pushed his plate with his finger. "Well, I'm here to help those who have come back from exile, right in the face of this war."

"We're going to meet them," I said. "Maybe meet someone from the guerrillas."

"Don't count on that," Evelyn said.

Jerry laughed. "Some groups do get to meet them. But we're here to see the refugees who have come from the U.N. camps in Honduras. They've taken apart their houses, and loaded them on trucks. The refugees didn't even know if they could leave the camp."

"That sounds like desperation," Bev said.

"People said they began to build and they couldn't finish what they started," Jerry said. "I guess that's bad."

"No!" Evelyn joined in. "It's not bad. The refugees are doing the right thing. Our organization supports them, raises money for them. Repatriation is key to everything. It has superseded the Sanctuary Movement as the way to change things."

"The killing goes on," Bev said to no one in particular, clearly tired of Evelyn's platitudes.

"The church has been responsible for the refugee movement," Evelyn continued. "Your son became involved with the refugees. He knew what the risks were."

Bev turned sharply. "Don't push what you don't know," she said. "David wasn't doing anything wrong and I'm not going to hear that from you or anyone. His death wasn't his fault."

"I didn't mean that," Evelyn said. "I heard he was involved in other aspects of the work of the church. I'm sorry you misunderstood."

After a silence, I felt like I needed to preach a sermon, and so I said, "I don't know if this helps explain things, but a family I know lost their home in a fire. I mean, they lost everything. I took them into my house until the insurance company provided temporary housing."

"How much insurance do refugees have?" Evelyn asked.

"That's just one difference," I said, nodding. "My church, the one before St. John's, and other groups helped, and they have replaced what they lost. Except for heirlooms and personal memories. Those are gone. But the thing that bothers me, the reality I'm talking about, is that three weeks after the fire, I had not gone out to see the damage."

"What's the point of seeing what's left after a fire?" Evelyn asked.

"I didn't see their burned-out house because I was afraid. Afraid of death. These were my friends —God fearing, decent people, almost family, but I couldn't look at how close to death they came. They thanked God, said they were blessed when God protected them. But I couldn't go out to the house."

"Seems to me, Charles," Bev said, "it's difficult to explain how a tragedy happens to some people and not to others, both of whom are following God's word."

"You don't think God killed your son?" Jerry asked.

"It was you who let him come to El Salvador," Evelyn added. "You allowed him to get involved. You knew the risks."

"She has enough guilt about this," I snapped, not feeling like a pastor at the moment.

"This is too much," Evelyn said, rising from the table. "I'm sorry if I've spoken too freely. It's just that I take this trip most seriously. I've got to get ready. I'm going into the market area to see what poverty is like for a day." Evelyn strode from the room, leaving her dishes on the table.

"Please don't be hard on Evelyn," Jerry said. "She tries to do what's right."

"She has been nice to Bev back in Philly, but she can see the danger and poverty here, too. Speaking of God, Jerry," I said, "have you seen Padre Rafael?"

"Not yet. But we'll meet him soon. He's on the list of people we'll be seeing. Speaking of which, I need to be arranging things." Jerry stood up. "A bigger truck for one, and the van for a meeting later."

As Jerry went across the open area and down the stairs, I stepped over to the common wall, tracing my hands along cracks in the cement. "This is a church," I said to Bev, "where they have not simply built a structure. They built a place where good things can happen." Bev sat, silent. "I know you're hurting, and I can't help you while you hurt so much."

"I know," Bev said. "You try to give me comfort."

"I feel so helpless," I said.

"I want to go to the street where it happened," Bev said, "where they murdered David. I was thinking, I should do something like Evelyn is, spend time with the poor in the market. I could use that as an excuse to watch."

"Watch what, Bev?"

"Where David died."

◯

Frustrated by her conversation with Bev and Charles that morning, Evelyn Gillespie left the church, determined to meet poverty. She tied a silk scarf around her neck, up high so her gold crucifix hung down on her blouse, parallel to the top two buttons she had left unbuttoned. Trusting her Spanish and the directions from Jerry Shields, she caught a bus from near St. Oscar's, changed to another, and arrived without a hitch at the designated intersection.

Alícia Ramos recognized her immediately —the only *gringa* getting off the bus. She greeted Evelyn with a polite bow and introduced herself. Alícia had some of her children and the morning's corn with her. The youngest, Miguelito stood quietly between older sisters Sonia and Marina. Daniela, the oldest child at fifteen, usually carried the corn but had gone on an errand to the market on this morning. Alícia said her older sons, Guillermo and Luis, were at an uncle's shop, helping to repair bicycles.

After introductions, Evelyn offered to carry the corn. Evelyn felt a skip in her step. A goodhearted woman, a person who cared about the world's less fortunate, she believed her experiences this day, when shared with others back home, would become a meaningful encounter. She didn't mind even when Miguelito, named for his father, darted in front of Evelyn, causing her to stumble. "Miguelito," Alícia spoke sharply, "you must be careful." Alícia shook her son gently. "He means no disrespect," she said to Evelyn.

Evelyn's Spanish contained little of the peasant vocabulary. Conversation toward her goal of learning the tortilla business progressed slowly. Alícia pointed to illustrate nouns, acted out to explain verbs. Carefully explaining each step of the process, she also talked about the never-changing daily routine.

Before Evelyn had arrived, whole ears of corn had been soaked in lye, to break down the corn into digestible form, then shucked from the cob. The first task for Evelyn took place at the fountain in the square where Alícia's children helped to wash the kernels. Sonia and Marina sat beneath the fountain where the water flowed as it rinsed out the lye, using the skirts of their dresses as filters to catch the bleached corn. Evelyn enjoyed the delight of the little girls when the fountain's cool water splashed on them. She noticed the giggling and playfulness didn't interrupt the nicely choreographed tasks. She also began to feel the warmth of the sun. A walk to the grinder came next. The corn had to be ground into wet flour so it could be made into tortillas. A trickle of water kept the friction from cooking the corn.

Then the reality of the work set in. Evelyn and Alícia crouched around a hot fire in Alícia's small wooden shack, shaping balls of dough, flattening them into patties and cooking them on a sheet metal griddle, turning and taking them off by hand. Daniela, back from the market, now joined them. She said nothing to Evelyn who sat near the one framed window, trying to keep the smoke out of her eyes. The window looked out onto the street, and customers came, often with only a few coins to pay for the small supply of tortillas they bought. A crude chimney took most of the smoke from the room. A blanket hung on a rope, hiding the bedroom area, more to protect against the soot than for privacy.

Alícia's little children soon grew tired of snickering at the *gringa's* clumsy efforts to form the tortilla cakes, and concentrated on their chores. Miguelito sat on a box, watching, never saying a word. Marina and Sonia kept their eyes on him, taking turns running when asked to fetch cardboard and an occasional piece of wood for the fire. Alícia and Daniela made tortillas quickly, efficiently, no wasted motion, silently correcting Evelyn's less successful efforts. Sameness enveloped the hut.

At mid-morning, Alícia excused herself, leaving Daniela in charge. Evelyn stayed, knowing she witnessed the poverty she had come so far to take part in. In time, Alícia returned and said nothing, except she had been to the market.

Evelyn's frown grew and receded, causing her eye glasses to slip on her nose. This tortilla looked better, although anyone could see the imperfections.

Alícia took it from her. "No more work on this one," she said. "If you work it more, it will only get worse."

"Sort of like life," Evelyn said.

"What do you mean?"

"The tortilla, or life, gets better as you work at it. It gets good. We sometimes say it gets as good as it's going to be. And then, no matter what you do, it becomes worse."

"Oh yes, the tortillas will fall apart," Alícia said, and wiped her brow.

"So does life. I turned forty this year. God. If you don't have it by the time you are an adult, in your prime, you just don't get it."

"In the United States, it is true perhaps."

"Everywhere. I think." Evelyn's frown tightened and relaxed. "Of course, if the tortilla doesn't turn out, you can start over, at least before cooking it."

Alícia paused to put some cardboard on the fire, coughing gently and squinting in the smoke. "You are probably right. I haven't been to school. Being here is all I know. Life for me is more like the fire. It burns. You cook some tortillas. Then there are only ashes left and someone else takes your place."

For a moment, Evelyn said nothing. She looked at another of her failed tortillas, and started over. "That's too depressing, Alícia."

"This is how life is for us. Don't hold on to the dough so hard when you turn them," Alícia said.

After a while, Evelyn nodded at the small bit of corn meal still remaining in the bowl. Evelyn wiped her brow. "You've done well," Alícia said, and took the bowl out to the back of the shack.

"How do you feel?" Daniela asked Evelyn. "Did you learn about tortillas?"

"Yes, dear, I did. You know, I never felt overwhelmed by the work, not at any moment." Evelyn stood up. Then she said, "Oh no," as Alícia brought in another full bowl of corn. "I forgot that bowl."

"Again?" Alícia asked. "Twice a day, every day, every day. Now you see what I mean? Every day."

No one spoke as the work making tortillas started again. Evelyn poked at her glasses. Alícia tended the fire and made tortillas. Eventually, Alícia handed out a tortilla to each child for their noon meal. She gave three to Evelyn and kept one for herself. She brought a small pot of beans to warm on the fire.

That same morning when Evelyn went off to find poverty, I walked into the large gathering room from the kitchen at the church. Bev looked up expectantly. "No luck yet?" she asked.

"They seem to think Padre Rafael had some other business and will be here sometime this morning. Soon maybe, but then they speed up their Spanish and I get lost."

"You look anxious," Bev said.

"I'm fine." I shrugged, then said, "I just talked to a young man. One of the youth group, I think. I asked him if he knew David. When he nodded 'yes' his expression showed the pain he felt. Not only for his own memories, I think. For us, too."

"A lot of people miss David." She looked at me as if she saw something new. "You're taking on my grief."

I didn't answer. She was right, I realized. I am mourning David though I hardly knew him except for a few meetings. Plus the many things Bev has told me about him. I had been anxious for her to tell me more about her son.

As we talked, Padre Rafael came slowly up the stairway from the lower level, watching us across the room. When I noticed him, he had the same look of sadness, probably thinking about facing what he now must do, talk about an event that had shattered Bev's life. I kept talking to Bev, saying words that could never bring back her son.

As Rafael approached, Bev looked up expectantly, seeing the man she had been waiting for, dressed in an old but clean pair of black dress slacks and a dress shirt open at the collar. Dark by complexion and from being in the sun, he looked more weathered than healthy.

"Let's have a cup of coffee together."

"At the very least," Bev said, shifting in her seat, as if she expected the answers she ached to have.

As he sat at the table, Rafael said, "I know what you want, why you came so far." The priest rested his coffee cup in the palms of his hands, above the table. "The death of your son was an accident. And it was cold-blooded murder."

"What?" Bev said, as much to herself as to Rafael and me.

"Let's hear what else he has to say, Bev," I said, reaching for her arm. "Let's hear it, Padre."

"Yes," said Rafael quickly. "There is much more to tell. David worked with me, and I took him on delegations like the one you are here with, helped him learn to work with the people. My work is not popular with some elements of our society."

"What happened?" Bev said, staring at the priest. "What in hell happened to my son? My David?"

"Maybe you should get to the point and save the politics for later?" I got up from my chair,

"You are right," said Rafael, his voice raised. "David was shot by someone in the death squad, killed by a bullet aimed at me. I am so sorry."

"When?" Bev gasped. "Where? Why? How?"

"David met someone. A woman named Vitalina. My sister. He met her on the last delegation we had, where the army bombed the village. He wanted to learn more about the FMLN side of the fight. He wanted to talk to her, and I made arrangements for him to meet her at a hotel in the southwest part of the city. It was the anniversary. . . "

"We know which day," Bev cried. "What happened, Padre?"

"David wasn't going to his office in the Archdiocese."

"Where was he going?"

"To meet someone from the FMLN."

"The guerillas?"

"So someone killed him, just for a meeting?" Bev said, looking totally exasperated with Rafael.

"In some ways it was retaliation. Vitalina is quite a heroine among some of the people. She's made them pay."

"Pay?" Bev said.

"Killed them. With a gun."

"Padre, get to the point. David. How did he die?" I felt Bev's impatience now.

Rafael nodded. "A white Jeep Cherokee. With blackened windows. Suddenly, there it was. A window lowered. A gun came out. A shot,"

"David murdered," Bev said. "I've known that in my heart."

"How do you know." I added, "that the shot was intended for you like you say? Were you there?"

"Yes I was. David saw the gun before it was fired. He pushed me down, got in the way of the bullet."

"David's compassion killed him," said Bev, turning away, unable to face us. "This is just like being at home," she said. "There is no comfort, not anywhere. Nowhere."

"A murderer killed him," Rafael said. "Please. There is one more thing. On our walk, I showed David a piece of paper that had a death threat written on it, addressed to me. David knew I was a target. He tried to save my life, and it cost him his."

○

"Momá!" Daniela said suddenly. "Look out the window! It's the Cherokee, the white one. It's driving past us again."

"I should ask them about the death of my husband right this minute," Alícia said, mostly to herself. "You must stay away from them," she added, speaking to Daniela. "Rosalita said to wait. We can't go near them, not yet." The finality of Alícia's words ended the conversation but both mother and daughter continued to imagine confronting the ones who had taken Miguel from them, pulled him out of the shanty house where they slept. Alícia never saw her husband and the father of her children again, not even at the body dumps that she searched the weeks after he disappeared. Images of tortured, dead bodies flooded her mind.

"I need some air. I'd like to go outside for a moment, if you don't mind," said Evelyn, interrupting their thoughts.

"Of course. Please do," Alícia said.

Evelyn stepped over to a tree just outside the wooden shack and used a folded newspaper to fan herself in the shade. Almost as if it had been waiting for her, the white Cherokee drove up, stopping at the curb where she stood.

Daniela, watching from the window, felt panic not only at her own father's disappearance but at the still fresh memory of the shooting death of David Stevens. "Mama, will they kill another North American?" Slipping out the back, Daniela moved along the other side of her shack, hoping to go unnoticed.

Evelyn stared at the vehicle, feeling panic. She could not see the driver inside because of the blackened windows. Her reflection came back at her, as though she was standing in front of a mirror. "Is something wrong?" she said to her reflection. "From home?" She continued to peer at the blackened windows as the truck pulled away, seeing a smudge on her face in her reflection in the windows. Then she sat, suddenly, on the curb, unable to think, barely able to breathe.

○

The intense fear passed for Evelyn, and she hurried away from the street, shaking from what felt like a confrontation. She knew about death squads, and yet the reality of staring at one came as a realization that now was personal. She gulped the bottled water she had brought, fumbled with a tortilla, dropped the dough back into the bowl. "I need to buy some water," she said. She took the younger children with her, reflexively seeking safety in numbers.

"I saw her." Daniela said as soon as Evelyn left, "She was trying to see into the Cherokee."

"It is bad when that evil devil is near," said Alícia. "The people who ride in that machine are evil. When you said you saw the truck, I watched also. That is the one that followed Rosalita and me at the market."

"Mamá. I'm afraid."

"So am I, daughter." Alícia took Daniela in her arms, holding her tightly, fiercely. "I wanted so much to go up to him, to scream 'Murderer!' in his face, point him out for all to see. But when his soldiers came after us, Rosalita shook with fear. We must be stronger before we confront him, Rosalita had said, and that's why I held back."

"What can we do?" Daniela moved a pile of perfect tortillas to the edge of the heat.

"Be very careful. In the morning, I'll go to the Co-Madre office. I'll ask them for help. Perhaps if enough of them join me we can do something."

"Mamá," Daniela pleaded.

"Later, my dearest one. If anything bad happens to me, here is something you can do."

"Nothing will happen to you, mama. Nothing bad. Please!"

"If it does. Only if it does! Don't let the niños live here in the city. Take them to the mountains. Let them grow up with the ones who live in the mountains."

"Mamá, I will do as you ask, but I don't want anything to happen to you."

"Enough, daughter."

"Mamá." Tears streamed down Daniela's cheeks. "Mamá."

Ten

Sick of talking without action, Bev went for a short walk, promising Charles she would not get out of sight of the church and would run if she saw a white Jeep Cherokee. He really didn't want her to go out without him, but she insisted she had to be alone. A short block away, she saw a young man with the same hair David had, almost blond, combed neatly to flow back over his head, shorter than David's style. *It's David*, she thought. *He could have just had his hair cut. He's wearing a white shirt and blue jeans, like David wore. He even walks like David.*

Bev ran after him, slowly at first, not sure. *Maybe I'm dreaming*, she thought, *or maybe the other was a dream and this is the real David.* When she caught up with him and he turned around, she realized it wasn't David! She had followed someone she'd never seen before.

"You're not David," she said.

"Lady," he said, as he turned to her, "I'm sure not David, whoever he is." Then his eyes got big and he knew.

"You know my son David," Bev gasped.

"Maybe somebody killed a David. But he wasn't on my side."

Bev could hardly talk. The young man flagged a cab, and pointed at her as he got in. " I'm not on your side. I'm a loyal American and I love my country.

Bev could only say, "So did my son."

○

Rafael poured another cup of coffee for both of us as I watched Bev walk down the hall to the front of the church. "She says she's sick of talking," I said. "I guess I'm more used to that, being a minister."

"You care for her."

"It shows?"

"Not in a bad way. But right now she isn't going to want, or need, a relationship. Just a friend who can listen."

"I know. We talked about us, and I do mean talked, and didn't quite get past the religion thing. She's Catholic, and I'm Lutheran."

"The Lutherans are doing good things in El Salvador."

"I suppose, but only on a small scale."

"Small things matter. Archbishop Romero said, 'Everybody can do something.' and I believe that is true. But, I don't know about the death squad. They will wait, I hope, until things calm down, and then they will find me."

I had nothing to say to that. The priest stood up. "I need to see someone for a few moments. Will you excuse me?"

"Of course." When Rafael left, I went to the front door, saw Bev standing across the street. She wanted to be alone so I wandered about the church, walked along the sanctuary walls, studied the paintings and wood carvings that made up the stations of the cross. I walked up the center aisle to the communion rail, knelt, prayed, more feeling than thinking. Rising, I crossed himself and went back toward the open air room.

I noticed a smell of something cooking, then went into the kitchen. The small room had a large stove, with six burners. A woman stood at the stove. Short like most Salvadorans, she wore a thin cotton print dress with short sleeves and a 'v' collar. A heavier cotton apron covered her skirt. "*Buenos dias*," I said, then asked in Spanish what she was cooking.

"*Frijoles negros*," she said. "For dinner tonight."

I took out my notebook, asked her if I could look in the pot as she stirred it. The black beans, she told me, had been soaked over night in water. She had added chopped onion, minced garlic, chopped green pepper and a jalepeño pepper, seeds removed. A little olive oil and a bay leaf were the last ingredients. I asked her what her name was, adding that when I cooked this recipe back home at my church when I returned, I would tell people her name when I served it.

She said her name was Sonia. She looked pleased at the image of a priest, or whatever she thought I was, cooking beans and reciting her name. "You must serve it on rice, like I will tonight, and put chopped hard-boiled egg and chopped scallions on top. You need wedges of lime to squeeze over the beans on the plate."

"I will do that. I like to cook."

"Not many Salvadoran men cook. Women belong in the kitchen," Sonia said.

"And taking care of the children, and being pregnant," I said, hoping I didn't offend her.

"Padre Rafael says women are to be liberated, just like the poor who have no land here. In his sermons, he tells the men to be good to women, or we will be double oppressed."

"That sounds like a good sermon. Does your husband think so?"

"When he is here. He is with the muchachos, in the mountains. But he would not help me cook."

"I would," I said, stepping back when Sonia cried out in laughter. "I'll help you now. What else are you making?"

Sonia looked at me, then pointed to the refrigerator. "Get out the ground meat. It's in a big bag. And bring the milk." She took a bowl and ripped up bread and dropped the chunks into it. "Cover these with the milk and get a spoon to mash the bread until it is mushy. Do you know the word mushy," she asked when I frowned.

"My Spanish is fairly good, but my vocabulary is limited here in the kitchen."

When the bread became mushy, Sonia put in the ground meat. "A mix," she said, " of beef and chicken." She told me to get two eggs and beat them slightly while she added salt, pepper, chili powder, and oregano.

"Where did you get the spice?"

"From a gringo." Now, shape these into small balls. I'll make the sauce."

"Okay, but tell me what you're putting in."

Sonia stood back, hands on her hips, waited until I had the notebook out again. "Olive oil, cilantro, chopped onion, garlic, more chili powder and oregano, and tomatoes." She began to cook the onions and garlic in oil, then put the other ingredients in. "Put the meat balls in the pan over there," she said, "and turn on the oven. Do you know how?"

I reached for the matches, opened the oven door, turned on the pilot light and lit it, then turned on the oven.

"I like to cook them early, then warm them up in time for dinner tonight. It gives the sauce time to soak in."

Before I could reply, Padre Rafael came in, laughing at the scene he had found. "Men don't cook in El Salvador, Charles," he said. "Or they didn't." He paused. "Women didn't shoot soldiers either. I guess everything is changing."

I thanked Sonia, then both of us went back to the big room to wait for Bev.

"May I ask," Rafael finally said, "Charles, what else do you do for diversion? For a hobby, I think you call it."

"Besides cooking? I read. Novels. I like fiction. And theology."

"Is there theology in fiction?"

"Sure. People make moral choices. Do good. Or Bad. Sometimes I use something from a novel in my sermon."

"Don't take this wrong, my friend, but here in El Salvador reality is enough for sermon illustrations. And the Bible has the best stories, anyway."

"Sure, and when I preach, I look at the Bible story, ask what is the text saying about back in biblical days, then look at it again, ask what it says for today."

"Liberation theology."

"Right. Then I ask the congregation to think about what the text is asking them to do in their lives right now. Sometimes they surprise even themselves."

◯

When Bev came back to the church, she went straight to our room. When she didn't come out, I went to find her. She told me about her encounter with the young man she thought was David. When she finished, she looked up, then said, "Am I crazy?"

"No," I said. When she didn't say anything else, I asked her, "Do you want to know why?"

"Yes, tell me why I'm not crazy when I can't even tell the difference between a stranger and my son."

"You didn't see a stranger. One of the phases of grief, according to what I know, is denial."

"I know he's dead," she shouted, stood up.

"In your head you do. You buried him. But you also miss him tremendously and sometimes our minds do things, like clinging to the hope that this is a dream, that you'll wake up and David will be there."

"I do that," she said, calming some.

"The stranger had some characteristics that reminded you of your son who you miss so much. That triggered an association, a normal one, and the hope flared up."

"Okay, I'm not crazy. But I have a request," she said, motioning me to follow her. "Let's find Padre Rafael and see how we can get an appointment with the U.S. Embassy."

I mentally hit myself, realizing right away that this was a great idea. No matter what they said, no matter that U.S. policy was at best tolerant of the solidarity movement, they would give Bev another perspective on how a country can have death squads who kill with impunity. I hurried to keep up with her. After a brief conversation, we went to the church office where I called the embassy and made an appointment for tomorrow with a man named Special Consul Woodrow Wilson Roberts. I had to calm Bev, who wanted a meeting right then. "The man might be busy," I said.

"Too busy for a mother whose son died on his watch?" she said, then went back to her room.

While Charles made the call to the embassy, Rafael excused himself, said he would bring more coffee from the kitchen. He thought that David's mother, and the minister, and the others in the delegation as well, all seemed to be such nice folk. Rafael wondered how people could be so different from the government they elect?

Rafael understood the blue American passport would not provide immunity. Well, he would tell her, the mother of the martyred young man. What was the legal phrase? *Res ipsa loquitur?* The thing speaks for itself? So far, the murder of David Stevens didn't speak for itself. How could he be a martyr, painted as he was with the stain of random death. Rafael sighed and walked back to her room. Bev turned away, sat bent over, as though she were trying to hold herself from falling apart. She shook slightly as she silently wept. He put her cup of coffee on the table next to her.

"So you and David were just walking along?" she said, ignoring the coffee.

"A young man named Saul was trying to catch up with us, and saw the shooting. He's also from Santa Cruz. Where David's last delegation went."

"Didn't you try to get a doctor? Did you help David at all?" She shook her head as though she could not visualize the scene.

"Saul called the police, but both of us left. Honestly, we were afraid."

"You left him lying there?"

"Bev, I'm so sorry. He was dead. I checked for a pulse. He wasn't breathing. I couldn't do a thing." Bev stood up, covered her mouth with her hand, lurched toward the bathroom. Rafael ran out of the room to find Charles.

◯

Rafael found me, still in the church office. I had been imagining the conversation with Special Consul Roberts, anticipating what might happen. But I had no experience to fall back on. Rafael told me what had happened when he went to give her a cup of coffee, and that he thought Bev might be sick to her stomach. "I'm not surprised," I said when he told me about leaving David, dead on the street. "You're lucky they just didn't haul his body away to a dump."

"We were watching. Many were watching. The police had to take him and report the death. They couldn't just get rid of a North American. That's the real reason."

107

"What is?" Bev asked as she came into the room. "What is the real reason, Charles?"

"Rafael, tell her."

"When U.S.-backed *Contras* killed a U.S. citizen, Ben Linder, working on a Nicaraguan hydroelectric project, a year ago, your Congress cut aid to those terrorists. Linder was unarmed, too, I recall. The political pressure made quite a difference in that conflict. Actually, I believe military aid to the Salvadoran government might also all be stopped if it is learned that the military were responsible for his murder. If military aid is cut off, the current power structure couldn't survive. Even with less than a total halt of military assistance, I have no doubt your side will benefit greatly."

"I don't recall," I said, angry all of a sudden, "telling you we had a side." I had feared this, the ulterior motive behind everything.

Before I could say more, Bev spoke up. "We came here to learn the truth and expose it, not to become involved in a civil war."

"The truth?" said Rafael. "Is that really what you want? Your son took sides, Mrs. Stevens."

"David didn't support the violence!" Bev said "What are you saying?"

Rafael focused on Bev. "Your son is a martyr. What Charles is saying is that perhaps Saul and myself, and others, want to expose the truth and let the world know that he is a martyr to gain sympathy for our revolution."

"Perhaps?" I said.

"Perhaps the truth will be exposed. Often it is not. We are not devious. We are simple peasants."

We talked for a while, and Bev started to yawn. She left, saying she needed to rest, to find sanity in this insane country. Rafael and I had nothing more to say, so I went to the kitchen. I wanted to help Sonia finish fixing dinner. The rest of our delegation had been touring some resettlement and would be hungry.

○

After the dinner I helped to prepare, the delegation went down to the lower level for a meeting with the youth group. Seven young Salvadorans sat in a circle, off to one side of the large basement, talking and laughing. Rafael led us gringos to other chairs which we added to the circle. After Rafael opened with a prayer, I offered greetings to them in Spanish, then explained to my people what I had said. Daniela greeted Evelyn, telling the group that she had been in the tortilla business earlier that day. Evelyn blushed and said that she had a lot more to learn.

I then suggested that each one in the circle should introduce themselves, then say what ever was on their mind. Questions and observations were encouraged, I said, to encourage a dialogue. Sister Mary Ann Lucy wanted to know more about their schooling and several said they were going to college. Saul Flores, who came to the church despite Rafael's concern for his safety, said that he hoped next year to go to the UCA, the Jesuit run University, to study to be a priest. Daniela, who was sitting next to Saul, punched his arm playfully and asked, "Why would you do that? Don't you like me?"

We all laughed, and I whispered to Bev that she should punch my arm. She didn't react. When it came time for her to introduce herself, she pointed to Daniela and said that she, too, found religion to be in the way of her personal life, but that her faith was very important to her. "I am the mother of David Stevens, and I know that some of you knew him. Padre Rafael did. He was with him on that day...."

Daniela and another teenage girl rushed over to Bev, put their arms around her. Others in the circle expressed sorrow. Saul told the group about being in the countryside with David when the community was bombed, and how David had done so much to help rebuild what was damaged. Sister Regina said that she knew one of the nuns who helped take wounded to a hospital, and they also said that David had been a great help.

Bev encouraged everyone who spoke of David, storing every act of kindness or delivery of necessities in her memory bank. I asked follow-up questions to get more about David. But how do you reconstruct a life —one of service to the poor— to fully appreciate all that David, and other internationals, accomplished. Bev would later say that she better understood his work and felt real relief in knowing that it was humanitarian and not a basis for his being a target of an assassin. I thought of the words of Jesus, "You must pick up your cross and follow me," but didn't dare mention them to Bev.

Then Padre Rafael offered a prayer, for David, his mother, and also for young Arturo Chacon, who had been captured and killed by a death squad working out of the Treasury Police building. Arturo had been part of the youth group. For a while everyone sat as though in silent tribute to the dead. I wondered if Rafael saw a connection between Arturo's death and our delegation visit. Did they get the wrong young man? Did Arturo tell them where they could find Rafael?

When the group resumed the introductions and dialogue. Bev didn't say any more, just sat on the edge of the chair, her hands on her lap, looking at each speaker. When the meeting ended, the youth and the delegation exchanged handshakes and hugs, then went their separate ways. Tomorrow the delegation would have more meetings and briefings. We, Bev and I, were going to the embassy.

That night I slept downstairs with the rest of the delegates, giving Bev the space to process all she had heard.

○

The next morning, when Bev and I went out to find a cab to the embassy, we met several folks from our delegation. Evelyn Gillespie sat on the church steps. Evelyn wore a tan poplin skirt and a white blouse. Martin Sands and the two nuns, clad in non clerical clothing, chatted near the main entrance to the church. Jerry Shields, wearing jeans and a nylon pull-over sport shirt, its pocket bulging with pens, came over to us with a Salvadoran woman. So far no one has tried to dress like the Salvadorans, feeling, I suppose, more comfortable in wearing the clothes they wear at home for casual events.

Jerry said, "I'd like you to meet Rosalita Menéndez. She works with the organization known as the Co-Madre, the Committee of the Mothers of the Disappeared. They help women, mostly, to find out about the deaths and disappearances of their husbands and children. Rosalita asked to meet you."

"You asked for me?" Bev said.

I spoke up, "We're hoping to visit your office."

"I want to invite you to visit us," Rosalita said. She looked down, no longer politely smiling. "There is something I must say. I knew your son. David took delegations to visit us, translated for them. I remember him, and I wanted to meet you and tell you that. I am so sorry about David. I too have lost a son to the war."

"You remember David," Bev said. "Thank you so much for coming here. Can you tell me more?" The two women eased away, talking in broken Spanish and English, holding on to each other. I could hear Bev asking the woman what her son's name was. A big step, actually, by caring about someone else's loss. She was doing her grief work.

"Thanks for the introduction," I told Jerry, glad someone had befriended her. "Bev will appreciate talking with her." We walked to the curb where a flat bed, one-ton Toyota diesel truck had arrived. Food and farming supplies were being loaded over the make-shift sides. The truck would also transport medical supplies for the clinic at the repatriation community St. Oscar's supported. The church had purchased seed for planting, two bags of fertilizer and a few tools. The driver, Antonio, had

to make a list so officers at each checkpoint could review the supplies
as they scrutinized the safe conduct passes. We watched Antonio as he
methodically recorded each item.

"Seems like a lot of red tape," Jerry added.

"It is. They always claim the churches are helping the guerrillas so
we have to cooperate, if we can. We bring supplies to the people in the
resettlement camps, for the refugees. They say that some of the people in
the camps have been with the guerillas. The government also claims the
refugees are then giving the food and medicine to the guerrillas."

"Are they?"

"Talk to Fidencio about that," I said. "I'll introduce you." I pointed
at a Salvadoran man quietly loading fence wire. Fidencio wore blue
gabardine slacks, a cowboy shirt, and a straw hat. Thin and brown,
muscles hard and knotted, he moved easily as he worked. A peasant,
or campesino in Spanish, Fidencio looked like a displaced cowboy,
not someone who farmed and worked for the owners of a large farm.
"Fidencio is at least fifty. He's one of the directiva, the leadership counsel
of the community. He led them when they escaped into Honduras."

I saw a passing cab and hailed it. "Bev," I yelled, "here's our ride." She
looked at me, then at Rosalita, as if torn between two needs. "We've an
appointment at the embassy," I said to Jerry. "Go introduce yourself to
Fidencio." Jerry walked over as Bev waved good-bye to Rosalita. We got in
the cab and drove away.

O

Rosalita stood pensively as she watched the cab leave St. Oscar's for
the embassy. She said a prayer for Bev, asking that the reality awaiting her
would not be too painful.

Rosalita lived in one of the shanty houses nearby, in Colonia Bayco,
near the end of 5th Avenida. She left her bed early and eagerly this
morning to go to St. Oscar's to speak to the North American mother
whose son had been killed. Rosalita offered Bev understanding and gave
her a warning: a gesture of kindness and a part of her work she enjoyed,
giving comfort to someone.

She would do whatever anyone needed, she thought, but preferred
talking to other women, even about how much they missed their
children, rather than to scavenge through the body dumps to find and
identify victims of violence. The women who were the angriest did that
work, using their fury to push them past the pain of finding a victim

so the one's responsible can be called to account. The photographs at the Co-Madre office of bodies found and unclaimed were a constant reminder of her own pain. This errand of kindness away from the offices became her special way of honoring the disappearance of her own missing son.

Eleven

The engineers who built the United States Embassy in San Salvador boasted it could withstand anything including a natural disaster. To their embarrassment, the earthquake of 1986 caused substantial damage to the structure, nearly bringing it down; now, two years later, it remained only partially operational. Work had begun on a new building to be fortified against acts of God, as well as revolution, while the old one served as a temporary barrier to keep U.S. policy inside and victims outside.

The wealthy of El Salvador rarely had a reason to visit the embassy. Visas for those who wanted to shop in Miami on weekends are arranged socially, not by standing at the door, sombrero in hand like a peasant. El Salvador's poor, void of social access, waited in long lines for the tiny number of visa applications processed each day.

When United States citizens arrived at the embassy for the first time, seeing the lines of Salvadorans waiting, they hurried past the crowd to find the right gate, scurrying to take care of business. Typically, when citizens show embarrassment about entering without waiting in line—not remembering that every nation's embassy gives priority to its own citizens—the Salvadorans laugh, not out of meanness but as a way of sharing embarrassment.

Inside the embassy, Special Consul Woodrow Wilson Roberts quietly worked within a policy molded by the East/West conflict or Cold War that Ronald Reagan and Secretary of State George Schultz saw in every nation and which dominated their decisions. Being pragmatic, Roberts did nothing to interfere with the policy. A career diplomat, Roberts' reputation affirmed his loyalty, along with an ability to work behind the scenes. One of his duties would be to meet with the mother of David Stevens. Her priest or minister had called for an appointment. Roberts had done this before with others, and had no anticipation of doing more than setting out the facts as he knew them. He would of course also express official regrets.

If Roberts nursed ambitions beyond his service as Special Consul, they were not known. He came from a family of wealth and politics, Ivy League schools and discretion, and knew the people who were important in most parts of the world. He worked hard at being correct, "like I was made with a diplomatic mold," he would say. "Perhaps an expensive one," he might add to those he knew well. El Salvador appeared to be a low-ranking post for him. Observers in Washington speculated that he would retain the post only long enough to accomplish an important, yet unidentified purpose. In the news in the U.S., El Salvador once again had the serious attention of the U.S. Congress.

Ray Grant, a young marine on his first tour of duty, stood by at the entrance, grateful Bev didn't seem to recognize him from when she mistakenly saw him. Perhaps his full dress uniform made him look different from her son. Grant escorted them down a long corridor to a reception office. He had them sit, waiting in small chairs placed in front of a plain wood desk in a vacant embassy office. The yellow tile floor was covered by an inexpensive beige rug, the walls and ceiling painted a dull white. The U.S. flag and a portrait of President Reagan were the only ornamentations in the room.

◯

While we waited, I thought about what we might accomplish, and didn't see much. But we have to try to get them to use their resources, our resources really. Bev whispered, "I'm feeling panic."

"Relax. It's like being back home. This is the U. S. of A."

"That's what I mean," she said as the door to the left of the flag opened. "Welcome to the embassy, Mrs. Stevens, Reverend Silas. My name is Roberts," he said, smiling, polite and without warmth. He offered his hand, first to me, then to Bev. I thought back to the days when gentlemen waited for the lady to extend her hand. "I am the Special Consul here, representing our great nation. I'm at your service. Do come in."

We went into his office, a posh replica of the outer office. We sat on overstuffed, leather chairs facing the large polished walnut desk, Bev's expression as bare as the top of the desk. "It is almost noon," he said. "I have a luncheon meeting soon, but perhaps coffee or a drink would be in order," Roberts offered.

We both shook our heads to decline. "Mrs. Stevens," Roberts said, "let me extend to you not only our country's grief over the lamentable loss of David Stevens, but my own." Roberts, in the dark suit, starched white shirt and burgundy tie of his office, briefly glanced at me. Then Roberts retrieved a manila envelop from the desk drawer and proffered it to Bev. "Your son's passport," he said.

"Thank you, from both of us," I said. "What we would really like," pursuing the question I knew Bev wanted answered, "is for you to tell us precisely what happened to David."

"Reverend Silas," Roberts said, "I related everything we know when I called Mrs. Stevens." I thought back to when I met David, shook the strong, firm hand of the then twenty one-year-old. "Well, unfortunately, I have nothing to add to my verbal report, or to that of the San Salvadoran police. I wish I knew more. Perhaps it was random, or perhaps someone had a grievance against your son, or maybe he was involved in something."

"Involved in what? Bev asked."

"I'm simply listing possibilities. I, we at the embassy, have no knowledge of your son's activities other than he worked doing humanitarian aid distribution. What does it matter? The bottom line is—and I'm sure your son's motives were the best—he most likely was at the wrong place at the wrong time.

"Most likely?" Bev said, her voice soft. "He was most compassionate. But David wasn't involved in something," she added in a dull monotone. "God, what a phrase. What is this 'something?' "

"I didn't say he did anything. I merely suggest that there could be any number of reasons why someone shoots someone in this country. Any number."

"What are you doing to investigate the shooting?" I had to get to the point.

"People are not always who they claim to be," Roberts said. "The government is fighting Communists here, and they do not always identify themselves."

"David wasn't a Communist," Bev said, but no fire darted from her tongue, not even a faint spark.

"Your original call," I said, "mentioned nothing about Communists. Now, suddenly, you're bringing them up?"

"I am sorry," Roberts said. "I was attempting to make a point and did it clumsily. You're right, the police report says nothing about Communists, and there's nothing to indicate their involvement."

"We'd like to see the police report."

"Well, it is only a summary."

"Surely you can understand," I persisted. "We want to see it."

"It will be in Spanish." I stared at the man. "Of course," Roberts said, "I'll see that you receive a copy."

Are you going to investigate the murder?" I will ask this until he answers, I thought, glancing at Bev.

"Murder does happen, you realize, especially here, where the situation is so unsettled. Violence is, ah, the norm, not the exception." Roberts leaned on the desk. "Mr. Silas, the embassy is in an awkward position."

Awkward, I thought wryly. How I hate the bland coating diplomats spread around. The death of her son was awkward. But, ranting at Roberts would do no good. The Special Consul would simply distance himself further from the situation.

"Reverend Silas," Roberts continued, seeing from my expression that

I wouldn't easily be shunted aside. "Let me be direct. A civil war is raging in this country. An extremely bloody civil war, I might add. The police are part of this struggle. To them, this is one small incident out of many. Sad as it may be, as it is, I mean, they will do nothing."

"I'm sure if you lent your position to the effort," I suggested.

"Not necessarily. But, regardless, my hands are tied. Your son's death has been adjudged a criminal matter, not a political one, and thus is out of my circle of influence. Do you hear what I'm saying?"

Bev ignored his question. "You've given me David's passport," she said. "Where is his Bible?"

Roberts appeared grateful that the subject had changed, said, "The Bible could have been stolen," he said. "The apartment had been searched before we arrived."

"Who searched it?" I asked.

"The police, Reverend Silas. I'm afraid they weren't very tidy."

"One more thing I should mention," Roberts added. "You have to understand the Salvadoran authorities view this murder in a much dimmer light than we do. As I've emphasized, there is a nasty war going on." I wondered how much dimmer the light could be than what we were seeing from this diplomat.

Bev said, "I don't have to understand anything. I want my son's personal things, I'll take them home."

Roberts rose from behind his desk, accepting Bev's dismissal. "Yes. Take them home. Go back to Philadelphia. This is a dangerous country," he said. "I would be remiss in my duty if I didn't urge you to exercise great caution."

◯

In the late 1970s, when Monsignor Romero responded to the pleas of the growing number of women in agony over the loss of their children, he suggested they organize, and that's just what they did. These women —the Committee of Mothers of the Disappeared, or Co-Madre— were mothers, mostly, with a few spouses, of men and boys who had been disappeared. The vanished were not in hiding, nor had they left the country voluntarily, seeking a better economic life. They, and even some women, were taken forcibly, by the army, the police and the death squads, never again seen alive.

The suggestion Monsignor Romero made resulted in a political force of grieving women gathered together to locate those disappeared sons and husbands. More than 500 women organized, searching the body dumps, taking photographs and matching them with pictures of missing family members. Whenever a new body turned up on the street or in a vacant field, someone from the Co-Madre office helped to identify the victim.

The Co-Madre office began its day at about 8:30 A.M. every morning. Many of the women had families, and they rose early to get them started before coming to the office. Some women volunteered full time. Others had to work to support their families, stealing a rare moment to find a way to help. Rumors of vast prisons hidden in the mountains were dream castles built of desperate hope, not reality.

Alícia Ramos had risen earlier than usual, making tortillas before the sun came up, then left Daniela in charge of the children. She wanted to pay her first visit to the offices of the Co-Madre. She approached timidly, wondering if there was any hope to be found in this organization. They would know her pain, but could they help? At least she would be able to talk to her friend Rosalita about her anger and her need to confront the Jeep Cherokee.

Alícia climbed the stairs to the second floor office, hesitating, wondering if her promise to her daughter Daniela to make this visit would endanger them all. She cautiously entered the small room that served as the business center of the Co-Madre. Three typewriter desks sat in a line, and women worked busily revising lists. They looked up and greeted her when Alícia walked in.

Photographs of the many disappeared children and husbands of the mothers filled two walls. The images were graphic, ugly detailed testimony to the violence perpetrated on the death squad victims, showing mutilated, dismembered corpses that only a mother or a spouse could recognize. What clothing remained on the dead victims was blood smeared and torn, but none of the prints showed any uniforms. Some faces showed the eyes had been gouged out. The photos of women having been raped were taken after their clothing, or at least a covering, had been put on them. These men and women were civilian, as were 90% of the dead in this civil war. The obscene display's sole redeeming value —evidence of the crimes against civilians— supported the Co-Madre's cry of outrage, of indignation, and for the demand that the terror must stop.

A display of awards and international recognition of the organization stood on top of one of the several filing cabinets, including a bust of Robert. F. Kennedy and a framed letter awarding the Co-Madre the Robert F. Kennedy Human Rights Award of 1985. Hand-made crafts on small tables were offered for sale to raise money for their work. Mothers worked making the crafts in a room at the back that served as a sewing room.

Just as Alícia entered the room, she heard loud voices downstairs. As she turned to look, a Treasury Police soldier entered, pointing a rifle at her, and screamed, "Get back!" He shoved her toward the sewing room. "Sit on the floor!" he shouted. Alícia fell to the floor, banging her elbow. Another woman reached out to help her and was hit by the soldier.

Five more troops stormed into the room, guns pointed at the women. Colonel del Norte followed closely behind his men. The mothers were roughly searched, their breasts squeezed until they cried out, and their identifications taken but barely examined. Some of the soldiers lifted the skirts on the younger women. The men randomly struck some with rifle butts, in the head and in the back. Any women wearing the white scarf of the Co-Madre had theirs ripped from them. Shouting to his comrades, a heavyset private rammed his rifle into the Kennedy bust, shattering it. Others screamed curses, and threats. "Where is your FMLN flag?" one soldier demanded.

Two other men carrying boxes joined the soldiers. Del Norte began searching files, ordering his men to help. "Look for letters. We don't need the stinking photographs of the dead fools they look for. They won't either when we're done." A soldier began overturning furniture as the women cowered. "Tie them up," del Norte ordered.

The one who had pushed Alícia knocked her to the floor, then hit her with his gun. He pulled her legs apart, flipped up her skirt.

"Not her," the women next to her pleaded. "She came here this morning, just a few moments ago. For the first time. She doesn't work here." The soldier grabbed her hair and twisted it until she screamed.

"That is her bad luck, old whore," del Norte said. "Tie them together so they can die in solidarity."

The soldier put a rope over Alícia and the woman who tried to help her, yanked it so tight both women gasped. The other women were also quickly, brutally roped together in pairs, back to back. When they strained to get free, they were hit with a rifle. Alícia prayed. She first prayed that Daniela would find strength to raise the children. Then she prayed she would soon be with Miguel.

Moments later, the soldiers had loaded what they wanted into boxes. The women's identification cards were tossed in the boxes as well. Two privates remained on guard, pointing their M-16's at the women. "Are you afraid of us still?" one of the women asked, still defiant.

"This is an outrage," another woman said.

"Shut up, dog of the FMLN," a soldier spat.

Del Norte came back into the room after making sure the boxes had been loaded on the truck outside. "Shoot them all," del Norte ordered.

He turned, left not waiting to see his orders carried out. The women screamed, some pleading for life and others defiant to their end.

The two soldiers fired their guns at the huddled women, each emptying a full clip from the assault rifles. One of them reloaded and fired his rifle again. Both were grinning as they poked the dead or dying bodies, making sure every one of the women had been hit.

All of the women died from the gunfire, though several lingered on, finally bleeding to death after the soldiers were gone. Alícia, and the woman who spoke up for her, perished immediately, being shot at close range. Silence filled the room as the bodies, limp and lifeless, seeped blood on the floor. A gust of wind pushed the door to the offices closed, banging an end to the horror.

○

Because she had gone to St. Oscar's to offer comfort to Bev, Rosalita escaped the massacre at the Co-Madre building. But news travels fast in El Salvador when tragedy strikes as hard as it did at those offices. Rosalita hurried as fast as she could. She had visions of other carnage. A cousin had died when the army bombed the National University. Every day she met someone who had a story that seemed worse than the last one.

Those who first ventured in, who saw the butchery, told her of the victims, then held her back, keeping her from seeing the slaughter. She strained, unaware that she hurt the other women as they kept her from going into the office. She realized that looking at dead bodies never brought them back to life. They couldn't testify against the perpetrators. When the names of the murdered Co-Madre were recited, Rosalita slumped to the street curb, burying her head in her hands.

She sobbed quietly, and one by one the others left her. Amid their sorrow, these women had to contact the families of the slain mothers. They were keeping busy, postponing their own grief and helping those who needed them now. The other leaders, those who survived by being absent, also talked of organizing a protest march. Rosalita just sat on the curb. Later, she would want to join them in their work, once again determined to fight back. Now, she only wanted to sit. Alícia's voice echoed in her heart, asking, then begging for help she had been unable to give. The white Jeep Cherokee and a truck full of troops, murdered these women whose crime was grieving the deaths those same troops caused.

Eventually, Rosalita became aware that someone had joined her on the concrete. An arm touched hers, reached over her shoulder, gently stroking her. Rosalita looked up. Daniela, Alícia's oldest daughter, sat next to her, now orphaned by yet one more act of cruelty. "Daniela, I'm so sorry. I should have come to you."

"The soldiers came to our place. When they told me Mamá had been killed, I threw up. I retched until I couldn't stand. They said something, I don't know what, and left. Then I did what I had to do. You have said I could not join the Co-Madre, that I'm too young. Now I am as old as you are, Rosalita. I am as old as anyone in this world."

"Don't say that. Don't despair."

"I don't know what despair is. I have no hope to give up."

No more words came as each felt sorrow that overwhelmed their ability to respond. Then Rosalita realized that Daniela was alone. "Daniela, dear." Rosalita stood up, brushing her skirt, looking around. "Daniela, where are your brothers and sisters? Who is with them? Let me go with you to get them."

"They are safe. I took Miguelito and Sonia to the orphanage up the hill, by the Presidential Palace."

"Oh, Daniela, are you sure this is right for the children?"

"The children are safer at the orphanage than with me. Mamá and Papá weren't safe."

"What about Marina and the boys? And you? Where are they going to stay?"

"Guillermo and Luis have gone into the country, and they took Marina with them."

"Into the country? They are so young."

"The boys are 12 and 13 years old, and Marina is 10. They are old enough to learn to shoot a gun. All three will do that."

"Daniela. No. Say it isn't true."

"There is nothing else for us. Someone —God, the government, those dirty soldiers— has taken all we have. At least those in the mountains can choose the reason for their death. That choice will not be denied them."

"It is wrong. To kill is a sin."

"To live in a place where the government can kill you whenever it wants is a bigger sin. Now, the army will have to go where it is not so convenient for them. Anyway, it is done. They have gone already." Daniela looked so old. "Let's walk to the Cathedral," she said, "to Monsignor Romero's tomb. It may be a long time before the children go into combat. What could you offer them that's as safe?"

"I don't know," said Rosalita. The two women, old as the earth, began to walk. "There isn't anyone to talk to," said Rosalita. "Even Monsignor Romero would not have known what to say to you now. But he would ask you to wait."

"They shot the Monsignor, Rosalita."

"But he died for a reason."

"Rosalita, did Mamá die for no reason? Did Papá?" Daniela reached into the folds of her dress. "This is Papá's Bible. Mamá gave it to me yesterday and told me it was her comfort. She said I should read it every day if anything happened to her. But, no words, nothing in the world can bring Mamá back."

"My God, it is so very, very wrong that she had to die here."

"Mamá had a strong faith." Daniela said.

"I know." Rosalita took Daniela's hand. "And now we must find Padre Rafael. Right now we'll need all the wisdom of God to do what must be done."

"What is that, Rosalita?"

"I will help you find and talk to the Padre. God will help."

"I want you to help me, Rosalita, not God." Daniela squeezed Rosalita's arm hard. "Let's go light a candle at the Monsignor's tomb. Let's see if this God who allowed the killing will give us a plan."

O

Daniela and Rosalita reluctantly left the Co-Madre office, leaving the work to those strong women who had begun finding a burial for the murdered women. They walked at a steady pace that made Rosalita strain but she didn't complain, knowing that Daniela needed to burn up her nervous tension. Daniela would have months, even years, of pain from the savage death of her mother and the breakup of her family. Rosalita knew, and vowed to protect the girl. She would love her as a daughter, because love kept victims from becoming second victims to evil acts.

When they arrived at the big church on the *Plaza Civica*, they walked straight down the center aisle, past scaffolding for the recently-begun repair work. The women reached the main altar, genuflected and made the sign of the cross. They paused briefly, Rosalita saying the rote prayers she always said, Daniela silent. Then they turned right to the tomb of Monsignor Romero. Each lit a candle at the Archbishop's cement-cased tomb.

International visitors on both sides of the conflict had made the shrine a "must see" sight, and usually were disappointed in the Cathedral's condition. Plaster had fallen from the wall in several places, and everything seemed old, neglected. Romero had said the building would not be repaired until all the poor had a home, but his death in 1980 and the 1986 earthquake had changed that policy. The Archdiocese had begun repairing and beautifying, and those with money were glad to contribute to this worthy cause. Some day it would again be a proper place for a wedding.

Rosalita, a regular at the tomb, followed her own personal ritual. She always wore the same plain white scarf on her head, a badge proclaiming her involvement with the Co-Madre. She stood as she lit the candle, knelt during the rosary she prayed, sat as she spoke from her heart with silent prayers. Monsignor Romero himself had told her that her own prayers were important to God. He didn't look down from his position of holy power to decide what God wanted to hear from supplicants.

Daniela was too young to remember that much about the actual man. But her mother, Alícia, had often talked about Oscar Arnulfo Romero as if he were still alive. Some said he *was* alive, born again in the poor of El Salvador. Many baby boys had been christened Oscar Arnulfo. Unlike Rosalita, Daniela did not have a ritual when she visited the tomb. Sometimes she said the rosary. More often, she tried to picture him preaching the sermons that people had learned and now recited, over and over. "I beg you, I implore you, I order you, stop the repression."

Did those words please God? Were they words of prayer now? Daniela sat, her hands clasped. "Are you still in this church, Monsignor? Or are you safe with God? Are there prayers to bring the war to an end? Heavenly Father, I don't know what to do. Protect me, at least until I can do what is right." Tears streamed down her cheeks, a sight so very common at the tomb of Monsignor Romero.

As the two started to leave the cathedral, a woman selling crafts whispered to Rosalita as she passed, "The white Jeep Cherokee is on the street leading to the market."

Pulling her scarf over her head, Rosalita said to Daniela, "We must go a different way, my dear. Come. I know where we can stay tonight, then we can go to Saint Oscar's church tomorrow. I think God wants us to find Padre Rafael."

"We will need God's help to find him before they find us."

"Once, Daniela, we could have gone to the Archbishop. He would have done something. When I said my prayers, I hope he heard them and helps us now."

"I pray for that too."

Soon they were safe, lost in the crowd in the *Plaza Civica.*

Twelve

We got back to St. Oscar's from the embassy too late for lunch and the delegation that left for a meeting at a re-settlement in the city. They were also going to the craft market, a place Bev couldn't face. "I have all the souvenirs I'll ever want from this country."

Although no one met us, Padre Rafael did leave a message for us that intrigued me. He had arranged for us to meet with someone from the guerillas. His idea was that we would go to a hotel bar, would be met by someone who would buy us a drink, then we'd talk. He felt it was safe because guerillas weren't known for frequenting public places.

I found a taxi to take us to the Hotel Alemeda, located two blocks off the Avenida de los Heroes, on Franklin Delano Roosevelt Boulevard. We drove by the military hospital where wounded soldiers lolled about outside during the day, watching traffic, and smoking cigarettes. I didn't know if I could feel sorry for the wounded, just following orders. Stories of the cruelty of the Salvadoran military didn't portray them as deserving sympathy.

We arrived at the Hotel Alemeda and paid the cab driver. The building had been damaged in the 1986 earthquake, and the restaurant portion closed for several months. Now open, it remained a favorite of delegations hungry for a moderately upscale meal, plus reasonable security and accommodations fairly close to what one could expect back home. The second-floor restaurant served good food and very cold beer, and offered an additional dining room on the third floor for larger gatherings or private dinners.

As we entered the lobby, I looked at the faded furniture, the aging elevators. "This is a step down from the Sheraton," I said, not having been to that hotel in San Salvador.

"It's okay. I could like it," said Bev. "David probably came here to talk to delegations."

"The beer is cold, I'm told."

"Let's have one."

We walked through the lobby, passing a couple watching television, into a darkened cocktail lounge back-lit by a drape-covered window along an outside wall. Without looking around at others in the room, we took a seat at a table away from the entrance. No one came to take our order, but after a moment the couple from the lobby entered. The woman took a place at the bar. Her dark-featured companion approached. "May I buy you a beer?" he said, in unaccented English.

"It's early but why not?" I said. "One comes here to drink."

"And for other reasons. I see you have followed Padre Rafael's suggestion." He paused, as three beers were placed on the table by his companion, who then returned to her stool at the bar. "You have a tragedy in your life, I'm told. My name is Carlos. Vitalina is with me, he said, pointing to her."

"Yes, Carlos," Bev said, "if having a son murdered in this country while trying to help its poor is a tragedy. The more I see, the more I think David's life, and death, are part of life here in this godless country."

We had just begun to talk about what he knew about David when Vitalina received a phone call, then came to the table. She whispered quietly to Carlos in rapid Spanish neither of us could follow, except Bev later said she heard the name "Rafael" spoken twice.

"I have bad news," Carlos announced. "Padre Rafael says there has been a massacre at the Co-Madre's office. All are dead. You must go back to St. Oscar's. Padre Rafael will need you."

Later, in the taxi headed to the church, I started to sweat. "Are you all right?" Bev asked.

I took a deep breath. "I'll have to be."

"Pray," Bev said, and slid across the seat close to me.

"Good idea."

◯

The whole delegation waited for us in the open room of the church. Some had already called back home to get the protest calls started. Others paced about, demanding justice. Evelyn sat alone, obviously weeping. Jerry had washed some clothes and was hanging them on a line. Rafael came in right after we did and announced that there would be a protest march by the surviving Co-Madre, almost 500 women.

Bev looked straight ahead. "I really do belong with the victims. They are standing up to the world, and I'm going to walk with these women. My place is there." The mother she met shared a loss as great as hers, had been so kind, so understanding of her own burden. How could she not accompany them?

Rafael agreed. "Many internationals will be present and it should be relatively safe because of the press and television. Even those not in solidarity with us are outraged by this slaughter."

"You're promising that Bev will be protected there?"

"As much as one can be in El Salvador. There are times when no one is free from risk. It should be secure for Bev if she stays with the others."

I could see that her mind was made up, and I would only upset her if I complained. The whole delegation would be going with us, and the only difference would be that Bev would be at the front of the procession, and the other internationals would bring up the back. I would be separated from her, by a crowd of women who felt the same loss and pain that she did.

When the time came to go, we took the van and she and I sat in front. Antonio drove as usual.

Bev got out of the van when it stopped at the crowd by the Co-Madre office. "You asked me to do my grief work," Bev said. "Here is where I belong." Bev waved at the tropical heat as she stepped out of the taxi. She turned after closing the door, smiling at me, waving her handkerchief, then wiping her brow. Many greeted her as if her arrival signified something about to happen. The crowd filled in around her.

She seemed dwarfed by the crowd as it came upon her like a strong wind on sugar cane before the harvest. Would that she bends, not breaks, I prayed.

A few moments later, Rosalita found Bev, then introduced her to Elena, another who had not been at the office. Others urged the three women to the front to form the spearhead of the march.

"I spent some time with your son in *Santa Cruz*, Bev," Elena said.

"The time with the bombs?" Bev gasped.

"After. We helped the wounded. I'm a doctor." Elena said. "Your delegation is not with you now?"

"They're in the back with the other internationals. I just had to be with Rosalita, and the others."

"We're glad you can be with," Rosalita said. The women began moving forward.

"I'm sad," Rosalita said. "Daniela went to the mountains to be with her brothers and sisters. She is very unhappy. She wants to do nothing, just be with the other children."

"She'll find help in the mountains," Elena said.

"And you, Bev?" Rosalita asked. "What about you?"

"Well, Rosalita, Charles told me to do my grief work."

"Today is as good a day as any, then," said Elena.

"Yes, and God bless you for joining us," Rosalita added.

"I hope that is enough," Elena answered.

"It is, my friend," Rosalita said. "God's blessing is always enough."

"It wasn't enough for David," Bev replied.

"That Monsignor Romero would not agree with."

○

The march proceeded from the Co-Madre office on 5th Avenida nearly two kilometers to the Cathedral. Police and army soldiers watched, parking jeeps or troop trucks at various intersections, showing their weapons but not interfering. The Co-Madre women they pulled down their white scarves over their faces when the military came close with video cameras. North Americans brought up the back, carrying banners, moved between the military and the women. Many on the streets watched the solemn, peaceful procession. Some waved support, others shook their head.

The group entered the Cathedral by crossing in front of the main entrance, across the Plaza Civica where the riots took place in 1980 when the army fired on the mourners at Monsignor Romero's funeral. Many remembered and some wondered who would die today.

Bev, Elena and Rosalita stayed at the front, entering the church with the first of the women. Pausing again, they filed into the pews and waited, remembering those they mourned.

Rosalita sat quietly beside Bev, praying her rosary, waiting for the others. She wondered as she prayed if she would have the courage to say anything to the group. What could she say?

Elena, formidable jaw thrust out, also sat quietly, on Bev's other side, praying without a rosary. 'I don't have my vaccine, she thought, and I don't have my rifle. But I have faith in you, God.' She looked up at the altar.

Bev didn't pray. She stared intently at the women moving past Romero's tomb, tried to memorize their faces. Each seemed the same, yet each so very different. I, too, am one of you, she thought. The pews at the front of the church were filled, and she realized that though she was the only gringa in the church whose son had been killed in this senseless land, she now sat as *one of a church full of women* whose sons and loved ones had been murdered. At last Bev noticed the noise from the two army helicopters hovering over the roof of the Cathedral, noise beating down like a hammer on their heads.

The North Americans and other internationals including Charles bunched up at the entrance of the completely filled church. The women were the first to see the Treasury Police troops march in from the side aisle near Romero's tomb. They stared in horror at Colonel del Norte, who stopped directly in front of the altar. He drew out his gun. "You!" he shouted. "You are under arrest!" Del Norte had his pistol pointed directly at Rosalita. "And you!" he shouted, pointing at Elena.

Before del Norte could add Bev's name to the list, she stood up, a hand on the shoulder of each woman. She spoke to a hushed cathedral.

"You cannot take these women!"

Del Norte aimed his gun at Bev.

"You have no right to be here!" Bev shouted, seeing the knuckle on his trigger finger tighten. She thought of David and the thousands murdered in El Salvador, and her voice echoed as she spoke, loudly for all to hear. "Do you see Monsignor Romero! His body lies right here! His soul is in the people of this country. It will not rest until there is justice."

Bev, looking at the barrel of the gun, spoke again, quietly but clearly so everyone in the church could hear. "It is time that you are held accountable. Murderer! This church is filled with witnesses. Let them hear your answer. Tell us now, in front of Romero's tomb, in this house of God. Answer me! Why did you slaughter defenseless women this week? Who, in God's name, gave you the right to take all those lives?"

The entire church seemed to come alive. The presence of the mothers and the others in solidarity took on a living force, straining forward. Colonel del Norte lowered his gun. "Arrest these three women!" he ordered. "Let the U.S. Embassy know we have the American. The other two will go with her. Take them away."

Bev said nothing, walking calmly to the Colonel and then with him as he led the three women away out the side door.

O

Of course I went crazy when I found out what happened inside the Cathedral. I could hardly move in the thick crowd, everyone straining to see. Rumors came back saying people had been shot, then, no, they weren't shot. Ten were arrested, then only one, then someone shouted that the *gringa* and two Co-Madre had been taken away. I stumbled on the stairs, scraped my elbow on the stones. I couldn't get to the side door. Fortunately Jerry Shields and Martin Sands from the delegation grabbed my arms, shook me.

"Let go!" I shouted.

"No, Charles, you have to go to the embassy. We'll get a taxi and get you there." After what seemed like an eternity we found the taxi. One of them pushed some money into my hand, then told the driver to get going.

Reaction to the abduction came immediately. Reporters at the Presidential Palace news conference were told the women were safe, and that the allegations against del Norte would be investigated. Yes, he likely would soon be under house arrest. Yes, they were aware no army officer had ever been convicted of a murder in El Salvador. None had been guilty, and perhaps not even now had the Colonel been guilty of anything. Yes, they understood the concern for the safety of those arrested. No, President Duarte could not comment until he had finished consulting with legal experts to make sure justice would be carried out. Yes they had been receiving an overwhelming number of phone calls from the United States. No, those calls would not make a difference in the policy of the Salvadoran government.

A smaller but similar press conference took place at the U. S. Embassy. Special Consul Roberts assured reporters every resource at his disposal would be used to protect Mrs. Stevens. Roberts pointed out that the two Salvadoran women with her were obviously not citizens of the United States and confirmed the embassy had no reason to work for their release. No, he responded to a question, the actual proof had not been evaluated. Justice would be left to the Salvadoran judicial system. And yes, he knew of its reputation. Mrs. Stevens would be safe. No, he didn't think her detainment had any connection with the death of her son. Yes the phone calls from the United States were unending. Of course the embassy would protect its citizens. When someone asked about the Salvadoran women, Roberts just shrugged, then said, "What about them? They are not United States citizens."

I arrived at the embassy, barged ahead to the gate, shoved my passport at the guard and demanded to see Roberts. I expected a hassle but he let me in right away. I was taken to the reception room where we had been before. I didn't have to wait at all. Special Consul Roberts and another man he introduced as Joe Colangalo came up to me.

"We've made calls. Mrs. Stevens is safe. Mr. Colangalo will take you to the Treasury Police and they will release her to you."

O

The three women had not spoken when they walked out of the Cathedral and were herded into the army truck, not even when they were pushed and touched and pawed by the rough hands of the soldiers, then transported to the Treasury Police building. They said nothing to the guards, nor to the soldiers who mocked them, then locked them in a small room with a steel door. They were three rooms down from where Arturo died, a fact they would never know.

Now locked in the cell, Elena broke the silence. "I feel defiant," she said, thrusting out her jaw emphatically. "This takes me back to another time and place. Long ago." Elena leaned on the door. "My father, a doctor too, treated some people in our home. In our kitchen, a secret, almost. The people never paid for their treatment, and we always had to clean up a lot of blood and mess afterward."

"Did you live in El Salvador?" Bev asked.

"Chile. I grew up in Chile."

"Her accent tells," said Rosalita.

"One day the army came and took my Father away in the back of a truck, like the ones that brought us here.

"Why did they take him?" asked Bev.

"They told Mother he had been charged with treason. They executed him after the trial, all according to military justice."

"Let's hope things will be a lot different here," Bev said, shivering.

"Things are never different when you work for the poor," Elena continued. "No one represented Father at the trial because he confessed to treating enemies of the state, guerrillas who tried to overthrow the government. Father said we knew nothing about their identities."

"I'm sorry," Bev said.

"I went to medical school in Spain. In his memory."

"It isn't that we may be dead soon," Rosalita said, "here in this temple of death. There is heaven for the dead. I cry because my son obeyed his father when he lived with us, and he obeyed me, his mother. The soldiers of the death squad even took away my pictures of him."

"If your son is dead," said Elena, "and I pray to God he is not, then perhaps he is in heaven. Is that not good?"

"Yes," Rosalita said, "heaven is where he is."

"David is in heaven," Bev added.

Elena sighed. "I spent my time as an atheist, in my day, and that wasn't all that long ago. What could God do?"

Bev said, "I know I would have gone crazy if I didn't have my faith. Maybe I'm crazy anyway." She laughed.

Rosalita agreed. "It took great faith to risk your life, like you did in the Cathedral. I thought he was going to shoot. I really did." She stood just a bit taller as she spoke.

Screams, cries and moans from outside their cell shattered the conversation. The women could hear scuffling, as though someone was being dragged past their door. Fear chilled them as a voice cried out, begging for help.

○

I arrived at the Treasury Police building with Colangalo. I had expected a foreign service civil servant to be in a suit and tie like Roberts. I was not prepared for a man who wouldn't stop talking and looked almost ugly in his rumpled, sweat-stained suit. Colangalo said something in rapid Spanish to the guard outside who then let us in. We were led to the lobby just inside the main gate and asked to wait. Lieutenant Taylor, who drove, stayed with the car.

An armed soldier sat at the only desk watching television. He knew nothing about any women. Colangalo asked to speak to him privately, and then the guard excused himself. In the background the sound of phones ringing seemed to be a necessary accessory, a force in themselves, to the drama being played out in this habitat of terror.

The desk officer came back into the lobby with his superior, a Captain Alvarez. "Your acquaintance is here, Mr. Silas. We had confusion because of the last names."

"I didn't give her name," I said. Now she's my acquaintance. I thanked Colangalo for that euphemism.

"Easy, Charles," Colangalo said. "So, Captain Alvarez, release her and we'll be out of your hair."

"I will arrange that."

"And the two who were with her," I added as Alvarez turned to leave.

"That is impossible," the Captain said.

"Are they still here?"

"Perhaps."

"Then it's possible. We don't leave without them."

Turning to Colangalo, I said, "Word has gone out already. The phones haven't stopped ringing since we got here."

"Captain Alvarez. Perhaps we too could make a call. Special Consul Roberts has been in touch with the President's office and with the Chief of Staff at Illopango. Which one should I call?"

Alvarez stared at us. "I will make my own call. Wait here," he said, and left the room.

"Charles, isn't getting Bev enough?" Colangalo asked.

"It's only the beginning. Wait until you hear what she wants." I looked around at the cheap furniture. "Maybe we should think about getting comfortable."

"Charles, don't be greedy. You're getting your way about this."

"My way? She's a U.S. citizen. I have no illusions about you or what you did."

"Whatever."

"Here comes Alvarez," I said as I sat in the chair.

Soon after, Bev and I were reunited in the lobby of the Treasury Police building. Elena and Rosalita were also released.

Part III
Death Of Impunity

Thirteen

Back at St. Oscar's, the three women sat with Rafael, Saul and me at the long table, a cold beer in front of each of us. A helicopter could be heard in the distance. Elena played with the bottle cap, turning it over and over in her hand.

"Do you think they'll cut the military aid to El Salvador?" asked Bev. "I'd like to think David's death did that much."

"Perhaps," Rafael said, though he didn't seem at all confident.

He looked at me as if to say he didn't want to spoil her hope. I just shrugged and said, "We aren't in any position to bargain any more, Bev. There'll be some pressure on the Salvadoran Government, and feelers out to the FMLN. That's progress."

"Nobody has been arrested for the Co-Madre murders," said Elena. "Nobody will, either."

"We must pray for Daniela," Rosalita said, clasping her still full bottle of beer. "I am not used to drinking this, so I am going. There is much to do. The answers about our disappeared sons have not yet been given to us. We will organize another march, and rebuild our offices."

Rosalita went around the table, exchanging handshakes. Bev stood up to hug her. "I'm so glad to have met you," Bev said. "I really needed your help."

The kind woman put a hand softly on Bev's cheek. "God bless you," Rosalita said as she left.

"And you," the group responded together.

Elena stood up. "I am going too. There is much a doctor can do in the city. I must find a house with a big kitchen, like I had when I grew up. And a table like my father had." Elena also went around the table, touching each person, giving and receiving a good-bye blessing.

"It seems like one at a time we leave this church to go back into the world," said Rafael. "I too have much to do to help the poor. It is what I do, you know."

"The poor and the poor in spirit," Bev said. "We might find a way to keep in touch. You should come to the States to tell your story."

"Perhaps," he said. "That mission field is too dangerous for me, I think, but perhaps. If I can do some good."

"You can see some important people," I said.

"Charles and my pastor, Father Jimmy, can find lots of people for you to meet," Bev added. That would help change things."

"Bev," said Rafael, "you are more perceptive than Charles. Tell him that the bottom is where the change will come from."

"From the people." I replied. This is what the liberation theologians
have said for a long time. "I should know better."

Bev stood and hugged the priest. "You have done so much. I'm afraid
for you. Take care of yourself."

"I will. I'm going to start now." He laughed. "I have an appointment."

"Where?" Bev asked.

"In the park. To get my shoes shined." He laughed, happy for at least
a moment.

Saul sat at the end of the table, alone now with us. Bev looked at him,
her lips compressed as if she had clenched her teeth. A vein pulsed in
her temple. "You gave me a great gift, telling me about David and his life
here."

"You've done the hard part. You stood up to one death squad, one
murderous Colonel."

"That's all we did, isn't it?" Bev asked.

"That's a lot. It gives hope to us, and we will work even harder. Right
now, I am going to a meeting of our youth to join with another protest
to help the Co-Madre. And I'm going to work even closer with Padre
Rafael. But I wanted to spend this time with you before I left."

"You aren't going to take up a gun?" Bev asked.

"It would dishonor David's memory. I am seriously considering
becoming a priest. No guns are needed if we have enough faith. I will try
to convince Daniela of that, too."

"I'll shake your hand on that," I said, "and I look forward to you
being my colleague. Same God, different denomination. I really mean
that. It is the same God, and the more I work with the priests, the less
difference I see."

"I get to hug you before you go, Saul," said Bev.

I put my arms around both of them, then gently took Bev from the
young Salvadoran man. We held each other for a long time after Saul left
the church.

O

Later that evening, Bev and I packed for our return flight to
Philadelphia. We were alone in her room in St. Oscar's. Bev folded
clothes, smoothing them, arranging them. I sat on the other cot next to
the open suitcases, watching her add things to her luggage from the neat
piles of clothes on the cot. She is much neater than I.

We almost refused to see Colangalo from the embassy when he came
to St. Oscar's that evening, but he had only a brief message. He spoke
in generalities of changes, and then reached into his briefcase. "This

is David's Bible," he said. "We should have returned it to you at the beginning." Bev stared at him, and continued staring until he left the church.

Finally Bev completed packing. "I think I'll take this in the carry-on bag," she said, picking up David's Bible. "I might read it." Bev opened the Bible, leafing through the pages, not reading but just looking. "And I might just put it on the shelf, in the kitchen."

I moved over to her cot, putting my arm around her as I sat next to her. "I don't have any magic words. But I'm still here."

"You'll always be here, Charles." Bev closed the Bible, setting it aside. "I'll be okay. I have some thoughts, maybe trying to help others. I can, if I stop crying." She laughed. "And I'll be here for you. You taught me something, Reverend Silas. You, Rosalita, Elena, Rafael and Saul and all these beautiful, suffering people."

"What's that?"

"Just being there, I guess."

"Rafael calls it accompaniment."

"David won't ever come back, I know that now. But if I can't have him back, I want to be healed. I know he'd want me to be healed." Bev picked up David's Bible. "There're no magic words in here." She hesitated, nodded, then said, "I think I want to have a life. With you. Let's go home. I feel like having chicken soup again. I can get some *cilantro*," she said, now smiling, and you can cook for me."

"Cilantro's a magic word," I said, helping her stand, holding on to her, turning her toward me as we hugged.

"It might be magic, Charles. It's from El Salvador, and is a memory of David. He would like your soup. If it's as good as you say it is."

○

When the delegation returned to Philadelphia, Father Jimmy and others met our plane. We all went to St. John's because most of the delegation came from there, and those with families had reunions. We went up the staircase to the Sanctuary, took places facing each other. Someone said we were heroes. At least Bev got that treatment and had to tell her story of the arrest and cell time over and over. I watched her talk, flush with excitement of taking part in what the solidarity movement called a victory.

After half an hour, Sister Mary Ann Lucy and Sister Regina left with other nuns who had come to get them, and that started the exodus for the others. Within minutes, there were just three of us. Father Jimmy sat across the aisle from Bev and me, smiling.

"It appears that other borders have been crossed by you two," he said, leaning back in the pew. "I'm happy for you."

"Father," Bev said, then turned to me. "We haven't talked about anything. I did tell him I want to be with him. I mean, I realized in that prison cell that I wanted to keep on living, have a good life, even with David dead. David would want that for me."

"Of course, Bev," he said. "I pray that you do. Charles has gone through this with you. You have that to share."

"I haven't even asked him if he feels the same," she said.

I just sat there, as if they were talking about me, or us, and I was invisible. Or, I was the elephant in the room, maybe. They talked about the Catholic Church, and the way some people resolve conflicts as a matter of individual conscience as the final determination. I stopped listening, thought of my reasons for wanting her in my life. I don't want to be her permanent grief counselor, or her pastor either. I care about her. I slapped my forehead, and thought, "I think I love her." Then I heard Bev's voice.

"Charles, are you alright? Haven't you been listening?

"Your frown is the cutest thing I ever saw," I said.

Jimmy laughed and clapped his hands. "Charles, you look like a lovesick teenager. Or maybe a puppy." Still laughing, he stood up. "I'm going. Bev said that you haven't talked about your future. Together. Maybe it's time you started. Don't get up," he said as he walked closer. "May God the Father, the Son and the Holy Spirit bless you both," he said, making the sign of the cross. "I expect to be invited to the wedding."

Bev and I looked at each other, still sitting on the same pew but apart.

○

We didn't live together right away. I still felt nervous about keeping my celibacy promise to the call to serve in ministry, and Bev still felt nervous about being partnered with a divorced man, but neither of these reasons stopped us. Finally I told her, "I hug you when you're sad, when you are thinking about David. I don't want him in our bed."

"What a thing to say," she said, looking both angry and confused.

"No. Listen. Making love can be simple self-gratification. We'd have done that if that is all it is for us. What I like to think is that it is like the Bible says, 'A man and a woman cleave together and become one flesh.' No one else is present. When you and I need each other in that way, for that reason, it will be the right time."

In time it was the right time, and we made plans for a wedding. When I announced our engagement from the pulpit on a Sunday at St.

John's, the congregation applauded, something decidedly not the normal Lutheran reserve. Bev went to visit her parents who, thankfully, were so grateful that she had come back safely in spite of the danger that they affirmed her decision. Her father even said he wanted to talk politics with me.

The major issue for us became housing, not as a conflict but because we wanted to do the right thing, avoid mistakes. Bev didn't want us to live in her house, but she didn't want to leave the memories. My townhouse didn't have much room and there wasn't a yard for her gardening. We put them both up for sale, and when mine sold, we bought a dream house in Drexel Hill, near Clifton Heights and Bev's old neighborhood and church and close to the trolley line I could use to commute to St. John's if I didn't want to drive.

A week after we moved in, we had our wedding in the living room, in front of the stone mantled fire place. As a compromise to my Lutheran calling and Bev's Catholic faith, we had a judge I knew perform the ceremony. I invited a few people from St. John's who had been on the delegation, and Bev only invited her parents. Father Jimmy came, and stole the show by coming up to us after the judge pronounced us 'husband and wife' to read the Catholic ritual for blessing a marriage. He couldn't marry us, but he gave us the church's blessing. We're not to tell anyone.

When everyone left, we sat in front of the fire I had built in the fireplace. I had one of the two overstuffed chairs I bought for the house and Bev sat in the rocker her grandmother had nursed her mother in. This time she didn't tell me that she had nursed David in that family heirloom. "Would you like more wine?" I asked. We had discovered a wine cellar under the back porch with a rack that would hold four hundred bottles. We tried the 'buy two, drink one' plan, but that didn't work.

"No wine. You intoxicate me," Bev said. She looked at the marriage certificate the judge had left. "I'm hyphenated. Mrs. Stevens-Silas. Why did you do that?

"David," I said. So much of our lives would involve him.

○

The pages of the calendar flew by that first year. Bev seemed to function well again, as I did, which I would call the healing phase of mourning. She didn't "get over" David's death, but found a way to accept his absence. Each of us, but Bev in particular, can say, "I feel good about how I did today." We had a reason to want a good life again, and that involved more than wanting each other. It's more than functioning again in society, too. We were able to find meaning in our life again.

But as Bev became more active in solidarity work, her need for justice became a weight on her back, holding her down. At St. John's I found myself preaching about justice more, until Jerry Shields offhandedly said one Sunday that I sounded like a prosecutor. He had a point.

In the spring, I arranged to have a meeting in Washington, D.C. at the State Department building on Pennsylvania Avenue. I was brought to a room with a long conference table. I met with a man named William Hoffman, an Assistant to an Under Secretary of State. He looked just like the dozen or so others I saw in the hallways, same dark suit, almost purple but blue, same white starched shirt. Hoffman sat at the head of the table, while I took a seat along one side.

I stared at Hoffman, then said, "I thought time would heal me, and Bev. Grief is one ugly son of a bitch. And that's why I want answers. Do you have a clue about what I'm saying?"

When Hoffman said nothing, I pushed back from the table, getting up. "Wait," Hoffman said. "There is someone here to speak to you, to give you some background."

A door behind Hoffman opened, and I watched a man enter the room. He was given a brief introduction as Edward Isaacs, a United States State Department representative from the Office of Planning. The briefing would be "on background" which meant that the speaker would not be identified by name and title. The man sauntered into the briefing room. Unlike the others wearing conservative suit and tie attire, this man wore a scuffed leather flight jacket, dark glasses, fatigue pants and a gold watch. As he introduced himself and his think-tank affiliation, he sat down in a chair across from me and unfolded into a casual position of indifference. I looked at him in amazement. The guy was not as alert as Harrison Ford playing Indiana Jones, not quite as cool as Bogart playing himself, but he seemed to have both in mind as he created his self image.

The "State Department Official", as I was instructed to identify him if I thought about quoting him at any time in the future, characterized Central America as a region of the world where violence is unusually severe. He began to explain how he had studied the region, traveled there regularly, and was taking his important time to brief me because of my special circumstance. I listened for a while, hearing standard ideology, ordinary patriotism and allusions to inside but classified information. I interrupted finally, reminding the man how we had been through enough to know the specifics of our case. "I'm not interested in generalities, or theories about Latin America and the domino effect. I want to know about the man who shot David."

The man adjusted his gold watch, leaned further back, and continued to lecture. "Violence," he said, "is a subject in which I specialize. For example, do you understand that in El Salvador, violence is internally generated and externally supported."

"I can't believe this," I answered. "David was murdered by a death squad, part of the military, though everyone denies that now. Damn it, the violence they internally generated is a crime. The external support is those people who won't bring him to justice."

"Justice is only part of the equation," the man went on. "Sometimes other matters —national security for one— takes precedence."

"Wrong," I shot back, "unless we need to rely on injustice to preserve our security. Is that what you're saying?"

The man just looked at me, stared for a long time. "I didn't expect you to understand," he said finally, and got up, sauntering out of the room as he pulled on the sleeves of his leather jacket.

I sat back in the chair, playing with a pencil. "If that last statement," I said to Hoffman, "is true, then he's a damn fool who knows nothing. If it's a lie, as I suspect it is, then everything he said is probably a lie as well. Doesn't say much for your resources, does it?"

Hoffman studied the now closed door. He turned back to me. "Reverend Silas, your cause is compellingly tragic. But I believe there's no way at all for you to bring this murderer to justice." He shook his head sadly, showing regret and said, "Someone, I can't say who and shouldn't even admit this, is protecting the man. He's just out there and you, me too for that matter, can't touch him."

Fourteen

On the day Charles went to the State Department, Bev traveled with him on the Amtrak train. She no longer had patience for diplomacy and political intrigue, however, and, instead of going with Charles to State, she walked over to the Capital Building, promising to either stay there or go back to a specified cafe in Union Station to wait until Charles found her. Bev had wanted to see the hunger-striking veterans, members of Veterans for Peace who were camped on the steps of the Capital, fasting in protest of the U.S. policy in Nicaragua. It had nothing to do with El Salvador, and everything if the government's domino theory had any viability.

The trip to DC had not renewed the deep-felt sadness when Bev thought about the injustice that pervaded her every experience in El Salvador; that never left her. Someday, she prayed to herself as she walked along, God will explain it all to me. Someday, she thought, looking up at the heavens reflexively, saddened by the lack of certainty in this world. When I see God, or better than that, when I see my son David again, I will have answers. But until then, I really don't know.

The fasting veterans were on the east steps of the Capital Building, and a small crowd stood near, listening to someone talk about the reasons why aid to the Contras should be halted. A young girl was playing a guitar, hinting at protest songs but not playing any melody long enough for others to sing along with the familiar fragments. Bev watched for a while, then wandered nearer to the rotunda, a hundred feet or so from the strikers.

A tall, fair-haired, older man with a sun-flushed, weathered face sat on the stone steps near where Bev stopped. As she approached him, Bev thought he had a faint resemblance to David's father, her first husband, and it surprised her that she would even think of him. Long gone from her life, more than twenty some years, she long ago stopped keeping track of the years or him, for that matter. "This is how David might look twenty years from now," she thought.

"The fasting isn't pretty," the man said, "especially when there's no response from Congress."

"If the politicians would listen to me," she replied, "I'd tell them a thing or two."

"I've tried. Few, if any, listen to anything they don't want to hear. But that's the same everywhere. In the churches, too, people aren't open to the facts, even when those of us who've been there tell what we've seen and done."

"Have you been to Central America?" Bev asked.

"I've worked there. Twenty years, in Guatemala and Nicaragua, and also some in Mexico. I'm a missioner, what we used to call missionaries, with the Presbyterian Church. My name is Jack."

"Hello Jack. I'm Bev and I've been to El Salvador, once, and Guatemala, once, with my son."

"I've been to Salvador too, on delegations. I was on the Presbyterian Church's national task force on Central America, in 1986 and 1988. Our reports were accepted at the General Assembly. Most of the folks in the pews back home ignored them."

"They probably think you're too political. But I've read them. My husband is a Lutheran Minister. Charles Silas."

He laughed. "I met Charles a few times. Good preacher. Good thinker, too. For me, I am so naive about politics. I had my chance, once, to tell the government what I thought, but then nothing ever came of it. But it's a good story."

They both turned to look again at the fasting veterans as applause rang out for a new speaker being introduced. Bev glanced at Jack, wondering why she had begun talking with this stranger. David would have liked him, talked with him about missioners they both knew. He reminded her of the kind of person David sought out, tried to be like. Charles will like this too, she thought, wondering why she didn't think of him first. "I'd listen to your story," she said, wanting to preserve the moment. "If you have time, I mean." She paused. "I'm waiting for my husband. He's in a meeting. You said it's a good story." Lord I hope I don't sound too eager, Bev thought.

"Sure. I've the time to talk about my moment in the political world. Once upon a time," Jack laughed, "actually late one night in July, 1987, I was sitting on my porch, enjoying the summer warmth and talking with my wife, Fran, about our efforts for peace in Central America. I'd been leading a week of talks at a church, trying to have a dialogue. Attendance was poor. I felt shunned. Some questioned my patriotism. I found myself at the emotional bottom of my efforts to communicate. The phone rang, and I did not expect good news. Who calls with joy late at night?"

"I can't imagine," Bev said, knowing how the telephone would never ring the same way for her.

"The call was from a secretary in the office where I'm based. She is the most reliable worker in the office, and never puts things off. This night, however, she had just remembered that she had taken a call at the office for me, from California, from a Presbyterian Church secretary, who wanted to know if I would be able to go to the White House in August to discuss the 1987 Task Force report. It seems that President Reagan had been given a copy of our denomination's report by a minister he calls pastor. In California. He had sent the report with a short cover note after it was adopted. Reagan had asked the man, 'How can this be?' After some discussion, they invited part of the task force to the White House. Including me. Six of us in all."

"And you went, obviously." Bev began to envy him for having the opportunity to speak to the most powerful person in the world.

"Initially, we met with Frank Carlucci, the National Security Adviser, and several aides including General Colin Powell. Carlucci said he took issue with some of our conclusions. For example, he said, he objected to our statement that there was no democracy in El Salvador. He mentioned elections. I said the Salvadoran Government using torture to obtain confessions couldn't be a democracy."

I know about torture, Bev thought, nodding for Jack to continue.

"After this dialogue, we were taken to the Roosevelt Room, where we met Secretary of State George Schultz, Vice President George Bush, and others in the cabinet. President Reagan entered, spoke momentarily with each of us while the photographer took pictures. Then we all took our assigned places at the conference table. The pastor introduced the group and led us in prayer. Reagan opened with prepared remarks, using three-by-five note cards. Schultz then added additional background and policy remarks which were exclusively in east-west terms. A minister from California spoke for our group, focusing on the issue of religious freedom in Nicaragua, suggesting that our denomination stood ready to help bring about peace.

"Each of us spoke about what was most important for him or her to say. We all showed respect for the office and the man, President Reagan. He later sent a note to his minister that he 'appreciated the good discussion we had.' We did too."

"That's quite a story," Bev said. She had listened to every word, knowing that David had been alive in 1987, in Guatemala perfecting his Spanish skills. If policy had really changed, maybe David would still be here, she briefly thought, then rejected. 'What if's' were something she put out of her mind as soon as they came. Bev looked to the west, toward the White House. Oh, if I could get in there, I'd demand justice, not peace, she thought. She remembered Fidencio and the other Salvadorans who refused to fight. Bev asked, "What did you accomplish by the visit?"

"We don't take credit for the peace efforts, nor do we actually think our words had any major effect," Jack answered.

"Still," Bev added, "you can't be sure. Your obligation was to speak out then and you did."

"We have continued to speak," Jack said, "for what that's worth. I really don't know. And, three of the six of us were audited by the IRS."

A silence followed, as Bev let her imagination take her back to David, to the response he would have said to this man who had a window of opportunity to influence his government. He probably knew David, she thought. But I'm not going to tell him. He's sad. He's tried to change the world, make it a better place. He's put his faith in God. I've done that too, she reminded herself. "I appreciate your story," she said. "Keep on telling it. Keep on with what you're doing. And God bless you." Tears had started to form in her eyes.

"Thanks for listening," Jack said as he got up. "It's been a long time since I have been given a blessing by someone from my congregation. You did just that. Thank you." He stepped away. "I've got to go. Time to be in another meeting." Knowing there was nothing more to say, Jack walked away, toward the fasting veterans, walking just a bit lighter after having told his story.

Bev found Charles and they exchanged stories of who they met and what they had learned on the train back to Drexel Hill. Life went on, but both of them felt that they were waiting. For what, they didn't know.

O

Time passed after that trip to DC, but little helped them learn anything about David's murder. They wrote letters, made calls, but nothing happened. Then El Salvador made the world news again. The first day of a major offensive, November 11, 1989, began with coordinated attacks in San Salvador by the Farabundo Martí National Liberation Front guerrillas, giving them control of parts of the capital city for the first time in the ten-year-old civil war. The FMLN forces dug in, awaiting a popular uprising to support them. Death struck randomly as the fighting escalated terribly.

The government responded by raining down bombs and artillery fire on any suspected entrenchment. Innocents and combatants alike were killed. Overnight a whole nation became paralyzed with fear. Frustrated by the inability of its forces to enter the zones controlled by the FMLN, the government struck where it always had, bringing the violence to those who worked within the law to bring change. Priests, other religious and human rights workers were threatened, if not actually harmed, and whole communities were pillaged and persecuted.

The University of Central America *José Simeón Cañas*, was a frequent target of response by those in power who wanted to punish someone, anyone, for any threat to the status quo. The UCA, as it is known, is situated south of the capital, San Salvador, along the Southern Highway, close to the notorious bank of the Military, named the Tower of Democracy. Repeated bombing by the rebels had rendered the bank unusable.

The main gate at the UCA opens to the highway, giving access to a driveway up a small hill, stopping at a gatehouse on the left or entering the parking level on the right. The driveway leads higher to cement buildings and walkways amid tropical flowering plants and trees, then still higher to the chapel and the residences of the Jesuits, priests who founded the University and serve as its faculty. Above the UCA are the houses of *Jardines de Guadalupe*, the residential neighborhood where two additional houses were used by some of the Jesuits, at 16 Calle Cantábrico and 50 Calle Mediterráneo. An upper pedestrian entrance provided access between the neighborhood and the school property.

Classes at the UCA were canceled, of course, as soon as the fighting began. A curfew was installed by the government that prohibited any civilian activity after 6 o'clock in the evening. Students and staff went home, leaving only the priests and a few others who tried to maintain the necessary services. As the FMLN offensive and the government's response intensified, UCA became a university under virtual siege by the Salvadoran military.

As the offensive began on that Saturday, several fighters from the FMLN blew open a gate with a bomb, entered into the campus and disappeared from sight. An army patrol set up heavy guard. A military guard drastically restricted entry and egress.

○

Four days later, on November 15, Padre Rafael walked out the front door of Saint Oscar's church, to the corner and down the street to the trolley he took to the central part of the capital. In spite of the conflict, some services were running during the day when both sides seemed to ease their maneuvers. At the produce market, Rafael changed to a taxi he was lucky to catch, riding as far as a clinic on *Calle Poniente*, near the U.S. Embassy. There Rafael spoke with a catechist who was to accompany a doctor going back into the mountains. The catechist would take the Holy Eucharist to isolated communities near Chalatenango. After his brief meeting, Rafael hitched a ride in the other direction with a Lutheran church worker who could bring him directly south on *Avenida De Los Heroes*, within two miles of the UCA. The rest of the way would be on foot, mostly along the Southern Highway.

Rafael didn't mind the walk, looking forward to prayer and reflection as he went, finding comfort in a dialogue with God that helped him to understand, or more accurately, accept the ongoing struggle. Rafael found the notion of God siding with the poor as key to his understanding of liberation theology.

A preferential option, to him, meant that those who had a choice also had an obligation to help the poor, to raise up the abysmal standard of living—almost a standard of dying for the really poor—of those less fortunate. The responsibility was not for the poor to raise themselves, for they would have done so if they could. The rich, those well off enough to have to have a choice, were called to work for justice. If this word was subversive, he didn't know, but he did understand how change had to come if those who called him *Padre* were to have any kind of life in this world. A calmness came to his face as it did each time he came to this point in his logic. A life in this world should be good if God is in this world and God is with the poor. How could it be any other way?

As Rafael walked along the side of the road, a White Jeep Cherokee eased up along side him, then pulled in front and stopped with the blackened windows of the passenger side in his path. Fear struck Rafael as he recognized first the vehicle, then the driver. Colonel Juan del Norte showed Rafael his automatic pistol, almost waving, then leaned on the hood, aiming at the priest's heart. The former head of the Treasury Police, he had retired and stayed out of headlines after the massacre at the Co-Madre offices the year before. Rafael had heard rumors that the Colonel had gone to Georgia, to the infamous School of the Americas at Fort Benning.

"At last we meet again," del Norte said, pulling back the slide to cock the gun and chamber a round.

"Haven't you killed enough?" Rafael kept his eyes on the gun as his mind raced, trying to think of a place to run, to hide. Maybe he could dive forward, against the truck. But then where would he go?

"A long time ago, before the whole mess started with the kid from the U.S., I knew you were a problem. You were the one I meant to take out."

Rafael listened to the occasional car passing, hoping that one might be the military and stop, wishing he could be arrested, taken to the safety of the political prisons. "I have done no crime. I have sought justice and truth."

Del Norte closed his eyes for a moment, as if remembering the trouble in 1988 when it all came undone. "There's no other way."

"Here? On the highway?" Rafael looked away finally, pulling his gaze from the gun and up to the heavens. A prayer formed in his mind. He thought of his father, Alejandro, and his sister, Vitalina. So much sadness had come into their lives. He thought about his parish, and the work he still had to do. He thought about justice and truth, wondering if either would come to this land named after the Savior he served. Time seemed to stand still as he prayed. "God," was the only word he spoke. A welcoming filled him as the first bullet struck him, then the second and third. Rafael was dead before the shooting ended, at home now with his God and his Monsignor. Del Norte could do no more harm to this priest.

Del Norte could prevent closure for those who knew him, however, and create a mystery that might even bring him to those he also wanted to remove. He came around to the side door, heaved the body into the back seat, and drove off. Later that day he would strip the clothes and dump the naked priest in a ravine. A soldier on patrol would find the body and have it disposed of, not making any effort to determine the identity of just one more casualty among so many.

Then del Norte returned the Jeep Cherokee, reloaded his gun, and went about the other off-the-record tasks he had on his agenda. He would leave El Salvador in three days, amid the confusion of the conflict, taking with him a watch and a prayer book that belonged to the now dead priest. And he would not return to use them for almost a year.

O

In his first year at the UCA, Saul Flores lived just outside the campus itself. The young protégé of Padre Rafael had been meeting with him from time to time at the UCA. Saul planned to talk with Rafael today, late in the afternoon, just outside the upper gate. Both men knew the danger they faced as the priest made his way to the UCA from his safe places. It was a risk among many risks they had taken during the ten years of El Salvador's civil war.

Saul grew up in Agilares, a town north of the capital. This middle-sized city had been the site of the assassination of the Jesuit Rutilio Grande in 1977, when Saul was twelve years old. Even at that age the death of a priest impacted on his life, as it did in everyone's life who knew and followed the voice of a new church.

Saul's parents had been hurt by Padre Grande's death because he preached a new gospel in which justice would be found in this life, not only in heaven. People were moved to work for change in society, seeking education, vaccination, sanitation, and fair wages. Saul's father, Luis Flores, joined a labor union and worked tirelessly at his job in a factory and as a union organizer, until his death by disappearance in 1981. Saul's mother, Gertrudis, and his two brothers continued to work in the factory, no longer belonging to the union. From time to time, Saul would visit his extended family in Agilares, enjoying the special food Gertrudis cooked for him.

Saul moved to San Salvador in 1983 after his parish priest found work for him with the Archdiocese offices. Saul had felt a calling to the priesthood, but was uncertain. Saul soon found a church home at St. Oscar's, meeting and joining the youth group that belonged to that church, getting to know Padre Rafael, who taught them theology between trips to and from his own congregation in the countryside.

Saul arrived at the now closed refreshment stand just outside the UCA. The only persons he saw were Salvadoran Army soldiers, blocking the turnstile gate and relaxing, arms not at the ready. One soldier gazed idly in Saul's direction, not seeing him, not concerned. Saul waited, wondering how long it would be before Rafael arrived. His closest mentor would find a way, Saul felt confident, to get past the check points, to be invisible to those who tried to control the streets. Rafael was an expert in clandestinity. But as time went on and Rafael didn't show, Saul began to worry.

Saul remembered the many times Rafael came to meetings, in the country and in the city, showing up when the others had given up expectations. He felt excitement at being able to share the latest letter from Bev in the United States. Keeping in touch with his dead friend's parents helped Saul through the bad days of his grief, such as when he felt guilty that he, not his trusting friend, should have been the one shot. David's mother—the one who most felt the grief and pain of such a senseless murder—always uplifted Saul, so much so that his decision to enter the priesthood flowed, to a significant extent, from Bev's willingness to place others ahead of herself. Saul's long talks with Padre Rafael, reflecting on the events in 1988 and the theological significance they had for Saul and his nation, could have no other logical conclusion for him.

The hours and minutes continued to go by without his friend's arrival, however, and at the last moment that he could be sure to make it back to his safe house, Saul regretfully left the campus entrance.

That evening Saul tried to study, working on class assignments that might not be due until the fighting stopped, needing to be busy to keep from worrying. Rafael had still not contacted him, couldn't now during the curfew. The conflict raged across the city and into the countryside, and the deaths of so many innocent people gripped Saul's heart like tongs in a block of ice. Saul also found himself thinking back to the murder of his good friend, David Stevens in March, 1988.

The evening grew late, well after midnight. Suddenly, Saul's
studying and reminiscing were interrupted by sounds of closer than
normal gunfire. Saul raced to his window after quickly turning out his
study lamp. Shattering glass and loud shouting tempered his desire to
investigate further. Carefully peeking from behind the curtained front
window, Saul could see part of the passageway that led from the Romero
Chapel to the new Jesuit residence. Five men were standing by the gate,
three hidden by shadows and two clearly visible in the moonlight.

Then he heard a voice he recognized, Padre Ignacio Martín-Baró,
Nacho as the others called him, cry out, "This is an injustice! This is an
abomination." Saul looked intently but could not see the priest. They
were pleading for their lives, yet still challenging the injustice confronting
them. Another voice, Saul couldn't be sure who, said something but all
Saul could hear was the word "God."

Shots rang out and Saul knew that death had once again taken those
who worked so hard for peace in El Salvador, those who inspired him.
One, maybe several of the theological lights in El Salvador had been
blown out, literally by the guns of the army. Saul slumped by the window,
no longer looking for signs of life, not even able to move.

Dead were Ignacio Ellecuría, Rector of the University; Ignacio Martín-
Baró, Vice-Rector; Segundo Montes, Director of the Human Rights
Institute; and Amando López, Joaquín López y López and Juan Ramón
Moreno, all teachers at UCA. The soldiers went into the building,
looking for proof of a connection to the guerrillas, Saul would later
learn. Also murdered that night were Julia Elva Ramos, who was working
in the residence, and her 16-year-old daughter, Celina Mariceth Ramos.
The soldiers came upon them hiding in the kitchen and shot them
without hesitation, eliminating witnesses to their terror.

Saul didn't know what to do. If he went to where the Jesuits were, he
might be shot. He wondered if one or more was not dead, waiting to be
rescued. His stomach churned, then he left his room, trying to stay in the
shadows. When he got to the scene, all of the priests were dead. Blood
spattered on the wall of the building and pooled on the lawn. Eye glasses
of one of the Jesuits lay twisted, one lens broken. Another priest still held
a book, it too now blood stained. Saul left when he heard others coming.
They turned out to be security people who would report the massacre.

It would not be until the funeral that Saul would be able to speak
at all. He stayed in his room, only eating one meal a day. Sitting in the
pew with fellow seminarians, even more worried because his friend and
mentor, Padre Rafael had not contacted him. Saul buried his head in
his arms, defeated in sorrow and pain. He watched the funeral service,
listened to the speeches and prayers, not joining in any of the common

prayers and songs. He remained frozen, as dead as the dead ones, until
he heard a young girl barely able to see over the pulpit from which
she spoke. Her words rang out, giving meaning to the deaths of Saul's
martyrs and meaning to his life: "Do not weep for them," she would cry.
"Imitate them!" Finally Saul had heard a prayer to which he would be
able to say, "Amen."

Fifteen

November 16, 1989, the day that the six Jesuits and two women were martyred in San Salvador, will long live in the memory of those whose hearts and feelings are with El Salvador. Just as many who were adults in the 1960s can tell you exactly where they were and what they were doing when they heard that President John F. Kennedy and Martin Luther King had been shot, many who were active in peace and justice issues in the 1980s remember when and where they received the news of the massacre of the Jesuits in El Salvador.

On the 16th, I had been at my office at St. John's when I received a phone call from Jerry Shields, who had seen it on television. I immediately went to find Bev at her office. She worked as a paralegal just ten blocks from the church, and I wanted to break the news to her in person. The receptionist had seen me before when I had to see Bev, so she went to get her. Bev looked panic stricken when she came to the lobby. "It's news from El Salvador," I said, to anticipate fears about family or friends here in the U.S.

"Tell me," Bev whispered, then burst into tears when I told her about the assassinations at the UCA. She calmed down, trying to be professional in an office that occasionally had to adjust to her emotional responses to life. I had said several times that, for lawyers and for most employers, they were more understanding than I would have expected.

We stayed up late that night, watching TV news programs and making phone calls. Anger flared in both of us, along with a sense of helplessness that virtually paralyzed our ability to think of anything we could try to do about the events in El Salvador. Exhausted finally, we ended our vigil with a promise to keep committed to finding a way to end the injustice, and to end the terror from the war. The fires of anger were banked, no longer flaming but still so hot, so ready to burst again to consume what is placed on them. We went to bed, zombie like. Neither of us voiced the ever-present reality of merely a year and a half ago, of David's death.

○

Bev wanted to go to the funeral of the Jesuits, even as she admitted it would be far too dangerous. We watched the news coverage, read the papers, met with everyone from El Salvador who came through Philadelphia. Our basement conference room served as a base for an entire community of people like us who felt the pain of the war and lacked any constructive plan to make a difference. Almost every meeting included some reference to Archbishop Romero's statement that, "Everybody can do something." We wished it were true, but for a long while, that "something" seemed to elusive for any of us.

If the slaughter of the Jesuit priests took El Salvador to a new low, down into the infamous places in history, it also served as the point where change finally took place. The FMLN learned that the popular uprising they sought to gain control of the nation didn't happen. The majority of the population did not take up arms. Those in control of the government, including the military, saw decreased international support for their war against communism. The people, sick of murder and destruction, simply resisted. One time when we talked about El Salvador, Bev said that David was like the majority of Salvadorans who could not participate in the violence themselves but who also were victims of it.

Of course Bev, and myself as well now, were still on the early part of the path to healing, whatever that might have been back then. Often when we sat together, in the living room in front of the fire in the cold months, on the patio under the canvas awing in nice weather, Bev would tell me stories of David, sharing memories that kept them fresh for her and brought me to know her son well enough to refer to him as my stepson. If he were alive, I could call him that, and I did, more and more, during that year. Bev took pleasure now in having her son for even those short, short twenty-three years, and sharing that with me gave her a vehicle to reconstruct his life. Once in a while she would interrupt a story to dash off to the area upstairs where she kept many of his things, then return with a school paper, drawing or piece of clothing that confirmed this latest memory.

Bev also found her anger to be strong, always present, seldom far below the surface. Bev began to judge everything against the rules that she had learned as a child, from her parents, at school, in church. Thou shalt not kill stood foremost for her of course, but coveting and stealing, lying, doing evil generally could not be tolerated in her presence. In some instances her vigilance brought satisfaction, like when she reported seeing an act of vandalism or when she honked her car horn as a driver made an illegal turn, only to see a police car following along to give the offender a traffic ticket. In many cases, unfortunately, her new, stronger sense of justice brought frustration when others ignore an act of injustice, not protesting nor speaking up.

○

Life was not all mourning and emotional pain. We were busy, Bev with her work as a paralegal, her gardening and, finally, some crafts. We had a glass or two of red wine most evenings, and she bought a super large hose clamp that she put around some corks we saved, then covered the clamp with hemp, making a hot pad. We took time to cook together whenever we could, though there were evening when I had to be at church and didn't come home until 9:00 or so.

The summer of 1990 lasted longer than normal, even for Philadelphia, and we spent quiet time on the patio under the awning. I called it our de-briefing time because we seemed to need to process the day together. There were times when I thought that heaven wouldn't be any better than our life together. We lived a very good, loving life, at first in spite of David's death, then because of how we preserved the memories.

We also talked about finding an opportunity to return to El Salvador. When we learned of a planned celebration in November, commemorating the first anniversary of the atrocity at the UCA, we decided to join that event. We would have the opportunity to visit with the rural community of Las Anonas, be part of what David would have been doing if he were still alive. Bev called our decision to go a "no-brainer" and made flight reservations the next day.

○

Three young men sat in front of us on the flight from Philadelphia to Miami, talking of parties and girls. One, in the middle, showed the others a magazine of soft pornography, pointing to one photo and then to the stewardess. The three could be brothers, Bev whispered, saying she saw a strong resemblance in their faces as they twisted and turned in their seats. Another put on earphones, bobbing to the music on the tape player. His head looks like a city pigeon walking after popcorn, she said. When another one took the earphones, his head swayed in the same manner. Bev quietly asked me if instructions on how to bob one's head came with the music. She seemed to be pleased at being able to joke about men who were about her son's age —her dead son's age she added— without feeling totally shattered.

The scars were healing, as she had been told would happen, wounds no longer raw and open. Padre Rafael in San Salvador had been the first to tell her. Or had it been me? Maybe both and maybe others too had told her she would begin to heal, and they were right. Bev had once survived her own confrontation with death, willing to give her own life so others might live. Even now, she would trade her life for having David back, alive. But that wasn't possible.

In the two years, seven months and seventeen days since the murder of her son, David Stevens, in the tiny Central American nation of El Salvador, Bev had found her way out of the deepest intensity of her grief by helping others. This day, November 10, 1990, as we began our travel, the adventure of conversion some would say, Bev spoke positively about how she had fulfilled a promise she had made to David, many years before, when he had been similarly converted amid the violence, murder and devastation that spewed out of El Salvador.

○

Our plane left Miami an hour late, on the second leg to San Salvador, bringing a first vivid moment of culture shock. As we boarded the plane, I felt a chill as I made eye contact with a heavy man, obviously Salvadoran, sitting in first class, in the very seat where Bev had sat next to me two plus years ago, his jacket tossed over the next seat to claim even more space. His eyes flattened, looking fierce and disdainful at us as we walked by, as if to say, "I don't want you *gringos* in my country. You're up to no good." I held his gaze as I walked by his seat to the tourist class section. I have seen that look, I thought, as if he thought he could do anything he wanted, just because of who he thought he was. More than contempt, he emanated impunity, above responsibility.

Bev hooked her arm around me as the plane climbed away from the Florida coast and out over the water, smiling at me, searching my eyes for confirmation of my well being. Bev hugged me, rested her head on my shoulder, squeezed her affection into me. Several times she has said that she cares about me, more now because we had gone through the death of her son together. She knew I had tried so hard to reach her those first months, promising whatever she asked for, and, mostly, delivering. She has told me that she would always treasure my presence, the strength I gave her until she could stand again on her own.

And now, together as always, we were on our way once again to the land that had claimed her only child, her David. Bev spoke the words of a poem I had given her, words that talked about looking forward in good memories, a memorial to a life, not backward in pain. "You saved my life," she whispered, "gave me permission to do whatever I needed in order to understand and ultimately accept David's death." She hugged my arm again, smiling at me as I lost my concentration on whatever I was thinking about. I too felt the love and joy of being with her.

As the plane droned on, we settled into our seats, each absorbed with our own thoughts. The talking, joking, reviewing plans of the first leg of the trip were done and now it was time to get ready for the challenges that we could anticipate and brace against the ones we could not foresee. El Salvador was at war with itself, and tensions were high as the threat of a second offensive loomed. In six days it would be the first anniversary of the assassination of the six Jesuits and two woman. A march had been planned in commemoration of the anniversary. Who could know what lay ahead?

O

The next morning, I sat in our room at the Hotel Alemeda, waiting for Bev to finish her shower, watching the sky cloud up with an impending storm. Last night's reunion with Saul, with the devastating news of Padre Rafael's disappearance, had stunned us both, leaving me, at least, almost unable to function, as if we were drunk. Saul had also made plans for us to go to the country the next day for an overnight trip to meet Rafael's family, and then return for the anniversary celebration and mass at the UCA.

Waking and remembering the priest, I felt shrouded in a hangover of fresh grief. "I never blamed him for David's death," Bev said when she got out of bed. "I sort of blame David for being a hero, saving Rafael's life you know. Sad, not blame like with anger and all that." Then she disappeared into the bathroom to get ready.

When the rain arrived, I turned my chair around to face the window. I shut off the air conditioner, opened the windows and looked out on the roof tops and walls of nearby buildings. The sky had closed in so that the sheets of driven rain seemed like waves in a sea, no clouds now but one huge enveloping gray mass of water like the hull of a great ship coming into harbor. When the rainfall diminished, individual darker portions re-formed into ominous shapes moving across lighter, higher gray. Several times, the rain intensified, enclosed and re-formed.

After a bit, the dormant volcano reappeared on the horizon, lit by lightening that struck like a child tossing pebbles at a sleeping dog. The countryside has always given us answers, I thought, but I really don't want to go. This is going to be a difficult trip, if only because I'm not a country boy. I listened to the rain and thunder, watched the sky bright with lightening, and admitted to myself that I was afraid.

"I'm not doing well with this," I said out loud, talking only to myself, trying to find my orientation, "and I'm taking my wife, the treasure of my life, into the country. I really hope that I can find a way to calm my fear." My hands were shaking and I sat, feeling as if there was no strength in them. My forearms tingled, and I shook, feeling that I couldn't hold a thought. Silent, I prayed, no longer in control of this day.

After a moment, I stood up, picked up my change of clothes and went to hurry Bev so I could take my shower. "It may be my last moment of comfort and luxury for a few days," I said aloud, to the otherwise empty room. The thunder answered me.

○

Colonel Juan del Norte, retired, returned again to El Salvador in early November, 1990, coming from Fort Benning, Georgia, and the School of The Americas via Charlotte, North Carolina, and Houston, on a series of military flights. His straight, military posture and half closed eyes invited no contact from others on the planes. If he had confided in anyone, he would have said he was coming to El Salvador for revenge.

In time, the Air Force transport landed at Ilopango Air Force Base, just inside San Salvador, and the Special Forces soldiers went their way. Del Norte quietly walked from the plane and through security. Del Norte went directly to the office of Colonel Sigifredo Ochoa, a close associate of retired Major Roberto D'Aubuisson, the evil one who would eventually be found to have ordered the assassination of Archbishop Romero. From there del Norte was taken by car to a house on Calle Mediterráneo, above the Jesuit-run University in San Salvador, the *Universidad de Simon Cañas*, known as the UCA. At the other end of the block, some of the priests lived in an off-campus Jesuit residence.

Colonel Ochoa did not live in this neighborhood but kept the house for guests. On a hill above the UCA, this neighborhood had many of the features of upper class residences, with high walls topped with razor wire or broken glass cemented on the top. A heavy steel gate covered the driveway, offering no opening even large enough to peek through. Inside, the car port held space for two large automobiles. The furnishings offered lavish comfort, with leather chairs and velvet couches, stark modern art and primitive paintings intermixed on the walls.

Three parrots in a large cage acted as sentries in the spacious, partially covered front yard. The living room at the other end ended with a view from the hillside on which the house sat, looking north and east over the main section of the capital. A small lawn and garden extended out from and below the living room. Ochoa had told del Norte several times that six turtles had been let loose in the yard, but, as the maid noticed, del Norte never bothered to look for them.

Del Norte went to the master bedroom, waiving away the maid who followed him through the house. "*Nada. Quiero nada* , he said. "I don't want anything." The maid shrugged, going back to the kitchen.

Del Norte unpacked quickly and stripped to his shorts. He began an exercise program of isometric stretching. He looked forward to dinner later that evening with the Colonel, when he would listen to each dinner guest describe the efforts made to contain Communism. In exchange for listening to their ideological patriotism, he would renew contacts and obtain the tacit permissions he needed. He would also pass on the response from his people in the States concerning the Jesuits.

Only the very powerful few, who used and protected him, a United States senator from the south, two very wealthy brothers, an aging entrepreneur with connections to a major fortune and a religious coalition, gave him access to some of the military apparatus, primarily of those who controlled the massive military aid that went to this country. In Honduras he had a well equipped country home with servants and military guards that served as his base of operation where he directed various factions of the Contras who sought to violently overthrow the Sandinista Government in Nicaragua.

○

The next day del Norte went for a walk through the nearby campus. Del Norte carried Rafael's watch and prayer book in his pocket. They now would be found, bringing others into his reach. He watched the growing crowds at the UCA as people gathered for a first anniversary commemoration of the Jesuit assassinations.

A fence had been put up around the area where the Jesuits had been shot in the head, splattering brains and blood on the wall. A rose garden grew there now, tended by the husband of Julia Elva Ramos and father of their 16-year-old daughter, Celina Mariceth Ramos. Both women had also been slaughtered in that massacre. Part of an office near the chapel had been made into a simple museum that displayed some of the blood soaked soil, an illusion to the Cane and Able story he overheard. The exhibit cases held books, pipes, eye glasses and other mementos of the dead priests. There were photographs too, showing the death and life of these men.

Casually, del Norte stopped a young man as he walked from the offices of the school. "Are you a student? A seminarian?" When del Norte confirmed what he expected, he handed the seminarian the watch he had taken from Padre Rafael. "This is also a souvenir of a martyrdom. Perhaps you can help it get to someone who might know the family?"

"Did it belong to one of them?" the student priest asked, pointing to the museum.

"No. I believe it was on the wrist of a priest, not a Jesuit but a priest, non-the-less. His name might have been Rafael." Del Norte placed the watch in the young man's hand and nodded. He turned sharply and walked off, knowing that another seed had been planted.

As del Norte expected, the young seminarian took Rafael's watch to his faculty advisor. The watch, not ornate or gaudy, was still expensive and had an engraving —RAC '75— on the back of the case. Padre Rafael Anaya Chavéz was ordained in 1975, and so the watch was identified, first by Saul, who the advisor knew had been a friend of the missing priest, then by several priests from the Archdiocese who were on campus to take part in the mass later that day. Later Saul found someone from the community where Rafael's father, Alejandro Chícas Anaya, lived, and where his sister, Vitalina Anaya Chavéz, came to visit.

Sixteen

Bev and I met up with Saul and others who were going to Las
Anonas. I drove a rented pickup. The rain had ended and the day began
to look like it might turn out nice. Bev sat next to me. Saul occasionally
broke the silence to point out a landmark as we drove along CA-1, the
Pan-American Highway, slowing for towns and cattle crossing, and
broken trucks or cars. When we reached San Miguel, I braked for the
inevitable tumulos. "Pull over," Saul said, "by those women under the
tree. It's lunch time and they make great pupusas. We can get out and
stretch." Saul immediately began negotiating with two of the women.

Saul bought two apples and polished them on his shirt as he joined
us at the tree where we had walked. We had started to eat the cheese
filled tortillas. "Did you like the pupusas?" he asked. "Here is an apple I
bought for you. It will taste clean and fresh."

Bev took the apple, polished it on her skirt, took a bite. "This is
what I miss, not having David any more." Saul's loss, too, I thought,
because David and Saul would have been very good friends. "You are
a good person," she said. "Someday you will be a fine priest and help
many people. Maybe you will be the one to bring sense to those who are
fighting."

"I am trying to help, but the poor mostly. I want to be a man of God,
of the church. Do you know what I mean?"

"You don't have to convince me. My husband is a man of God," Bev
said, putting a hand on my shoulder. "I know you are a man of God. You
are a very good person."

"You are kind." Saul tossed aside his apple core. "David was so proud
about how kind you are. And he was right."

"I miss him," she said, pulling into herself as though she felt a chill.

"So do I, and that's another reason why I am studying to be a priest.
David was ten times more a person of faith than I am or ever will be."

"He wasn't that religious," Bev said, wiping her lips with a tissue.

"Padre Rafael always told me, 'Saul, at best the church reaches the
ethical but not the prophetic level.' I told him he was prophetic..."
Saul stopped, his face contorted. After a moment, sighing, he went on,
"My professors talk about this at the seminary. There is no Archbishop
Romero, no prophet to challenge the conscience of those who are
responsible for so much death. Like Padre Rafael. I really miss him. He
is, was a prophet."

"I miss him too. He taught me much, even in the short time we were
together. I remember him saying that when people admit they have no

answer," Bev said, "that walking with the people —the poor, mostly,
but others who are victims— is all they suggest, they do the most good.
Accompaniment, as Charles calls it, is an answer in a way. Not an answer,
really, because we don't know why David had to be at that place at
that time. But comfort. Maybe that's enough." Bev looked down at the
ground. "Since the Jesuits were killed, aren't priests really afraid? Look
what we think happened to Padre Rafael."

Saul's hand went to his watch, remembering the watch that had been
recovered at UCA. His face turned white as he spoke of his mentor, his
friend. "We know what happened. Padre Rafael is dead. But we don't
know how or why."

O

News of the appearance of Rafael's watch traveled fast, straight to
the community of *Las Anonas*, and to Rafael's sister. Vitalina held a
photograph of her brother close to her heart. Beyond tears, she squeezed
herself, hurt herself as she sat. "Such a waste of a life," she cried. "It has
never, ever been what we should have had. My brother, Rafael my dear."
Vitalina continued to cry, to hold the photo, to rock herself gently.

As Vitalina sat wrapped in her agony, she thought of ways to find the
killer, to get revenge. Her friends and co-combatants would investigate
Rafael's death, and she would learn who had done it and why, but it was
already clear to her that del Norte had killed him. When she heard about
Rafael's watch and the man who stood so straight, so military, she knew.
It didn't take magic to know some things.

As she sat, thinking, Vitalina toyed with the idea of seeing a witch.
Not a farfetched idea, either, she knew there were people in El Salvador
who claimed they could do some strange, almost black magic things, like
make a loved one come to you or put worms in someone's body. Many
of her family and those she knew growing up in the city believe in a
kind of spirit working. It's so sad, she thought, that my dear brother had
all that faith in God and now he's dead. And I, who know not what to
believe, the church or witches or in my rifle, am left here to wonder. "My
poor, dead brother," she said aloud, feeling anger flowing in her veins,
no longer sad but wanting to savage the man who had taken Rafael from
her.

O

Long after dark, I stopped the truck at the dead end of the dirt path Saul called a road. We had arrived at our destination, the community of *Las Anonas*, a repatriation settlement in an area where the rebel soldiers freely visited. A flashlight glimmered as we got out of the truck, and a Salvadoran man came from behind the trees to greet us. He was dressed in the traditional white fieldworker clothing, and carried a towel around his neck. He led us down the footpath, up a steep hill, coming to the common building which served as meeting hall and church, among other things.

We were given a quick bite to eat by one of the women, and slowly more of the people began to file into the hall. Two men with guitars were joined by a violinist, then a tambourine player, forming a band and playing. Some of the community were dancing. Others talked or just sat, listening and watching.

As the music played, Bev sat along one wall. She played with a young child who flirted with her, then sought the safety of his mother's skirts. She looked out on the dance floor and saw a young man in green fatigues and a black tee shirt. He was dancing with a young woman from the community. Next to him was a girl also in a black tee shirt, who was dancing with the man who had met them at their truck. They were obviously having fun and no one paid special attention to us.

One of the group who had been outside came over to us, saying, "The *Muchachoes* are here. If you want to talk to them, come on out."

Bev went on ahead of me. Outside, a group was talking next to a cement wall which had been decorated with FMLN graffiti. Several men and one more woman were dressed in the black tee shirts. Each had a gun, which they were very careful with, so as not to threaten the rest of the group. In time, they stacked the weapons at the ready.

The conversation was easy as they talked about families and events. No one mentioned the conflict. Bev asked, "What message do you have for me to take back to the United States?"

A young man s said, "We will never stop fighting until there is justice in El Salvador." Others clapped or shouted agreement. Then he asked, "Do you have children?"

"Not any more," she responded. Saul overheard her answer and came over to stand next to her.

The young man hesitated, not sure of what he heard, then pressed on with his proposition. "Do you want another one?"

"Why do you ask," she said, smiling at Saul, shaking her head quickly, as if to warn him from speaking.

"I will be your son. I will come to the United States with you and go to school. I will be your son and go to U.C.L.A." He laughed. "I will even study."

"Then you will stop fighting?" Bev said, holding her hand up to stop Saul from interrupting, not telling the young man about David.

"For a while. I'll study and come back here, better prepared." Someone else asked a question and the moment was gone. No one mentioned David, and Bev remained silent. I had come over too, and Saul whispered what had happened into my ear.

As they talked, a woman in combat clothes, named Vitalina, joined the group. She stared hard at me, almost contemptuous, waiting to see if I would recognize her.

"You?" I said, the moment after she walked up. "You were in the bar, at the Hotel Alemeda in 1988, with, wasn't it Carlos?"

"Your memory is good. Such a pity."

"Why is it a pity?"

Vitalina paused for a moment, studying me, as though I don't know something that I should. "Don't you know that we can't find my brother, my beautiful priest brother. Haven't you asked? Rafael said you wrote, that you understood each other," she said.

When I said I did know that Padre Rafael was missing, she moved away from the group to an alcove where she backed herself against the cold cement wall, pushing her back into the wall and stretching.

I walked over to her as she relaxed. "Is your back bothering you. I couldn't help notice you against the wall, trying to get taller."

"Are you asking me to dance?"

"I wasn't but I will," I replied. We went to the dance floor, and I tried getting a sense of the music, not sure of myself, while Vitalina danced as she had from childhood. Moments later one of the men from the community broke in, rescuing me. "I tried," I said, as they danced away. Vitalina ignored me.

Bev joined me, and we watched Vitalina dance with several of the other muchachos, and with several of the men from the community who were not armed or in uniform. Finally, an older man, Don Alejandro, came over to her, broke in to her dance. Vitalina let him take her in his arms. She stiffened, then went on with the dance. When the music stopped, Bev went across the floor to intercept Vitalina. "Will you talk to me about your brother?" Bev whispered.

At first Vitalina ignored Bev, as though she had moved beyond the present, or had gone back in time to better memories. Coming suddenly back to the present, from the remembered childhood happiness with her brother to the present knowledge that Rafael had been disappeared, certainly dead, her whole being ached for her brother, what was left of her brother, memories. And now, she thought, he can never keep his promise to me.

Of course he agreed and would have kept his promise if she had found that good man. Here, in the middle of a war, in the middle of a nation shattered by fighting and conflict, Vitalina knew she'd never see Rafael again. For a long time she continued to sit, to endure the pain.

Once the two women were in the cooler night air, they walked away from the main building. "It's quieter out here," Vitalina said, "away from the group."

"I wanted you to know how we feel about Rafael. He's so special."

Vitalina stared hard at Bev. "He's dead. I just don't know when or where, but he was disappeared."

"You can hope."

"I have hoped, for a whole year. And I've been in the city and all over, and no one knows where he went. So many times we never get answers. But I still might find out."

"Knowing helps, maybe some, but the death is still a death."

Vitalina's pained expression proclaimed her obviously fresh grief for her brother. "I know you know about it. I heard about you being with Elena and Rosalita in the prison. But my brother is most certainly dead. We both know that."

I'm so sorry," Bev said. Silence overtook them until finally the music from the dance penetrated their thoughts. "What about the rest of your family?" Bev asked. The two sat on a bench near a store room. "Are you from this community."

"I am, now. It didn't exist when I was young. The old one, Don Alejandro, is my father, and he and my mother didn't make it together. He likes the women, always has," she said, voice trailing off.

"Tell me about it. I want to know about your life. How did you come to this?"

Vitalina laughed. "To this? To carrying a rifle and shooting the enemy and sticking my gun in the face of men who bother me? You want to know about me?"

"Sure." Bev pulled her collar up in back of her neck, and shivered. "I'd like to know what led you to carry the gun." Her gaze was fixed on her companion, continuing to ask all the questions she needed desperately to ask. "I have to understand."

"My life story would take too long to tell. But I will tell you this. I was born in the country, north of the capital, one of six. I just danced with Papá." Vitalina thought back to the time she lived in the capital with her father. I'm not going to talk about this, she thought. Not about being thirteen and locked in a shanty all day long because he —the old lecher— thought all women were vulnerable to any man. I remember the keyhole, my only window to the world, and I remember wanting to kill him.

"Did he, um, abuse you?"

"Not that way. He likes women, not girls, and I left when I was thirteen. He didn't know what to do, and when I got my first menstruation, he took me back to my mother. They had separated. The only work she could get was in a house, as a maid or nanny, and the owners didn't want a lot of her kids around. Then, when my brother Rafael came back from Los Angeles, and started to study to be a priest, I went on my own. I worked and I had a tiny apartment. Rafael was the steady influence in my life, always saying that I could handle any problem, offering encouragement. He was proud of me too, when I moved from a job in a kitchen at La Comida Primera to other jobs for better pay."

"You were free," Bev commented, hoping the conversation would continue. I can learn more about Rafael, she thought.

Vitalina shrugged her shoulders. She had always been willing to test authority. Before she took up arms, before her father and her people were hounded to death, she had been working in the city. "Not freedom, not like now where I go where I want. Working is a trap for us in El Salvador. I have a sister who has worked for eight years at a factory for the same wage the whole time."

Bev stared, as if she wondered how that could be.

"If my sister couldn't keep up at her job, someone else would step in her place. Same with me. I needed money to live." Vitalina picked up her rifle and set it across her knees. "This is a tool of death, I know that. But it also is a choice I've made not be chained to a house and not to belong to a man who has no respect for me. Rafael had respect for me, as his sister. I don't know where he got it, because Papá never did have consideration for women, not even Mamá. But anyway, most men I met before I joined the fighting were only interested in one thing. Not that I'm against that," she added.

Bev simply nodded, then sad, "Go on."

"I told Rafael how I felt. He took me to a nun who tried to convert me, tried to get me to become a nun, really, but I couldn't do that. One religious in the family was enough, because Rafael knew about God and I really didn't. And I didn't want to. I wanted freedom, and all I saw in the nuns was a different master. Finally one of the sisters took me to meet a woman. She's famous now. Her name is Comandante Mari Carmen. I talked to her, and she told me to take a bus into the countryside and wait. They found me. That's when I became a *muchacha*, and that's when I learned how to make any man back down. Rafael was furious, quoting from Archbishop Romero and going on about God and love. He was really mad at the Comandante but I made him understand."

"How did you make him understand? I've gotten to know him a little bit and I'm surprised. How did you?"

"My brother couldn't give me anything better. Nothing. I said I couldn't live in a house all my life serving a man and raising his kids, unless he showed me respect and was faithful. I couldn't protect myself in the city, and he couldn't be around all the time. I said I didn't want to be a whore."

"What did he say," Bev asked, thinking that she had that with Charles. Respect.

"He said, if I didn't want to do all those things, then I should probably get a gun and shoot people because life was going to be that way until someone changed them." Vitalina was laughing herself, now.

"Rafael said that?"

"Almost. Everything but actually shooting people. Anyway, I spend most of my time in charge of a radio, not in actual combat. But I have shot some people I think were bad, were part of the problem as the *gringos* say, so when I shot them the problem became simpler. Anyway, our *muchachos* don't have many battles. But here I am, I've talked your ears off." Vitalina stood up. "Let's get back. I want to see if Papá has found someone." The two women went back to the party.

○

Saul and I were sitting by the band when Bev and Vitalina came up to them. "What's Alejandro doing? Vitalina asked."

"Getting drunk", Saul answered. "He's grieving."

"That won't help," I added.

"Charles," Bev said, I was telling Vitalina that if I can't have David back, I want to be healed."

"I want to kill the murderer of my brother," Vitalina said quickly.

"Healing is important," Bev said, talking directly to Vitalina. She had been talking to me about this idea of healing, and obviously had given a lot of thought to what she felt. "Life is meant to go on, I believe, though

I never thought I'd say that." She paused, trying not to cry. "And now I tell people who are hurting like I did that I want to be healed. Charles tells me my wound will scab over, form a scar that isn't an open sore, if I do my grief work. I do want to go on living, though I didn't care at all about dying when I looked at Del Norte and his gun."

I made an exaggerated sigh of relief that was only partly an attempt to be humorous. "I'm not kidding when I say that I'm glad you've started to heal. Really." I shook my head at the feelings I felt for her.

Bev turned to look at me. "Can you hear me say 'if I can't have David back I want to forgive who killed him?' "

"Lord, no," I replied and so did Saul.

"That really sounds phony," Vitalina added.

"It sounds forced," I said, "maybe because not having David back is tied to being healed but I don't know how to put forgiveness in the equation. We both know what they say about vengeance not working."

"It probably doesn't work," Bev nodded. "I don't suppose someone else's death would make it easier for me. I'd worry about the creep's mother."

"Right," Vitalina snorted in disbelief. "I suppose you worry about the scumbag's dog, too."

"Well I know the pain and if David had been a criminal, even a murderer. . ."

"Instead of a martyr?" I asked.

"Yes. Even then, I'd hurt just as bad as I do now. The pain is the same for everyone. But David's killer took my son's life from me —from both of us— and I'm not going to let him take mine."

"I want vengeance," Vitalina interrupted. "Rafael is my brother, and I want revenge."

Seventeen

The next morning, Bev, Saul and I returned to the capital, going directly to the UCA and a campus buzzing with activity. Almost three thousand people had arrived for the events commemorating the murder of the six Jesuit priests and two women, exactly one year ago.

At one end of a parking lot, preparations were being made for an outdoor mass. Small groups of international visitors and campesinos from the countryside made visits to the tombs of the priests in the Romero Chapel, offering up prayers for justice and the well being of the martyrs. Visitors shed tears as they passed through the small exhibit of the personal effects of the murder victims, seeing broken eye glasses, a pipe, books and blood soaked soil. Some ventured behind the buildings to the roped-off garden and wall where the final killings were carried out. The rose garden in full bloom presented a stark contrast to the deaths to which they gave tribute.

I had a brief conversation with Padre Jon de Cortina, S.J., in the park. Father de Cortina had visited St. John's some months before. On sabbatical from the University, he had been working in *Chalatenango* when his six co-workers were murdered. He told me of yesterday's journey from "*Chalate*" and his accompaniment of several hundred campesino families for the commemorative events. It was nice to see him again.

I walked aimlessly for a while, unable to focus on any agenda. What would happen next? Music played over a loudspeaker by *Grupo Teosinte*, providing a background of song and guitars. Visitors mixed with students and with Salvadorans from the city and from the campo. The song *Sombero Azul*, or Blue Sombrero, proclaiming the sky to be the hat of El Salvador, had become my favorite. I found a patch of grass and sat down, laying back, listening to the music and the voices of those who walked by. I looked up at the bright blue sky and the sparse high clouds. I wished I had known David the young boy who knew clouds and sky but none of the horror of murdered priests. David belonged in my memory, when he was young so long ago.

As I lay under the tree, listening to the music, watching the clouds, the Simon and Garfunkle song of the 1960's, *The Boxer*, came over the speakers, also sung by *Grupo Teosinte*, in Spanish. The song broke my reverie. The music sounded so right as I lay there, echoing years off my own life. The words were for today, however, for the Salvadorans of the 1990's, not a translation but an encouragement to persevere. I thought about how being here at the University of Central America contrasted with where we lived in the United States. The words of the song had new meaning, translated from one boxer's struggle to a whole people striving for dignity.

I continued to stare at the blue sky, looking into its depth, remembering the words Padre de Cortina had spoken to the group at St. John's. "If God is not with the people of El Salvador, then God is nowhere." Now much more significant than when I preached about them, the words seemed to pull me into the depth of the sky above, lifting my soul to where there is a God, not quite to where David, now resided. Where is that, I thought, blinking then staring harder, trying to penetrate the infinite blue.

The priest's words rang true. As Padre Cortina added when he spoke at my church, "God is very present in El Salvador." He went on to say that those who visit El Salvador can meet God. He invited them, not only to hear the Gospel but see and taste and smell it being lived by the people with whom God lives. He promised a transforming experience. In this world of much confusion and rapidly changing events, I felt comfort in knowing that God could be near. If that were true, then David was close as well. "This is as close as I get," I thought, "lost in that damn sky. If only I could fly up there and reach into its depth. If only the blue sky wasn't a wall instead of a window to heaven."

◯

That evening, Bev and Vitalina sat together again, this time on the steps of a building near the chapel at the UCA. Their eyes still shone with the excitement of the march from the city, and the moving words that had been spoken during the brief service. Vitalina leaned over to Bev, taking her arm in friendship. "There is so much emotion here," she said. "I can feel it deep down in me."

"There sure is. During the march, the girl with the megaphone had me shouting right with her," Bev answered.

"It has a strength," Vitalina replied. "*¡No a la guerra! ¡Si a la paz!* No to war! Yes to peace! It sounds better in Spanish."

"I tried to watch the people," Bev said. "The bystanders seem to be smiling, some of them, and a few have scowled, but for the most part the march seemed to be okay with them. Do you think they support the protest?"

"Some do, some not so much," Vitalina said. "A lot of the people in El Salvador don't like the war and blame both sides for it. They understand our protest, and a lot are really outraged at the killings of the priests. But most of them didn't join the offensive last year and wouldn't today if we started another one. We have support for protests, but not for the fighting."

"Then what's your strategy? How can the war end?" I should know this, too, Bev thought. It's why David got involved.

"We do things like blowing up power lines. It's been a very effective stratagem for us, because it's one way we reach the rich, cutting off electricity to their factories and offices."

"Charles thinks the war will only end when economics force one or both sides to change their strategy."

"Bev, one side —the oligarchy and the military— is making so much money from the U.S. fighting Communism, they can afford to keep this going for a very long time. When the military aid gets cut, the rich will find another way to exploit us."

"How is that?"

"We can't fight forever. That boy who joked about college said some truth too. We want normal lives. At least after I kill del Norte. But normal has to be different and we know that menial farm work is a thing of the past. We'll want schooling, health care, jobs, opportunities to join the rest of the world. My father, Don Alejandro, thinks the world will be just fine if he gets a small plot of land, and for him it will be fine. But not for the next generations. There isn't enough land as it is, and we can't survive on tortillas and beans any more. The revolution is about survival. Can you see that?"

As the two women talked, a short, bent-over man in peasant's clothing came up to them, saying, "Señoras, did one of you drop this book?" He handed Vitalina a prayer book which she immediately recognized as belonging to Rafael.

"Where did you get this," she demanded, grabbing him, then looking around frantically.

"I don't know," the man stammered. "Please, don't hurt me."

"Tell the truth," Vitalina shouted, shaking him.

"What is it?" Bev interjected.

"It's my brother's prayer book. Who gave it to you? she repeated.

"A man. Tall. Not heavy, in a suit. I didn't see him too well. He was in the shadows. He gave me some money. Do you want the money?"

"Where?" Vitalina said, letting go of him and putting her hand on a pistol in the bag she carried. "Where is he? When did it happen?"

"I don't know. He left, through the upper gate. He made me walk in front of him after he pointed you out, so he could go out. I don't know where he went," the man pleaded.

Vitalina continued to look around, trying to spot someone in a crowd of both Salvadorans and internationals.

Bev had not moved after the man began to describe what had happened to him. Finally she spoke. "I have to find Charles. It's del Norte, and he was here. I have to find my husband."

Vitalina pushed the man away, waiving him to leave. "The prayer book is an announcement, Bev. He wants us to know he's here. And I will be ready," she said.

○

We argued long into the night. We had been asked to go with Saul and others to a repopulation movement, transporting building materials and people to an abandoned area in the war zone where a new community would be set up. The community would be named after Rafael, and Bev could not stay away.

Twice I started to call an airline to book flights home, twice Bev threatened to leave the hotel and go back to the UCA. Finally I relented, agreeing while every nerve in my body said no to the pleas my wife made. The reverie of the day before, and the joy of the mass, went down with the sun that night. Bev would not stay away.

"We're going to go with the people tomorrow," she had said, and we're going to help them dedicate the land. It will be a monument to someone who helped us when we needed it the most. And besides," she added, "Vitalina and her friends will be there, at least if she doesn't find del Norte."

○

The next morning, I rolled over in bed, still trying to get comfortable, scratching an ankle, not looking forward to a journey of accompaniment for which I could find no energy. My watch showed 7:30 AM, not early but too soon to get started on another effort of uncertainty. I was fighting an illness, both stomach and fever, and wanted to go home. I didn't like the stink of garbage, and not being able to sleep. I added cold showers and mosquitoes to the growing list of dislikes, ending with an unpleasant thought for all the people, including myself, who preach one thing and do another.

And most of all, I felt fear that del Norte would be there, somewhere. I rolled again, reached out, then peeked with one eye to find that Bev had gotten up, presumably washing up, getting dressed. This time, I thought, at least there are others who offer some protection. Not even I could imagine fifty or sixty North Americans being killed.

Bev came out of the bathroom, smiling as she did more often now in the morning. "Getting up, sleepy?"

I just nodded. I felt sick and considered using it as an excuse for not going, but I had to do what I'd promised. There would be no replay of last night's argument. Slowly and deliberately, I got up, showered and had one more attack of stomach trouble, dressed and ate breakfast. Finally I carried the two bags Bev had packed for the day and got ready to drive.

○

I eased the pickup into the southbound traffic from the hotel, found the left hand turn I needed. A short ride later I turned right onto *Avenida de los Heroes*, drove past the Camino Real Hotel and finally to Calle Poniente. Virtually no room remained for me to park as vehicles for the caravan were everywhere.

Several hours later, the caravan left. After a long drive —55 kilometers and several stops— news came of the truck having been captured by the army. I almost declined when Saul insisted that I be part of the negotiating team, but Bev pleaded and logic said that I should be there, if only for my experience as a lawyer. Former lawyer, I reminded her. I didn't appreciate this unpleasant surprise on a day that had no joy. I finally agreed, still uncomfortable, but unwilling to voice my worries even to myself.

A short while later, we drove to a cross road on the Pan American Highway, CA 1, driving down into the valley and the city of San Vicente, capital of the province by that name. San Vicente is a beautiful city nestled among the mountains, filled with century old houses and stores, and a military base.

Dennis, from Minnesota, and I formed part of the negotiating team, joined by two Jesuit priests from California. Saul, who had been selected to be the translator, directed us to the center of the city, staying on the main road. As we passed the Salvadoran Telephone Company Office,

Dennis pointed, "Over there," indicating a barricaded road. As we pulled up, we could see a flatbed truck, obviously our vehicle and loaded with supplies, being guarded by armed soldiers. A civilian leaned on the door, chatting with the guards.

The five of us walked around the barricade and up to the truck, which had been parked on the south side of the street, across from an open garage door. The heavily guarded and armed building, not quite a fort, seemed capable of withstanding an attack. The windows and other smaller doors were barred. A sign over the open double doors identified the building as the headquarters of the Fourth Brigade of the Salvadoran Army. Four guards with automatic weapons stood at ease.

"This is our vehicle," Saul said, translating after Dennis spoke in English to the guard. Other soldiers gathered around. A brief discussion in Spanish ensued, then Saul said that we were to go into the main building. We entered through the large double door, walking back to an office in relative privacy to meet Major Monico. One aide remained when the escort guards left.

The plain office had a mixture of ordinary wood and metal furniture, no personal items visible. A portrait of President Alfredo Cristiani hung behind the desk. We took our places in a row of chairs spread in a semicircle in from of the desk. I watched the two Jesuits, wondered how they felt being inside a military base, possibly with someone who had something to do with the murders of their colleagues one year ago. We knew the military had killed them, but did not know which ones. Neither priest showed signs of concern, but neither were smiling.

The Major spoke politely yet firmly, giving Saul plenty of time to translate, explaining why it was impossible for us to take the truck. The argument reduced itself to a question of ownership.

Dennis correctly claimed that we represented the ones who purchased the material and thus had a right to have it returned. Major Monico remained polite, wanting to know who personally paid for the material. Over and over, Dennis insisted that it wasn't illegal under El Salvador law to buy building materials and drive around on the roads. "So, why was the truck detained?" I asked at the end of each round of dialogue. Monico ignored the question each time.

After further debate, it was clear an impasse had been reached, and other strategy became necessary. Politely saying we would return, we went to make phone calls to people in the United States who would initiate a telephone tree, where each person called had agreed to contact two or three others until several hundred people would be notified of the situation. Everyone had promised to make known their concern about the situation to the State Department, to the U.S. Embassy in El Salvador, and to the Salvadoran Government. Chain letters may be illegal but chain telephones got results, I thought, surprised I could find anything to think positively about at this time. All circuits would soon be busy.

Of course, I had been wondering about Bev and the others. Were they still parked up on the Pan American Highway? As the five of us rounded the corner to find the public telephones, our delegation of 15 vehicles arrived, accompanied by an escort of Salvadoran soldiers in two jeeps. The caravan parked along the west side of the headquarters, U.S. citizens at the head of the cavalcade, followed by the Salvadorans.

As the people emptied out of their vehicles, they greeted the negotiators with much shouting. I found Bev and quickly learned that the caravan had been detained and held captive by the army, not allowed to go anywhere. "We were surrounded by soldiers with guns, machine guns or automatic rifles," Bev told me, "and they looked at us like we were the enemy."

"We are," I said, relieved that she was with me again, and I filled Bev in on what had happened inside the fort.

Whispering, she told me, "Vitalina's in the caravan, and wants to ride with us when we leave." Speaking louder, she asked "What's it like in there?"

"Not bad. Some jeeps, a truck, a bunch more soldiers with M-16s. We went back into an office, had a bit of an argument with the Major over a photograph."

Bev stared at me, moved closer. "Don't you get hurt," she said, holding my arm close to her.

"We called the States, and we'll see what that does." I eased my arm from Bev. "Stay close to someone big," I said. "Looks like the negotiators are going in again."

"Charles. See if I can use the bathroom."

"Sure," I laughed. "Come on."

I joined the other men at the large door to the headquarters as Major Monico arrived. "Who are these people," Monico asked, glaring at me.

"This is my wife," I answered. "Say, where's the bathroom? She needs it."

"Down that way," Monico said in English, pointing back and to his right. He gave an order to a soldier in rapid Spanish.

Bev went off with him, glancing back at me. I watched them walk until they turned and were out of sight. More to worry about now, I thought. Saul tapped me on the arm, bringing me back to the issue at hand, and translated Major Monico's response that there had been no arrest. We had stayed in sight of the double doors.

Several of the group decided that we might be in danger and blocked the doorway, so that the soldiers with their M-16 rifles were unable to

close the doors. The North Americans formed a large circle and began
to sing. Major Monico was not happy. He had to raise his voice, almost
shout, as the group outside formed a large semicircle around the large
door and had begun to sing protest songs. Saul's translation blended
with 'We shall overcome' and Monico started to talk before Saul
finished.

"Let's do English," I interrupted, and Major Monico started over.

"You can't do this," he said.

"Can't do it?" Dennis asked. "We are doing it. And by the way, is your
phone ringing? It was true, the group could hear several phones ringing
in the background. The protesters remained in the circle and sang more
songs. It was like a movie set, where the army had all the guns and all the
power, and the North Americans were in control. Thank God they didn't
use the guns, I thought. It's no comfort to know that shooting is the only
way a gun matters if the threat of it is ignored.

"Wait outside," Monico said.

"Not till my wife comes back," I replied. Dennis, the two priests, Saul,
Major Monico and his two armed aides stood with me, waiting, listening
to the songs outside. Sweat had formed on the brow of one of the priests.
The other appeared to be praying.

After a few more minutes of sparing, the negotiations ended. Dennis
and the group were told to call the High Command, using a public
phone down the street. "No we don't have a phone for you," the Major
said."

I pointed to a phone and asked, "Why not that one? We could use
that while I wait for my wife."

"Find your own phone, gentlemen," was the reply.

When Bev came back, Monico again ordered us out. "And no one
else will be able to use the bathrooms. You have insulted us," he added.
"Wait outside while I make my own phone call." The doors were still
held open by unarmed women and men in the face of soldiers carrying
M-16s.

Eighteen

The group of Salvadorans and North Americans accompanying them on the repopulation began making a lot of noise, some singing and a few taunting the soldiers. Dennis and I were back inside trying to convince Major Monico to reconsider his refusal to let the truck go when two men arrived in a Salvadoran Army jeep. The driver jumped out of the vehicle and hurried up to the crowd that surrounded the door to the fort, pushing his way past those who stood in his way.

Entering the door, he walked up to Dennis and me as Major Monico walked away. "My name is Major Joseph Andrade, U.S. Army, attached to the U.S. Embassy. Who's in charge here?" He looked at the two of us, then at the two priests who stood silently near, then at the others who were still crowding into the doorway.

"Well," Dennis finally said, "we're ecumenical, so I guess no one's in charge. But those people out there, and a lot more back home, have asked the four of us to speak for them."

Andrade looked back at the jeep, signaling to the other man who just sat, ignoring the whole scene. "I'll talk to you then. You've got to call off these wild hippies. It's dangerous here in El Salvador. You don't know what you're doing."

"Are you here to protect us?" Dennis asked.

One of the North Americans heard that question and shouted, "Yeah. Protect us like you did Jean Donovan and the other murdered church women," laughing as he spoke.

Andrade turned to face him. Another protester spoke up, "You're an adviser? So advise them to give us our truck."

Another shouted, "Yeah. Advise them not to bomb us."

Andrade tried to speak, found no words, then broke away and went inside the building toward the office of Major Monico. I tapped Dennis on the arm. "He's not going to help. I'll go talk to the other one."

Bev stood in the large circle, now near the center and farthest from the door. She later told me that as I headed to the jeep, a woman she didn't know said, "Look. There's another from the CIA."

Bev laughed in spite of the tension, noting that the two who arrived in the jeep and I all had on jeans and a dress shirt open at the collar. Must be the uniform of the day, she thought, and said to the woman, "That's no CIA guy, that's my husband."

"It is?"

"Yes. He's been inside. He's one of the negotiators."

"Oh. Gee, maybe that's why they picked him." She frowned, then moved over to someone from her community delegation to report on the news.

Meanwhile, I approached the man sitting in the jeep and spoke, "Are you more composed than your partner?"

"*No habla Englais*," he said.

I looked at him, holding his stare. "Have it your way," I said. "Hope you don't miss anything." The man turned his gaze, looking up at the sky as I spoke, and continued to ignore the whole scene. I walked back to the door. I fleetingly remembered the first agent, Joe Colangalo, I had met when we went to the embassy and when he helped me free Bev from del Norte and the prison. They come and go, I thought, but now it's the military. I quickly dismissed the past.

Major Andrade came back out and tried to address the fifty North Americans amid hooting and mocking. "You are guests in this country. You have no right to speak out," he said.

"Sure we're guests," a woman shouted back, "and we're invited guests. Who invited you?"

Andrade's voice rose as he replied. "Leave this repopulation to us. We have the expertise in arms and guns."

Dennis immediately interrupted, "Are you threatening us with talks of guns?"

Andrade shook his head, "I'm not threatening you."

I moved up close to Andrade, standing face to face. "This is not a matter for guns but for the rights of the people," I said.

Andrade pushed his way back into the building. I tried to calm those near him in the crowd. Dennis motioned to him. The large double door had been shut and a small, side entry remained open briefly. Dennis followed Major Andrade inside, then I joined him. A soldier took his post at the door and no more North Americans were admitted.

The songs and prayers outside were drawing a crowd from the city. A military employee came with a video camera, and photographed the delegation. Telephone calls began coming from the United States, and other calls went from embassy to High Command to this military post in San Vicente.

The Salvadoran Commander, Major Monico, had now been joined by his superior officer, Colonel Carpio. I was fascinated as Colonel Carpio walked up to Monico, disdainfully waiving off a soldier trying to report. Carpio spoke sharply to Monico, eyes darting around briefly to take in those nearby, then closing, narrowing to slits. He looks like a big snapping turtle, I thought. This is the first man in El Salvador, aside from del Norte at least, who really scares me. He's like a reptile, totally without warmth, and has no feelings for us.

Major Monico pointed at Dennis and me, then outside. U.S. Major Andrade approached, spoke into his radio quickly, then whispered into Carpio's ear. When Carpio nodded, he motioned for Charles and Dennis to follow him back to the office where the negotiations had first begun with Major Monico. Salvadoran Colonel Carpio was now giving orders, quietly, although Major Monico remained the spokesman. Major Andrade was giving advice.

Andrade closed the door to the office, then pointed to a couch. "Sit, and relax," he said. "There's a call coming in from General Ponce that may resolve this," he added conspiratorially. The Jesuits froze, knowing now that the one who had ordered their colleagues killed was involved in our conflict.

After a while, the embassy called and spoke with Major Andrade. Major Monico was not in the office as the cards were being played out. Dennis and I sat back on the couch, watching and waiting, relying on the pressure coming from the United States and from the noisy group outside. It felt like a soup or stew just about coming to a boil. U.S. Major Andrade and Salvadoran Colonel Carpio were the only two others in the room, and Carpio took no notice of the North Americans.

Another call came in, and Major Andrade whispered to me. "It's a call from Colonel Ponce. Top military man in the whole country. Chief of Staff. It looks good," Andrade added. I already knew what Colonel Emilio Ponce represented. I also had been told that Ponce had ordered the killing of the Jesuits last year. I felt sympathy for my co-negotiators now, and had more anxiety myself now, simply because this man had decided to intervene. Colonel Carpio took the telephone, mostly listening, speaking occasionally as in a quiet conversation.

After that, it was all over. Colonel Carpio disappeared into the depths of the building and Major Monico reappeared. He went outside with the negotiators and said that the delegations had now been given permission to take the truck full of building supplies and go anywhere they wanted to go. "Someone must sign for the supplies," he said, and a Salvadoran woman, tears in her eyes, came forward to sign for them. They were free to leave.

One of the Salvadoran women who had been part of all the events of the last two days came up to me, shaking my hand. She said, "Yesterday you said some very nice things. Today you put it in practice. That is what is important." I stood a bit taller after hearing that.

I thought that simple solidarity was dangerous enough. Today this group had seen what happens when people come together with a goal, both Salvadoran and North American, both homeless who are displaced by a war and homeless who are displaced by a policy implementing that war. It was physical solidarity.

Other Salvadorans were congratulating the two Jesuits from California. One was breathing hard, not feeling well. His associate offered his water bottle, helping the priest to a bench. "It wasn't easy," he said, sitting. "After, my knees shook for five minutes. A year ago, they killed the six."

Someone yelled in Spanish, "*Viva* solidarity with the Internationals!" Everyone responded, "*¡Que Viva!*" The air was filled with shouts of "*¡Viva!*" during this victory.

As the celebration continued with cheers and shouts punctured the air, I walked back over to the jeep. Major Andrade was sitting back in the drivers seat, his silent companion still gazing at the sky. Andrade spoke quietly. Those leftists got me angry," he said. "I shouldn't lose control."

"No harm." I looked at the man, thinking. It was interesting that this bunch of North Americans could hold the 4th Brigade at bay and win a stand-off of power. To be delayed and detained and win with telephone calls and pressure was a victory of some kind. I saw it as a form of nonviolence that could succeed. The pressure and the threat of pressure was tough enough so that the ones with the guns didn't use them. "It was all right," I finally said. At least Andrade knew it was not a good thing to lose control and he was better for that, I thought. "Why do you think you lost it?" I asked, implying that a military advisor should have better control.

"Don't know," Andrade replied.

I wondered if Andrade had a guilty conscience about the death squad government. He had such a compelling need to explain the situation, almost a desperation that we believe the perception of reality he believed or tried to. Maybe he really believes the lies and he's frustrated that other North Americans don't see it his way. As the conversation ended, I asked Andrade a question. "Do you know someone named del Norte?"

"I never met him," Andrade replied.

"Never? He was head of the Treasury Police two years ago. Weren't you here then?"

"I haven't met him. Not since Fort Benning and the School of the Americas."

"Figures for him. You were there too?" I asked.

"He's a rogue."

"Stop him."

"Can't, but I can do this. He's coming for you." Andrade started the jeep.

"Why the warning?"

"You didn't insult me," he said and drove off.

○

The caravan left the town of San Vicente, driving off like a victory procession. Joyous shouts came from all the trucks and vans, mixed with laughter and more *"¡Viva!"* acknowledgments of the nonviolent defeat of the army. There was also more than normal admiration from the people on the streets, who waved and echoed the shouts.

The parade returned to the main highway, drove for barely five minutes and turned on to a gravel road that soon became dirt and mud, heading toward the small field where the food and water and building supplies were to be used to rebuild a community. It was to be called *Communidad Padre Rafael*, in memory of the priest who had given his life for his people.

I had pulled our pickup in at the very end of the long line. Saul had gone ahead with the Jesuits who would consecrate the land and the building materials. Bev sat in the middle again and Vitalina, who had a small canvas sack with her, sat in the truck with us, leaning forward as if to see into the future. She looked like a coiled spring about to expand. I hesitated with the news of del Norte, not wanting Bev to feel the terror that I felt. Then, stopping the truck, I told the two women, "I got a warning. Del Norte is coming for us."

Vitalina quickly pulled two pistols from the bag. "Insurance," she said. Bev watched, said nothing as our truck fell behind the caravan. Then I resumed speed, driving along a path next to the woods, trying to catch up to the fading lights of the others.

As I turned at the end of a field, it came —the white Jeep Cherokee— pulled out from a side road, blocking the tracks and isolating us from the group. Colonel del Norte quickly got out of the Jeep, pointed his gun at our windshield.

"We get out," Vitalina said quickly, shoving one of the pistols into my hand. I slowly eased myself out of the truck while Vitalina got out by the passenger's door. Del Norte kept his gun pointed at Vitalina, while she moved slowly to her right, showing her gun and separating herself from me and the truck, making it more difficult for del Norte to shoot us both.

Vitalina screamed at del Norte, using Spanish words I had never heard. Del Norte turned to me, as though he could only talk to a man, that a woman could not call him to account. "I'm going to shoot her, like I did her brother. I really like this."

"You! Murderer. Are you going to take her watch, too?" I shouted.

"Why not? I'll strip her, toss her body in a dump somewhere, like I did with the priest." Del Norte crouched, aimed at Vitalina. "Stay where you are," he shouted. "Then I shoot you, because I know you, and I owe you. Then the mother dies."

I quickly glanced at Vitalina, then back at del Norte, knowing one of them would soon shoot, realizing I would also have to fire, especially if Vitalina was hit. Could I save any of us? As I raised my pistol, a loud gunshot rang out from behind me. Del Norte froze as the bullet went by him.

When Vitalina heard the gun, she immediately fired at del Norte once, then ran up to him and put two more bullets in his chest, to be absolutely sure the man who killed her brother was dead. Then she kicked him, just to be sure.

I turned to see Bev holding a gun, tears streaming down her cheeks. "Another gun was in the sack," Bev said.

◯

Silence engulfed us as the three of us stood as witnesses to what we had done. Neither Bev nor I could speak. Vitalina took charge. "How long," she asked, "have you tried to get officials in the U.S., and in Salvador, to take legal action against your son's murderer? Cold blooded murder!" Neither of us answered, still motionless. "And now he's admitted he killed my brother," Vitalina went on, "stripped him naked, and tossed his body away. Well I have a place for this one's body, where nothing will remain. Mysteries can go both ways, my civilian *gringo* friends. Neither my government nor yours will do anything about the disappearance of this one. How can they? This is justice," she said, waiving the gun in the air.

Finally Bev spoke. "Remember once I told you an evil man murdered my only son, Charles," she said, "and I asked you, what did that make me? Now you know."

"Bev," I started to say.

"Listen to me. What have I done? I've done the last thing on earth I could do for my son."

I let the gun I held fall from my hand, then walked over to Bev. Vitalina turned back to the body of now dead Colonel del Norte, dispassionately pushed on his chest with her foot, seeing that he was truly dead, then came over to Bev. "That evil man murdered my brother," Vitalina replied. "And my bullets were the ones that killed him, finished him off. Your bullet distracted him, but didn't hit him. He would have shot us all."

"I don't know about those things," Bev said. "I just know we've stopped this murderer from ever killing again."

"We both did," Vitalina said, picking up both the borrowed pistols, wiping them clean and putting them with hers in the bag she had taken from the truck. "I'll get rid of the one you used Bev, just like I'm going to take care of this carcass. That's all it is anymore." She opened the door to the Cherokee, motioning for me to help her with the body, and the two of us stuffed del Norte's body on the seat. She picked up her bag. "I've got to leave before the others come to see about the shots. And, there's no need to tell anyone what happened. I won't, except for Papá. Alejandro. He needs to know."

"I suppose you're right," I said. "But Saul should know something. I can't think of how to tell him."

"I'll find him, when the war is over and he's a priest. I'll tell him in confession," Vitalina said, smiling finally at me. "I may make him keep my brother's promise too, if I find a good man to marry. Saul can do the ceremony like Rafael promised."

"I wish you luck," I said, speaking for both of us. "And I will pray for your safety through out the rest of the war, however long that will be."

Vitalina started the Jeep, drove around our pickup truck. "Come back when there is peace. We'll need people like you," she said, driving off without waiting for an answer.

○

We watched the Cherokee truck for the last time, holding each other. "Charles," Bev said, "let's go home, for good this time. I've had enough of El Salvador."

"Me too, for a long, long time. Except for Saul's ordination or Vitalina's wedding."

"Funny," Bev said. "Charles, aren't you going to say anything about the murder we just witnessed?"

"That was self defense. Anyway, in war, you shoot first or get shot by the other side."

"You're right, again. Anyway," she said, mimicking my use of the word, "I feel like eating chicken soup again. I can get some cilantro leaves and you can cook."

"Cilantro's the magic word," I said, holding her, turning her toward me as we hugged even harder.

"It might be magic, Charles." Bev held on to me, clutching me tightly, then pushed me away. "Where were you twenty-five years ago? I know this is silly but I would have married you instead of David's father back then.

"You might not have met a priest like Father Jimmy to bless us."

"You might have become Catholic." She moved closer, for a kiss now.

"I'd give up preaching for you?"

"There are other ways to be a minister, Reverend Charles. You could write."

"I love you."

Epilogue

Bev and I have a good life together. I am still the pastor at St. John's Lutheran Church, coming up on fourteen years of service. We've been back to El Salvador, most recently last year in 2000 for the twentieth anniversary of Romero's assassination. For David it was a dozen years.

The Lutherans in El Salvador were very kind, too, having a separate commemoration service at Resurrection Lutheran Church in San Salvador. Lutheran Bishop Medardo Gomez spoke at the outdoor service for Romero, a nice gesture, we thought.

2001 looks like a good year for the church. I'm not so sure about the political world. It is March again, and I'm making chicken soup in St. John's kitchen for the 21st anniversary of Romero's murder. It is thirteen years for David, though in ways it is like thirteen days or even hours. We talk about him

It's warmer this year, and Bev will be here soon. She will walk from her office. The law firm where she works has merged several times and has gotten quite large. She is the supervisor of a dozen or so paralegals. She has helped start a bereavement group in our neighborhood at home. She is so compassionate, so understanding, so spiritual. We have taken up ballroom dancing, and have found the ultimate joy when we move together, as a couple, as one.

She has made a small shrine by the baptismal font, using a print we have of an artist's rendition of Romero being shot while saying mass. Angels float over the archbishop's head and a crowd of peasants watch as the cowardly solder fires the gun from hiding. David's decoupage of the horrors of 1980 is next to it, as is a small photo of David. So is his Bible. Bev has made a banner, quoting Romero when he said, "Stop the repression" in English and Spanish. At the service, Bev will tell of the time David recited Romero's last sermon in the church in Antigua, Guatemala, and then she'll read it in both Spanish and English.

I'll preach a short sermon reminding folks as I often do of the words of Jesuit Jon de Cortina, "If God is not with the people of El Salvador, then God is nowhere."

About the Author

John S. (Jack) Munday is a writer and lawyer who lives with his wife, Fran, in their home in Isanti County, Minnesota. He has traveled to El Salvador and other Central American countries twelve times, including leading delegations to the region. Munday is the author of four nonfiction books, including *Surviving the Death of a Child* and *Justice For Marlys: A Family's Twenty Year Search for a Killer*. Jack's three children and Fran's two surviving children have given them twelve grandchildren. Jack and Fran enjoy ballroom dancing and being spoiled by their Papillon, Dreamer. Jack continues his passion for writing, which has been his dream since childhood.